Also by Catherine Bruns

Italian Chef Mysteries

Penne Dreadful

Cookies & Chance Mysteries

Tastes Like Murder

Baked to Death

Burned to a Crisp

Frosted with Revenge

Silenced by Sugar

Crumbled to Pieces

Sprinkled in Malice

Ginger Snapped to Death

Icing on the Casket

Cindy York Mysteries

Killer Transaction

Priced to Kill

For Sale by Killer

Aloha Lagoon Mysteries

Death of the Big Kahuna

Death of the Kona Man

IT CANNOLI BE MURDER

AN ITALIAN CHEF MYSTERY

CATHERINE
BRUNS

To my father, from whom I get my love of Italian food. You are always missed.

Published by Poisoned Pen Press, an imprint of Sourcebooks
P.O. Box 4410, Naperville, Illinois 60567-4410
(630) 961-3900
sourcebooks.com

Library of Congress Cataloging-in-Publication data is on file with the publisher

Printed and bound in Canada.
MBP 10 9 8 7 6 5 4 3 2 1

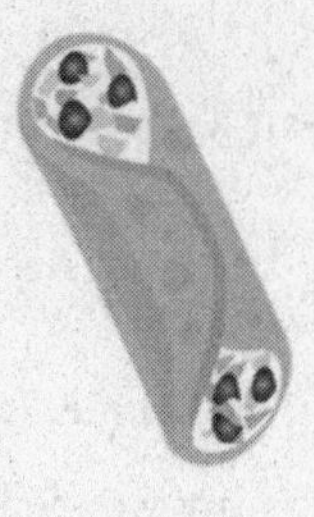

ONE

RAIN DRUMMED PLEASANTLY ON THE ROOF while I diced and sliced tomatoes with my serrated knife on the cutting board before me. Satisfied that I had chopped enough, I lowered the tantalizing red vegetables into the stainless-steel pot and added spices. There was no need to measure—I knew by sight how much was necessary. Three pinches of garlic powder. Two shakes of pepper. A handful of dried basil. Fortunately, the herbs from Spice and Nice's store in town were always fresh and perfectly accentuated my entrées.

Making tomato sauce was nothing new to me. As a trained chef, I'd been doing it for more than twenty years, practically at the knee of my talented grandmother, who'd created the original recipe that I'd tweaked over time. I took pride in the fact that it was an award-winning creation, voted number one at the New York State Fair a couple of summers back.

But this time, it was different. The fact that I was making sauce in my *own* restaurant was not lost on me. A tingle of excitement ran through my body as my wooden spoon went around the inside of the pot, and I inhaled the warm, rich, wonderful smell. I smiled at my surroundings with satisfaction.

My restaurant. I was the one in charge. I called all the shots. It was thrilling to be in control, but also a bit terrifying. In eight short days, I would throw open the front doors of my Italian restaurant, the first of its kind in our town, for the public eye. Given all that had happened in the past six months, this was nothing short of a miracle, and also a dream come true.

The front door opened, and a familiar female voice floated through the walls.

"Tess? You in the kitchen?"

"Where else would I be?" I called out grandly while stooping to adjust the burner.

My cousin Gabby appeared in the doorway. She was wearing a yellow, hooded slicker reminiscent of the Morton Salt Girl, but that was where the similarities ended. With her curvy figure and enormous dark eyes, Gabby could turn the head of any man in Harvest Park.

Gabby held a cardboard tray that contained two Java Time cups and a white bakery bag. In her other hand was a lumpy package. She sniffed the air and grinned. "Ah. It always smells so good when you make your sauce. But the restaurant's not even open yet, and I'm guessing that new freezer of yours is already piled high with enough to last through the summer. And it's only the end of April!"

I laughed and gave the sauce another quick stir before placing the lid on the pot. Gabby held out a cup to me and I took it gratefully. "Archie's famous dark roast. How'd you know I needed a caffeine fix?"

"Because I know you." Gabby hung her slicker on one of the metal hooks next to the door that led to the alley and took a moment to fluff her short, dark hair. "Tess, you're pushing yourself too hard. For someone who cooks all the time, you never seem to eat. You look like you've lost weight, so this should help." She handed me the bakery bag. "I stopped by Carlita's and picked up some apple fritters."

My mouth watered. I *was* hungry, but oddly enough, I rarely ate when I cooked, except for a sample taste here or there. Many chefs were like that. I laid the bag down on the new Formica countertops I'd recently had installed and reached inside, then took a large bite from the pastry. It was still warm, and I let out a moan as the taste of cinnamon and apples burst inside my mouth. "So good. You're right, I haven't eaten yet today. No time."

She wagged a finger in my face. "How are you going to keep up your strength to run a business if you don't take good care of yourself?"

"Have you been taking lessons from my mother?" I teased. "She'd be saying the same thing if she weren't out of town with your mom."

Gabby cocked an eyebrow. "Yeah, I can do a pretty good imitation of Aunt Fran, but all kidding aside, you should take a night off while you can. Your life is about to change big time."

She was right, of course, but I didn't mind. In fact, I welcomed the change. The restaurant had helped keep my mind busy over the winter and off other matters, specifically my husband's untimely death.

"I'm excited and nervous at the same time. You know what it's like—starting your own business. The dream is about to become a reality." I recalled vividly when Gabby had opened her store, Once Upon a Book, a cozy little bookstore that was her pride and joy. A flurry of anticipation soared through me. It was my turn now.

"Oh my gosh, yes," Gabby groaned. "I had the most awful butterflies for weeks. And now I'm having them again because of the signing tomorrow night. Tess, I've never had a bestseller in my store before. This is a huge deal. The waiting is killing me, so I decided to come bug you for a while."

"Well, I'm glad that you did."

Gabby's presence was always welcome. Even if we'd been born sisters, we couldn't have been any closer. I knew that Gabby had had a tough time getting her business off the ground. The bookstore had had its share of ups and downs but was now entering its second year and holding its own, or so I thought.

I went back to the stove to check on my sauce. When I took possession of the building in January, I knew it would take a good deal of money to remodel the restaurant how I'd always envisioned it. For starters, the roof had to be replaced, but thankfully, my landlord, Vince Falducci, had paid for that. The flooring and walk-in freezer, however, had come out of my own pocket. If things went well, I did plan to buy the building within the next year, and Vince had said he would deduct those costs from the sale. But if the restaurant soured, I'd be forced to return to employment in someone else's kitchen.

"Oh, I almost forgot." Gabby held out the lumpy package to me. "A little thank you gift."

Mystified, I grabbed it from her outstretched hands. "Thank you for what?"

She shot me a look of disbelief. "Are you kidding me? You've been crazy busy but are still going out of your way to make goodies for my book signing tomorrow night. I can't tell you how much I appreciate it."

"Oh, Gabs. This is fabulous!" It was a beige straw mat for the restaurant's front porch with a border of tomatoes around the words Welcome to Anything's Pastable. That was the name I'd chosen for my restaurant months ago, even before I'd signed the papers. Everyone had thought it was cute and especially fitting, given the blows life had dealt me lately. They didn't know I had another reason for the name as well.

"It's beautiful." I wrapped my arms around Gabby's thin shoulders and gave her a squeeze. When we moved apart, I noticed that her lips were pinched tightly together. "Something's bothering you. Come on, out with it."

She stared at me with concern in her eyes. "Tess, so much is riding on this book signing. Sales have been way down lately. If they don't improve soon, I don't know what's going to happen."

This was an unwelcome surprise. I knew Gabby barely broke even some months but had no idea that the store was doing so poorly. Gabby was too proud to ask for help, even from family. Still, I was ashamed I hadn't figured it out for myself. I'd been wrapped up in the restaurant lately with little time to think about anything else.

"But the signing should fix everything, right? I mean, this is Preston we're talking about." Preston Rigotta was a number one *New York Times* bestselling author who lived about a half hour away from our picturesque little town, in the elite Saratoga region of Upstate New York. He wrote suspense novels that critics called riveting, and unputdownable page turners. Gabby had devoured all of them, while I'd read none. She'd idolized the man for years, and when it came to favorite authors, Stephen King was the only one who eclipsed Preston in her mind.

So, when Gabby had discovered Preston had a new book coming out, she'd taken the bull by the horns and sent an impromptu message to his website, asking if he'd consider doing a signing at her store. She'd almost fallen through the floor when his daughter, Willow, who managed the site, had responded and invited her to come to their house and meet Preston in person.

"It's going to be the social event of the year," I assured her. "Do you know how many people are coming? I want to make sure I have enough treats."

Gabby fiddled with the lid on her cup. "I've asked people to RSVP, via the store's Facebook page or in person to me, but it's still difficult to say. Maybe between fifty and seventy-five? And I can't afford to turn away walk-ins. If I run out of books, I can always ship them out to people or have them picked up at the store later."

"He must have many tour dates scheduled since he's so popular," I commented.

She shook her head. "Not Preston. He has a few signings listed on his website, including my store, but most are within New York State. He doesn't need to trot all over the globe. His books sell themselves."

Gabby was a true fangirl, and I hoped it paid off for her. "Well, never fear. I'll make sure the food is covered. I'm going to bake all the sweets tomorrow morning so they're fresh. You said that cannoli were Preston's favorite, right?"

She nodded. "He told me that his entire family loves them. Say, can you make biscotti, too? Your chocolate is really yummy. I feel bad for asking, but I'm paying for your time and the ingredients, so please don't argue with me."

"Forget it. This is my treat."

"Come on," she implored. "I'm not about to take advantage. You've got your own business to worry about." She glanced around the room and beamed. "It looks so different in here. Dylan would be so proud of the restaurant—and you."

"He would be proud," I agreed. "Dylan shared my vision for this place." It had been six months since my husband was killed in a fiery car crash. A few weeks after his death I'd discovered from my cousin Gino, a detective on the local police force and also Gabby's brother, that his death hadn't been an accident. Dylan's car had deliberately been tampered with. After the shock wore off, I'd embarked on my own quest to find his killer and, with Gabby and Gino's help, had succeeded. The person was now behind bars and I'd gotten justice for my husband, but that wouldn't bring him back.

I tried to steer the conversation back to the restaurant itself. "I wish this place didn't feel like a money pit some days." It was the biggest gamble I'd ever taken in my thirty years because I couldn't be positive about how the place would fare. The building came with a sordid reputation, which didn't help. It had previously been called Slice, a pizza parlor fronting as a cover-up for some shady dealings.

Gabby was counting on her fingers. "So, we have cannoli—your vanilla crème ones decorated with chocolate chips, right? And chocolate biscotti?"

I waved a hand in dismissal. "Forget the chocolate biscotti. I have a recipe for cinnamon-chip-flavored ones I'll use instead." It had belonged to my maternal grandmother, the one whom I'd gotten my love of cooking from. "It's fabulous. The biscotti melt in your mouth. I'll make a batch of them. But I have to ask…why didn't you go to Carlita's for the cannoli? Hers are awesome."

Carlita Garcia owned Sweet Treats, the bakery next door to Gabby's shop, where the fritters had come from. She was a warm, wonderful woman who was also notorious for having the inside scoop on all of Harvest Park's gossip.

Gabby gave a sly wink. "When it comes to food, I'm always going to ask you first, Tess. I know dessert isn't your first love, but there's nothing you can't make. Besides, I thought it would be a good opportunity for you to pass out some of your business cards for the restaurant."

"I do like the way you think." I removed the pot of sauce from the burner. "Did you check out the dining room on your way in? Things have changed quite a bit since you were in here last."

She shook her head. "I was too busy trying to shake all the raindrops off. How about a tour, Julia Child?"

Gabby always knew the right thing to say. While Preston might be her idol, Julia was tops in my book. We walked out of the kitchen and into the main dining room, which Gabby had passed through on her way to the kitchen, located in the back of the building.

"How's Lou? I haven't seen him in a while."

Louis Sawyer, or Lou as everyone called him, was Gabby's boyfriend of five months and a member of the town's police force, along with Gino. Gino hadn't been particularly happy about the two of them dating but finally seemed to be accepting it.

"I haven't seen him all week either," Gabby confessed. "I've been crazy busy with Liza on vacation this week. It's not ideal to hold the signing tomorrow night with her out of town, but what else am I supposed to do? Preston picked the date he wanted and that's that. Wow, Tess." She glanced around the room in awe. "It doesn't even look like the same place."

"That's what I was hoping you'd say." Her remark gave me immense satisfaction. I'd worked at Slice for a brief time last fall and, despite the poor conditions, had seen the possibilities before me. My one regret was that my husband hadn't lived to see it, too.

My life had been incredibly lonely since Dylan's death. We hadn't gotten around to having children yet, and my only companion in our blue Cape Cod–style house was Luigi, our tuxedo cat, who did his best to keep me amused. It had helped immensely to have the remodeling project to keep my mind focused on other things—besides Dylan—during the long and dreary winter. This restaurant was my labor of love to him, and I could see his support in each remodel I made. Now, when patrons entered the main dining room from the front door, there was a hostess station directly to their right where I pictured Dylan greeting guests with a warm smile, guiding them to the built-in wooden bench to wait for available tables.

The orange plastic booths and cheap tables that had

previously dominated the dining room were long gone and had been replaced with square oak tables and matching chairs. There were fourteen in all, meaning I could accommodate fifty-six people at once. New Pergo flooring gleamed under our feet while looped cable lights hung from the beamed ceilings, echoing draped pasta noodles. The paneled walls were adorned with black-and-white photos my mother and father had snapped thirty-five years ago on their honeymoon in Italy—classic sites like the Leaning Tower of Pisa, Trevi Fountain, and the Coliseum.

I'd also added a collage of photos on one wall of the people nearest and dearest to me. There was a picture of Dylan and me on our wedding day, Gabby in front of the bookstore during her grand opening, a photo of my parents with me shortly after my birth, and one of Gino and his wife, Lucy, with their twins.

A small oak bar was situated along the back wall of the room with two rows of wineglasses suspended from a shelf above it. Permits and licenses had taken forever to obtain, with my liquor license only coming through last week. I'd been one of the lucky ones because depending on the time of year, it could take months or years to receive one. But now I was proudly ready to serve bold red wines and tart limoncello, displaying an array of corked bottles like artwork behind the dark wood surface.

I'd also ordered charming brass basket lamps for each of the red-checkered tablecloths, but they had not arrived yet. I'd been told they'd shipped two weeks ago and had received no updates since—one more thing causing my blood pressure to rise. There was a new gas fireplace next to the bar, because I loved the idea of a crackling fire on cozy nights in the winter, but now I wanted to kick myself for the extra expense. Perhaps I should have waited until the fall to install it. Who knew if I'd even make it till then?

No, I needed to stop the negative thinking. I was a good cook and the place looked beautiful. Besides, we didn't have an Italian restaurant in our small town. It was going to work. *Think positive.*

"Tess?" Gabby looked at me inquisitively.

I blinked. "Sorry. My mind was somewhere else. What did you say?"

She beamed. "I was saying how gorgeous everything looks. Now what about your staff? They're all set, right?"

"Not exactly." I exhaled sharply. "I have some interviews lined up for tomorrow and Sunday. So far, I've hired three part-time waitresses and need at least one more. A couple of the girls are in college and don't want to work five nights a week. One isn't sure if she's returning to her hometown for the summer so I'm taking a risk on her. I'd really love to find someone who has skills to help me in the kitchen and maybe play hostess on busy nights, but so far I haven't had much luck."

Gabby watched me with a thoughtful expression. "I did some waitressing in college, remember. I can help out if needed."

I made a face. "I'd love that, but you've got your own business to worry about."

She slung an arm around my shoulders. "If you find yourself shorthanded on opening night, let me know. I'll be here for most of it anyway. Liza can always close up the bookstore if needed. Hey, family over everything, right? And who knows if my store will be around by then anyway? If Preston decides to ditch me—"

"Stop talking like that," I scoffed. "It's going to work out fine."

My phone buzzed from my jeans pocket and I drew it out, praying that the repairman wasn't canceling. Hey Tess. Hope all is well. I'm back in town. Are you around tomorrow? I'm working tonight.

Gabby peered over my shoulder. "Everything okay with Justin?"

"Sounds like it. He's finally home." Justin Kelly had been my husband's college roommate and best friend for many years. Shortly after Dylan's murder, he'd confessed that he had feelings for me that ran deeper than friendship. Justin was handsome, kind, and caring, and I'd leaned on him heavily after Dylan's death. I was very fond of him but couldn't entertain the idea of anything more happening between us yet. He'd respected my wishes and asked if we could continue spending time together as friends.

After six months, it still felt at times that my husband had just passed away. Some days were better than others. Justin had always been there for me, and I appreciated him for it. We'd gone to the movies a couple of times, spending hours shopping, and I'd cooked him dinner at my house. These things had never been out of the ordinary for us. God knows I needed my family and friends around me now. I shot off a quick text to him.

"How's his mother doing?" Gabby asked.

"She's better, but I know that he feels guilty leaving her." At the beginning of February, Justin's father had passed away from a sudden stroke. He'd taken a leave of absence from his job at the fire station to fly to California, where his mother was now living alone.

"I'm so glad he's back. I told him to stop over at the signing or else I'll have to wait and see him the next day." I went back into the kitchen, grabbed the doormat and then laid it down on the front porch. I hurried down the steps, turned around, and surveyed the one-story building with immeasurable pride. It had been repainted last month to a tan shade instead of the former brown, and the blacktop of the adjacent parking lot resurfaced. "There. It's perfect now."

Gabby pointed at the blinking sign on top of my roof that read ANYTHING'S PASTABLE. "Hey, your *G* isn't lighting up."

"Yeah, I know. Vince has a repairman coming to fix it on Monday." Some days it was like I was beating my head against a brick wall, but these things were to be expected. Everything would sort itself out eventually, and I was excited to show my restaurant off. "I guess some days you take one step forward and then two steps back."

"Owning a business is like life, honey. You have good days and bad days. Loving what you do makes it all worthwhile, though." She looked at me and I spotted unshed tears in her dark eyes. "Tess, I'm so scared—scared that something is going to ruin the signing tomorrow night. This could make or break the store. I still can't believe that Preston agreed to it. This is a dream come true for me, and I can't afford to let anything mess it up."

"You need to stop worrying." It was so unlike Gabby's carefree, go-with-the-flow character and made me realize how anxious she was. As a new business owner, I understood her feelings more than ever, and the same thoughts were constantly running through my mind about the restaurant.

While I had no doubts about my cooking skills and had held every job possible in a restaurant before, that didn't guarantee Anything's Pastable's success. What if no one showed up on opening night? The sign on the front door had said that we were accepting reservations for next Saturday night. It had been up for two weeks, but no one had phoned yet. I'd mailed out over two hundred fliers as well.

"Stop worrying," I assured her. "The signing will go great, you'll sell lots of Preston's books and, everyone will be well sugared up, thanks to me. What could possibly go wrong?"

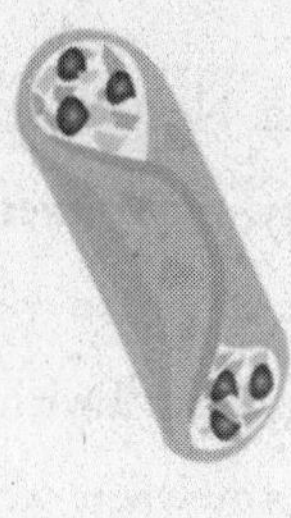

TWO

ALTHOUGH IT WAS MORE CONVENIENT AND spacious to bake in the restaurant's kitchen, I decided to make the desserts for the signing at my house. I was not home much lately and felt like a neglectful cat mom to Luigi. Some people might argue that he was only a pet, but he was so much more. Luigi was my solo roommate and a major source of comfort, especially since Dylan's death. He'd made the first six months of bereavement easier.

I'd set the alarm for six-thirty, but Luigi roused me at six with furry head butts looking for his breakfast. After I fed him, I brewed myself a cup of coffee from the Keurig and sipped it thoughtfully in my living room window seat, staring out into the deserted street. With a sigh I watched the sun break through the gray cloudless sky. It was still a bit chilly for late April, with a high of only fifty degrees expected today. But this was New York State. Next week, we might be looking at a sweltering ninety. One never knew.

My Cape Cod was only 1,400 square feet, but Dylan and I had both fallen in love with its charm when we purchased it three years ago. The hardwood floors underneath my bare feet were cold, and I'd forgotten my slippers upstairs. Oh well. No time for that. I had a lot to do this morning. I flipped through my day planner and ran my finger down the list of today's activities.

I had one interview scheduled for this afternoon and two for Sunday. That left me all morning to bake. Many interviewees preferred the weekend, especially if they were employed at other jobs. That was fine with me. I'd been at Anything's Pastable every day for the past three months, so the day and time didn't matter. I thought back to Gabby's admonishments the previous night. Did I need to push myself so hard before the place even opened? No, but I'd chosen to do this. It helped fill the yawning, empty gaps in my life, and I was ready to devote as much time as needed to the restaurant.

Somewhere in between my interview and Gabby's bookstore event, I was expecting my menus to be delivered and a couple of vendors to stop by. One was planning to give me samples of coffee to try, while the other was pitching their linen service. I'd briefly thought about doing the laundry myself to save money, but the idea was ridiculous. There weren't only tablecloths to be considered but aprons, clean cloths, napkins, and rugs. The restaurant would be open Tuesday through Saturday, and I'd only have Sundays and Mondays off, leaving little time to throw in countless loads of dirty linens.

Gabby had asked me if I could be at Once Upon a Book by five o'clock. Preston's talk didn't start until six forty-five, with the signing at seven. She needed help setting things up, especially with Liza gone.

After I'd showered and dressed, I went back down to the kitchen. Luigi trotted after me and jumped onto one of the stools at the breakfast counter, his enormous green eyes watching me intently. Motorized purrs filled the room as I mixed ingredients together and my Kitchen Aid began to whir.

At five years old, Luigi was in his prime of life and enjoyed sleeping in the window seat soaking up sunshine during the day or batting around the stuffed mice strewn around the floor. I'd thought about getting him a playmate, since I was away so much, but wasn't sure how he'd react. He seemed to enjoy being the one and only King of the Roost.

I made dough for one hundred and fifty cannoli. I shaped even more dough into one hundred cinnamon chip biscotti, which weren't hard or crunchy like the typical biscuit treat. My biscotti melted in the mouth like butter. I'd recently decided to feature cannoli on my menu in addition to four other desserts—cheesecake, tiramisu, genettis, and spumoni, but my grandmother's biscotti recipe was still just for me. While Italian entrées and sauce were my main passion, baking classic desserts always set my mind at ease.

Piping the cream into the shells and decorating the cannoli with chocolate chips was the most time-consuming part. After this phase, I placed them in the fridge while I cut the biscotti, my hands moving on autopilot as I worked my way through the morning.

It was almost one in the afternoon before I finished loading the dishwasher, and I remembered my interview was scheduled for two o'clock. My back ached from bending over to fill the cannoli, but this was important to Gabby, and despite being busy I was happy to do it. Although Gabby's bookstore was the only one in Harvest Park, many preferred to buy books online or e-book versions instead of supporting local business owners. If tonight's signing was a success, it might attract more authors and sales—something she sorely needed.

"It's going to be a huge success," I assured Luigi, who was busy cleaning his paw and seemed disinterested in Gabby and her plight. I checked my watch and raced upstairs to change, my mind already shifting gears back to the restaurant, my upcoming interview, and other items on my to-do list before Gabby's big night arrived.

It was shortly after five o'clock when I pulled up behind Gabby's store. She opened the back door before I had a chance to knock, so I assumed she'd been waiting for me. "Sorry I'm late."

"How'd the interview go?" she asked.

"It didn't. The woman never showed." This had been my third no-show. I'd hoped to have all my staff in place by now. Time was growing short.

Gabby helped unload my car. "Aw, her loss. Wow, Tess. These look terrific. How many did you make?"

"Two hundred and fifty." I glanced around at the

desserts, baffled. "Shoot. I think I forgot a tray of cannoli." How on earth had I done that? My mother had called while I was loading the car. It had taken me a few minutes to get her off the phone; then my neighbor Stacia had run over for a quick chat and Luigi had knocked over my purse, spilling the contents onto the floor. It was a wonder I hadn't forgotten my own head before rushing over.

At least the forgotten tray was still in the fridge or so I thought. "Maybe we won't need them," I said. I could always freeze them for the restaurant next week. Or, if we ran out, I could make a quick dash home.

Gabby waved a hand. "Don't worry. I'm short on space and not sure my fridge will hold all of this anyway." Gabby's back room, where we were standing, was designated for employees only. It had a tiny dorm-size fridge and a microwave stand on wheels with a drawer for silverware and a cabinet at the bottom. A ten-cup coffee pot was squeezed in next to the microwave. In the back corner of the room, which led to the alley, was a metal table loaded with a cardboard box of books. Two folding chairs sat at both sides.

Gabby pointed at the forty-cup coffee urn next to the box of books. "I rented this for the occasion. I'm using my ten-cup if anyone wants decaf." Her face reddened as she looked at me. "If we run low, do you mind making some? I hate to treat you like an unpaid employee, but you're all I've got tonight, kiddo. I'll be ringing up sales in the front and answering phones if people call to order a book."

"Use me and abuse me," I teased. "It's fine. Like I said, I'm all yours for the evening. Too bad our mothers are out of town. You could have put them to work, too." They'd gone to New Jersey for the weekend to visit a friend of Aunt Mona's. My mother had told me on the phone earlier that they expected to be back on Monday.

Gabby made a face. "Come on. You know it's better that they aren't here—well at least *my* mother. She'd ask Preston all kinds of rude, blunt questions. Mom received an early copy of his book *Destiny Calls,* and she's the type who'd go blabbing the ending to everyone." She sighed. "She means well, but some days her mouth has no filter."

I loved Aunt Mona, my father's younger sister, dearly, but she wasn't the most subtle of creatures. My mother, on the other hand, was very prim and proper. Although my father had been gone over five years, she had no interest in dating anyone else and had plenty of opportunities, too. At the age of fifty-five, she was attractive with a great figure and always knew when to turn on the charm. It was ironic because she seemed more interested in my non-existent dating status than her own.

Gabby helped me arrange a tray of cannoli and biscotti on a small table she'd set up in the back of the store, where Preston would give his talk and then sign books. She'd either rented or borrowed folding chairs, which were placed in rows around the author's speaking area to accommodate his guests. "Preston personally came out to the store last week with his daughter after I met them at their home. He said the place was positively charming."

"Preston has good taste." The store was indeed glorious—a 1920s one-story building with a high ceiling, Mediterranean-style floors, and bookshelves made of knotty pine. The former owners had operated a candy store for several years and were in their seventies when they'd decided to retire. They'd sold the building to Gabby at a very reasonable price, and everything had fallen right into place. "Stop worrying. It's going to be a huge success and give the store more exposure."

Lines of worry had etched themselves into Gabby's face. "Tess, if things don't pick up soon, I might have to let Liza go. Sales have been stagnant since Christmas.

Wouldn't that be a kick in the head? 'Hey welcome back from vacation. By the way, you're fired'."

Ouch. I'd hate to see that happen to anyone, especially Gabby's lone employee. Liza was as bookish as her employer and had told me that working at Once Upon a Book was her dream come true. "What if I loaned you a few grand to help tide you over? When I get home, I'll look over my numbers and—"

"No way," Gabby said sharply. "I know that the restaurant has cost you far more money than you planned on."

The silver bells attached to the front door began to jingle and Gabby gasped. "Holy cow. People are early!"

Gabby made a beeline for the register while I rushed into the back room to make sure she'd hit the switch on the coffee, since large urns took a while to brew. Fortunately, it was already percolating, so I started a pot of decaf. I gathered cream, sugar, and napkins from the back room and then placed them next to the tray of cannoli in the signing area.

"Is there any decaf? My husband prefers it to regular." An ethereal female voice spoke from behind me.

"It will be ready shortly." I turned around to see whom the voice belonged to. A tall, rail-thin woman with honey-colored hair pulled into a French twist stared at me. I recognized her immediately. "You're Sylvia Rigotta."

Preston's wife cocked her head proudly and adjusted the lapel on her designer pink suit. Her smile was thin and brittle, her blue eyes sharp and inquisitive as she extended a slender hand. "The one and only. Are you Miss Mancusi's salesgirl?"

Her condescending attitude wasn't lost on me. I'd seen Sylvia's cooking show, *Spice it Up with Sylvia,* on Channel 11 and hadn't been fooled. In fact, I secretly suspected that she couldn't even fry an egg. As a trained chef, I could easily spot the small mistakes that gave her lack of training away. For example, she'd once braised meat in a Crockpot, covering it completely with liquid, when anyone with cooking skills knew that only a little bit was permissible since her method would result in a stew.

Gabby had not mentioned that Preston's wife was attending the signing, and I wondered if she'd known ahead of time. I smiled pleasantly. "No. I'm Tessa Esposito, her cousin. I'm helping out with the refreshments tonight."

"Aren't those cute," Sylvia cooed as she eyed the pastries. "I meant to bring cannoli with me but forgot them at home. Well, they won't go to waste. I'll bring them to my show tomorrow morning." She gave a low giggle. "See, there isn't time to make them on the air, so I do it before the taping. Of course, mine are made from scratch, though. Did you buy these at a bakery?"

"No, they're homemade."

"Really?" She sounded unconvinced. "I never would have thought. Do you work at a bakery?"

Sadly, I'd dealt with her type before. Sylvia enjoyed belittling people she thought were beneath her. I had no desire to continue the conversation but for Gabby's sake didn't want to be rude, either. "No, I'm a chef."

Her eyes widened in surprise as she scanned me up and down. "Where did you do your training?"

Perhaps Sylvia planned to run a check on me? I smiled so wide that my cheeks hurt. "The Culinary Institute of America."

Sylvia put a hand to her delicate, swan-like neck. Maybe it was to feign enthusiasm, but I couldn't care less what she thought of me. The overhead lights reflected off the sizable diamond of her wedding ring. She glanced back at me, a smug smile in place. "Where do you work now?"

Maybe Gino could use Sylvia in the police department's interrogation unit. "As a matter of fact, I have a new Italian restaurant opening in Harvest Park, a week from tonight." I handed her one of my business cards that were lying next to the tray of cannoli. There was a picture of a tomato with ANYTHING'S PASTABLE across the front, and my name printed neatly underneath it, *Tessa Esposito, Proprietor.*

Sylvia gave a low snicker. "What an adorable name," she said then purposefully placed the card back on the table. "Be sure to catch my show if you need any recipes. They're so easy to follow that *anyone* can make them. In fact, I just featured an amazing eggplant parmigiana recipe last week. I hope it works out for you, darling. You do realize that approximately 60 percent of restaurants close their doors before the end of the first year, right?"

Irritation was simmering to a boil in my chest, but I made no comment. What was the point of wasting my time with an egomaniac? Although I'd been in this woman's presence for less than five minutes, I already disliked her. I knew from Gabby that after Preston became famous, he started touting his wife's so-called culinary talent to anyone who'd listen. He was the one who'd managed to wrangle a job for her on the local television station.

A broad-shouldered, silver-haired man with striking

sapphire eyes and a Mediterranean skin tone approached us. Gabby followed at a respectable distance behind him. The guest of honor had clearly arrived.

"Tessa," Gabby said excitedly, "may I present Mr. Preston Rigotta, *New York Times* bestselling author and legend."

Preston puffed out his chest and shook my hand. "A pleasure, indeed. Are you Gabriella's employee?"

I noticed Gabby wince in embarrassment, but I merely shook my head. "No, I'm her cousin and helping out tonight. It's very nice to meet you." I hoped he didn't ask me how I liked his books since I'd never read them.

"A cup of coffee. Cream, no sugar. And two of the cannoli," Preston said in a commanding voice. Surprised at the order, I started to get a plate ready, but he pointed at Gabby.

"Of course, right away." Gabby rushed into the back room for his coffee, while I loaded two cannoli onto a plate. She took the plate from me and carried it and the coffee over to the head of the table, where Preston was already seated. As she put the items down in front of him, he grimaced. "This won't do. I have a bad back. A couple of those pillows I saw in that armchair up front should help. Fetch them."

Gabby flushed slightly. "Oh, I'm sorry, Preston. I didn't know. Yes, right away."

She hurried up the aisle as I sucked in some air. I didn't like how this pretentious man was ordering my cousin around. Gabby wasn't his employee. I knew from my former days as a sous-chef at a high-priced restaurant that there were some celebrities who always expected to be treated as such. Well, not in *my* restaurant. Everyone would receive the same exemplary customer service. No one deserved to be treated better than anyone else.

A woman younger than myself stepped out of the *Self-Help* aisle where she'd been browsing and walked over to me. She had long, sleek dark hair and eyes like Preston's. "Hello, I'm Willow Rigotta." She extended her hand.

"My daughter," Preston said proudly as he stretched in the chair. "She runs my website and accompanies me to all signings." He bit into the cannoli, and a strange look came over his face as he turned to his wife and said, "Sylvia, this doesn't taste like yours."

She tossed her head. "That's because it's *not* mine. This woman made it. Tina, right?"

Really? She couldn't even remember my name after two minutes? Maybe it was deliberate. "My name is Tessa."

"This is incredible." He took another bite and dabbed at his lips with a napkin. "Maybe she should give you some pointers, Syl." With the snide remark, he finished off the pastry, stood, and strode into the restroom next to the *Employees Only* door.

Sylvia's complexion turned as red as a ripe tomato. She pressed her lips tightly together and marched straight up the aisle, almost running into Gabby.

Gabby handed me the pillows. "Tess, do you mind arranging them in the chair? People are arriving."

"Of course not. You go ahead."

"Well, well. Look who's here. Hired help for tonight? Or do you just work for food?" A woman my age set a box of bookmarks down on the table with a loud, deliberate thud.

Gabby's face immediately paled when she locked eyes with the woman. "What are *you* doing here, Daphne?" She practically spat the words out.

Daphne Daniels smiled in satisfaction. She was a striking blond with a perfect size four figure. I hadn't seen her since we'd graduated from high school twelve years earlier. She'd left town shortly afterward, and I hadn't known she'd returned.

"Hello, Gabby. What a pleasant surprise." Daphne's light brown tulip-sleeved sheath matched her eyes, which suddenly flicked over to me. Her generous mouth, coated in frothy pink lipstick, smirked. "Oh, my God. It's Tessa, Gabby's shadow. I see not much has changed."

Preston returned from the restroom, and Willow, who was still standing next to me, tugged on his sleeve as he passed by and spoke in a low voice. "Daddy, I thought you said she couldn't make it. Mother will *not* be happy."

"I'm your father's publicist and am always available whenever he needs me," Daphne said snidely.

Willow glared at her. "Believe me, my mother knows that."

The word *publicist* rooted itself in my mind. Oh boy. Suddenly, this book signing had disaster written all over it. Gabby and Daphne had been enemies throughout high school. Daphne was the popular, perfect girl who'd zeroed in on Gabby in the ninth grade and then proceeded to torture her for the next four years. Somehow, she'd always managed to be there to trip Gabby during soccer practice, humiliate her in the lunchroom, and had once even stolen her clothes out of a gym locker so Gabby would have nothing to wear after swim class. Things all came to a head on prom night, when she'd "accidentally" pushed Gabby into an outdoor pool at the country club and ruined her dress.

Somehow Daphne had gotten away with everything unscathed. Poor Gabby. After spending her high school days trying to hide from the queen of mean, she now had to face her as the employee of her literary idol.

"Publicist?" Gabby asked in a disbelieving tone. Her almond-shaped eyes never left Daphne's face as she addressed Preston. "I thought your publicist had accepted another job and that Willow was stepping into the role tonight."

Preston reached for another cannoli. "No. Daphne's been with me for about four months, since my last publicist moved on."

Daphne sniffed. "I was working at a boutique publishing company, and I've been living in Saratoga for several years. Not this hovel of a town."

I bit into my lower lip, trying to temper my reply. It didn't work. "It's plain to see you haven't changed much."

Preston narrowed his eyes. "Daphne will hand the books to me for autographs and take pictures of me with my fans." He turned to address her. "I plan to be out of here by nine, so if someone is taking up too much time, you'll have to move them along."

"Of course, Preston. Whatever you say." Daphne

laid a hand on his arm, but he immediately shook her off. She looked crushed by the action, which surprised me. I'd never thought of Daphne as having deep feelings for anyone besides herself, but she seemed in awe of her employer.

Daphne spotted the cannoli and reached for one. She closed her eyes as she chewed and let out a little moan. "Oh, this is delish!" She caught sight of Sylvia, who had returned from the front of the store and gave her a sly grin. "Did you make these?"

Sylvia's face looked as if it had been carved out of stone. After a few second of awkward silence, she pointed at me. "No, Tina did."

Good grief. I didn't even bother to correct her this time.

Sylvia pinned Preston with an angry glare. He shot her back one of clear contempt, and the room's temperature seemed to be approaching a freezing level. Sylvia walked to the door of the Employees Only room and looked over her shoulder at her husband. "Preston, I'd like a word with you. *Alone*."

Preston seemed annoyed by the request but dutifully followed his wife as he nodded to Gabby. "More coffee when I get back."

I was sorely tempted to tell the man to get his own darn coffee but didn't want to ruin the evening. Then again, I had a strong suspicion that might happen anyway.

Gabby and I went into the back room, and I filled a carafe with regular coffee while she grabbed the decaf. As Gabby refilled Preston's cup, I noticed that her hands were shaking slightly. We returned to the signing area, where Willow and Daphne exchanged a heated look, but no words. Willow looked away and then disappeared into the restroom.

Daphne seemed not to notice or care that the Rigotta women obviously detested her. She helped herself to another cannoli and then let out a low giggle. "If I keep eating like this, I might end up looking like you, Gabby."

Gabby's nostrils flared. "Look, just stay out of my way tonight, okay? This is my store, got it? And you are Preston's employee. He's the one I care about impressing, not you. We don't have to pretend that we like each other." Gabby had been a bit on the timid side in high school, nothing like her current outspoken self, and Daphne acted momentarily surprised before masking it beneath a concealed grin.

"No, we don't," Daphne said cheerfully. "But in case you're not aware, I'm calling the shots tonight. One word to Preston about your treatment of me and he's out of here."

Gabby forced back a laugh. "Oh really? I find it hard to believe you have that much influence on him."

"Preston adores me," she winked. "You have no idea how fond he is of me."

Oh boy. Too much information for my taste.

The bells on the front door suddenly rang out, and Gabby hurried up the aisle, but not before she shot Daphne another scathing look. Daphne's phone buzzed, and she strolled across the store to answer it. I started to grab more decaf and then remembered the back room was being used. Before I could back away, Sylvia's angry voice floated through the door.

"You promised me she wouldn't be here tonight. There was no need. Willow could have handled everything."

"You're overreacting as usual," Preston snarled. "She is an employee. That's all. I told you that I am not involved with her."

"Liar," Sylvia hissed, and I was shocked by the contempt in her tone. "Don't treat me like an idiot. I know you've been sleeping with her, Preston. I won't tolerate this *again*. You promised all those years ago—" She broke off suddenly. "After tonight, I don't want to see her anymore. *Ever.* Get rid of that floozy when the signing is over or trust me, you'll be very sorry."

Hair rose on the back of my neck. *Preston was having an affair with Daphne? Preston had cheated on Sylvia before?* So, Daphne's words about him being fond of her had been correct.

A step sounded behind me, and I turned around to meet Willow's sapphire eyes. I hadn't even heard her come out of the restroom. Great. Caught with my hand in the cookie jar, so to speak. This evening was shaping up to be a barrel of laughs, and the signing hadn't even started yet.

"Excuse me," she said politely and moved past me to enter the room. After a minute Preston emerged, completely unruffled, and started to greet his fans who were filtering through the store. I knocked on the door and then went in to grab more napkins, but the room was empty. Mother and daughter appeared to have split. Maybe it was for the best.

When every chair was occupied and there was standing room only, Preston immediately launched into a twenty-minute arrogant talk about himself, the book, and what inspired him to write it. He then mentioned how the trade publications had all praised it highly and hinted that a movie deal might be in the works, which delighted his readers. He'd failed to win me over, though. The thought that he'd been cheating on his wife with another woman was repulsive.

After the talk, people who had purchased the book lined up for Preston's autograph. Some wanted pictures, which Daphne took. Anyone who hadn't purchased the book yet went up front to see Gabby, who, from the continuous ringing of the phone and register, wasn't getting a moment's peace.

As I approached the back room, an elderly woman with gray hair and bifocals tapped me on the arm. "Excuse me, dear. Are there any more cannoli?"

I glanced over at the tray and was shocked to see that only biscotti remained. It was a compliment that they'd gone so fast. The woman looked at me expectantly and I hated to disappoint anyone, especially where food was concerned. "I'll get more if you can sit tight for about ten minutes."

"Oh yes," she said eagerly. "They were wonderful. The best I've ever had."

Music to my ears. "I'm so happy you enjoyed them."

Preston was still sitting at the table, a book in front of him to sign, while Daphne snapped a picture of him with a woman about our age. Willow and Sylvia had not reappeared, and I was curious where they'd gone. Gabby was chatting with someone up front, her voice light and excited. Sales must be good, and I was thrilled for her. She'd worked so hard on this event and deserved every dollar that it brought in.

I glanced at my watch. Eight o'clock. It would take me all of ten minutes to grab the cannoli out of my fridge at home and return—fifteen at most. Maybe I should tell Gabby? She was chatting with customers up front. I doubted anyone would miss me as I slipped out the back door that connected to the alley.

Gabby had two designated parking spots—one for herself and the other where my car was parked. Someone might grab my space before I returned, but it was a chance I'd have to take. Without further ado I started the engine, backed my car out of the spot, and drove off into the night.

A few minutes later I pulled into my driveway, welcomed by the lamp I'd left on in my living room window. Luigi greeted me at the front door with a plaintive meow. I patted him on the head, and he followed me into the kitchen. From the refrigerator I grabbed the missing twenty-five cannoli, which rested on a heavy steel platter that had belonged to my grandmother.

Luigi rubbed against my legs and I laughed, stooping down to pet him. "Hey, buddy, I'll be back in a little while. I promise." He still had food in his dish and plenty of water, but I felt like a mother leaving her child for work. Luigi flicked his tail and then trotted back up the stairs, with another meow. Someone was clearly annoyed with me. I locked the door and hurried out to my car, noting to give him an extra treat later.

When I returned to the bookstore, as expected, another car was parked in the spot I'd previously occupied. Just my luck. I didn't want people to see me entering the store with the cannoli, so I drove two doors down to Java Time, which was owned and operated by my good friend Archie Fenton. His Buick was parked in one spot while the other was empty. I was certain he wouldn't mind if I left my car there, and he knew it on sight. Like Carlita, not much in Harvest Park escaped his attention.

The sky had turned pitch black during my absence. I grabbed the tray from the seat next to me and walked toward Gabby's back door, noting that the dim bulb above it was on. I'd almost reached the dumpster when I heard a woman give a low chuckle and froze in my tracks. I knew that laugh. It had tortured Gabby through high school. What was Daphne doing outside? Shouldn't she be protecting her beloved Preston from his onslaught of fans?

The laugh came again, bitter and cold this time. "You're such a loser. How could you even think that I was serious about you?"

"Don't call me that," a deep male voice growled in return.

Holding my breath, I crouched down behind the dumpster, praying they hadn't seen me. The man's voice sounded familiar, but for the life of me I couldn't place it.

"But it's true." Daphne was clearly mocking him and enjoying it. "Hey, don't get me wrong. You're hot as sin, but that's all you've got going for you. I told you last week that it was over, so quit following me around. You can't hold a job and don't have two nickels to rub together. It was fun for a while, but I've got better opportunities waiting."

"Yeah, I get it. You must really think I'm stupid." Anger was evident in his tone. "I saw the way you looked at him tonight. You're cheating on me with the big-time author, aren't you?" To my surprise, he laughed suddenly. "You think he's going to leave his wife for you? Get real."

"That's none of your concern," Daphne snapped back. "And how exactly was I cheating on you? You were just a fling."

"It was more than one night," the man insisted. "We were together for four months."

"God, you're pathetic. You counted? Look, we had some good times, but it's over. Now, do me a favor and get lost. And don't go back in through the bookstore. I don't want people to know I'm associated with you."

An ominous silence followed, and I put a hand to my mouth to muffle my breathing as I waited for the man's response.

"You low-life tramp," he muttered. "All you care about is how much money a man has. I thought I meant something to you."

"Please," Daphne said. "The entire town knows that you're nothing but a joke."

"Careful, babe," he warned. "Karma is going to catch up with you. And when it does, I hope I'm around to see it."

I adjusted the tray in my hands and took a step forward. Something crunched loudly under my foot. I winced. A soda can. Of all the worst luck.

"Who's out there?" Daphne called.

Crap. I was busted. I straightened up and emerged from behind the dumpster, trying to act casual. "Oh, hi, Daphne. I had to run back to the house and get more cannoli—" My voice trailed off when I noticed whom she'd been talking to. It was none other than Carlita's son, Lorenzo.

Lorenzo Garcia was four years younger than me. His parents were a mixture of Italian and Spanish background, and he'd clearly gotten the best of both worlds. Lorenzo was movie-star handsome with tousled black hair, expressive dark eyes, and skin the color of cognac. Women between the ages of twenty and ninety stopped to look at him on the street. He was the youngest of Carlita's six children, the most attractive, and the most problematic.

Carlita had confided to me a couple of months ago that Lorenzo had no desire to work for a living, something she herself didn't understand. Despite his lazy, carefree attitude, he was a nice guy and seemed respectful of his elders. The thought of him being used by Daphne sickened me. If Carlita found out, she would go crazy.

The shock on Lorenzo's face must have mirrored my own. "Hello, Tessa." He stared from me to Daphne, as if unsure what to do next.

"You again," Daphne drawled. "Tessa, you were always such a nosy little thing in high school. Still trying to snoop around and get dirt on people?"

"I wasn't snooping," I lied. "I planned to slip in the back door so I wouldn't disturb the signing, and no one would see me bringing the cannoli. Speaking of which, aren't *you* supposed to be helping Preston?"

Even in the semidarkness, I noticed Lorenzo stiffen at the mention of Preston's name.

"It's Mr. Rigotta to you," Daphne sneered, "and I'm on a break." She turned to go back inside, but Lorenzo grabbed her roughly by the arm.

"Let go of me!" she snapped and shook him off. "Crawl back under your pathetic rock. I have nothing else to say to you."

She slammed the door, and Lorenzo and I were left alone in the night, an uncomfortable silence stretching between us. Lorenzo stuck his hands inside the pockets of his worn jean jacket and refused to look at me. "Guess I'd better shove off. See ya, Tessa."

His expression was forlorn, and it bothered me to see him so upset, especially over a woman who wasn't worth his affections. Daphne had obviously stomped all over his heart.

"Hey, Lorenzo," I called. "Why don't you hold up for a minute? I've got to run inside with the cannoli, but maybe we could have a talk afterward?"

He gave me a sad smile. "They were good, by the way.

I had one while I was waiting for Daphne. They're even better than my mom's. Don't tell her I said that, though."

I laughed, hoping to lighten the mood. "Thanks."

Lorenzo shifted his weight nervously from one foot to another. "Speaking of which, I didn't see you here tonight, Tessa."

A chill crept up my spine. "What are you talking about?"

His untrusting eyes searched mine. "This is between us, okay? I didn't see you, and you didn't see me. Trust me. It's better that way."

Before I could say anything further, he disappeared into the darkness.

THREE

DAPHNE HAD CONVENIENTLY LOCKED THE BACK door when she'd gone inside the bookstore. I rapped on it with my free hand, thinking the effort was futile, but it was opened in seconds by Gabby. She stared at me with a puzzled expression. "Where were you?"

I held up the tray. "Sorry, I ran back home for the rest of the cannoli because we were out. How's it going?"

Gabby moved out of the way to let me enter, then glanced out into the alley and scanned both sides. Satisfied, she shut the door and locked it. "We ran out of biscotti, too, so I brought the plate back." She grabbed a napkin and began to move the pastries from my steel tray to the empty china dish. "Except for our unpleasant blast from the past, the evening was a huge success."

"That's fantastic! I'm so happy for you. Hey, is it

normal for authors to bring their family to signings with them?"

"Some do," Gabby replied. "Personally, I think Sylvia uses it to her advantage to get more attention for her show. Willow is in charge of Preston's website, joined at the hip to her parents, and basically has no life from what I've heard. She's at her father's beck and call constantly."

"How old is Willow?" I asked. "She looks like she's still in high school."

"Her father mentioned that she'll be twenty-one this month." Gabby glanced around. "Where the heck did I leave my keys? Oh, never mind. They'll turn up eventually. Preston's still chatting with a couple of fans, but I sold the last of his books five minutes ago." She exhaled a sigh of relief. "This may get me out of the red for a little while, Tess."

I placed the tray down on the table and hugged her. "You worked hard on this event and I'm so proud of you." But my mind was still in the alley, recalling Daphne and Lorenzo's ugly exchange. Had he threatened her? It sure sounded that way.

Gabby was watching me intently. "What's wrong? You look like you've seen a ghost."

"Nothing. I'm fine." I didn't want to bring up Daphne's name again. Let Gabby enjoy her success for a little while. It could wait until tomorrow.

Her face glowed. "Lou's here—he's pulling a late shift tonight. I was just grabbing him a can of soda. He's the one that finished up the last of the biscotti."

"Is your brother with him?"

"No, he's not working tonight. The twins had a concert at school. Gino called me earlier and said he was sorry that he and Lucy couldn't make it to the signing, but I honestly didn't expect them. Gino barely has time to eat these days, let alone read a book."

As the sole police detective in Harvest Park, Gino was dedicated to his job, and the well-being of the town and his family. Although he drove Gabby nuts with his overprotective ways, she knew she was lucky to have him. I had no siblings, but Gino always looked out for me as well.

Gabby picked up a Snoopy mug with a picture of a red wagon filled with books. I sniffed the air. Her drink didn't smell like coffee. "Is that wine? Aren't you driving?"

Gabby grinned. "Oh, chill. Only one mug to celebrate. Want to join me?"

"Thanks, but I'm good."

She yawned. "Man, I'm drained. My adrenaline has been pumping all week for tonight, and now I'm so tired I can barely keep my eyes open." She glanced at the wall clock. It read five minutes to nine. "I'd better get back out there. I know Preston wants to leave." She moved my empty stainless-steel tray to the top of the microwave and picked up the plate of cannoli. "By the way, everyone was raving about the cannoli and biscotti. Lots of people took your card, too."

"That's wonderful!" I said excitedly. "Looks like it was a great night for both of us."

She gave me a high-five. "Darn straight it was." Gabby opened the door, and we walked back to Preston's signing table. He was chatting amiably with a couple of star-struck females while Sylvia stood stiffly a few feet away. I wondered when she had returned. Sylvia's eyes were glued on Daphne, who was giggling and touching Lou's arm as she chatted with him. I glanced around the store but didn't see Willow anywhere.

When Gabby saw Daphne talking to Lou, she froze. Lou smiled over at her and said something to Daphne, but she refused to let go.

"That does it," Gabby grumbled. "She's been trying to get under my skin all night long."

"Gabs—" I tried to hold her back, but it was no use. She walked over to Lou and put her arm around his shoulders, then shot Daphne a death glare. Daphne merely shrugged and went to refill her plate. She'd already eaten several, so it was evident that she was a fan of my cannoli.

"Gabs, I've been chatting with your hunky cop friend here." Daphne took a large bite of the pastry, then wiped her hands on a napkin. "My, isn't he a keeper!"

Gabby kept one hand protectively on Lou's arm. "Yes, I think so."

"How long have you two been together?"

"About five months." Lou ran a hand over his blond buzz cut and smiled at my cousin with warm green eyes. He was good-natured, easy to like, and, in my opinion, the perfect guy for Gabby. As a cop, Lou was also intuitive, and it seemed he had already gotten the message that there was no love lost between the two women. Gabby had never been the clingy type. She was simply doing it to make a point. This was also the longest relationship Gabby had ever been in. I knew she cared deeply for Lou and vice versa and secretly hoped they might tie the knot someday. Aunt Mona was not as subtle about it. Every morning she drew out her rosary beads and said a little prayer that her daughter wouldn't wind up an old spinster.

Daphne reached for another cannoli. "These are so good. Guess you can't eat them because they'd go straight to your hips, huh? Too bad you never lost that baby fat, Gabby."

I had started to clear the table of abandoned, empty coffee cups when a loud shriek punctuated the air. Gabby's cup of wine was all over the front of Daphne's dress. Preston's fans were gaping, and he looked livid. Gabby and Lou appeared shocked, as if they didn't understand what had just happened.

"You did that on purpose!" Daphne screamed.

Gabby put a hand to her mouth. "Oh, my goodness. Daphne, I'm so sorry! Your dress is ruined. Here, let me help." Gabby gingerly held out some paper napkins.

Everyone was staring at the ruined dress, except for me. I was focused on Gabby's face. For a split second I caught an expression of immense satisfaction in those wideset eyes of hers, and my suspicion was confirmed.

Daphne snatched the napkins from her angrily. "Baloney. That's the type of juvenile behavior I'd expect from someone like you. You've always been jealous of me."

"Jealous?" Gabby echoed in disbelief. "Why would I be jealous of a pretentious snob who thinks she's better than everyone else? I'd be happy never to set eyes on you again."

Daphne looked shell-shocked as she grabbed her purse off a nearby chair. "That does it. I'm leaving." She turned to Preston, who had a bewildered expression on his face. "I'll be in touch tomorrow about the sales." She shot Gabby a venomous glare and then stomped past us on her way to the front door. A second later bells jingled, and the door slammed loudly.

Color rose in Preston's angular face. He smiled cordially at the two readers, but they'd already figured out it was time to leave. One woman picked up two cannoli while the other one gave us a fleeting smile, and they hurried to the front door tightly clutching their copies of Preston's book.

Preston glowered at Gabby. "Miss Mancusi, your behavior toward my publicist was extremely unprofessional."

"I kind of liked it." A sly smile crossed Sylvia's face.

Preston glared at his wife but said nothing.

"I'll wait for you in the car, darling," Sylvia drawled. She moved to the front of the store without a single word to me or Gabby. I was starting to think I was invisible.

"Preston, I'm so sorry." Gabby said meekly. "It was an accident. Honest."

Preston puffed out his chest. "When more orders come in, we'll provide signed bookplates to ship. I don't care to set foot in your sordid little store again."

Gabby looked crestfallen, so I spoke up. "One minute, Mr. Rigotta. Gabby's been running herself ragged all week for your signing. There's no reason to treat her like this. Daphne has been trying to make trouble for her all evening. She had no right to talk to her like that, or anyone for that matter. Gabby only wanted to make this a successful evening for you and herself."

"Tess." Gabby's voice trembled, and I noticed that Lou, who wasn't usually demonstrative in public, had his arm around her. "It's all right. Really."

Preston looked at me like I was a piece of gum on the bottom of his shoe. "Tina, you might make excellent cannoli, but you should learn to keep your mouth shut in affairs that don't concern you. I'll never do another signing in this dump again." With that, he stuck his nose in the air and strode up the aisle. A few seconds later the bells announced his departure.

Gabby sank down into a chair and put her face in her

hands. "That's it. I'm ruined. When word gets out, no other authors will come here again."

Lou bent down next to her and squeezed her shoulders. "Come on, Gabs. It can't be that bad. The guy was a pompous jerk. Surely no one's going to believe him."

"You don't understand," she sighed. "He's a very powerful figure in the literary world. He'll tell fellow authors to avoid my store. And since he's local, he won't endorse it to his readers either."

"They won't believe him," I assured her. "Besides, that sounds very childish of him." Was the man really that petty?

"Babe, I've got to get back to work," Lou said. When Gabby rose from the chair, he planted a kiss on her cheek. "I'm off tomorrow. How about I pick you up about noon and we spend the day together? We'll do anything you want."

I turned and went into the back room, not wanting to intrude on their intimate moment. As I rinsed out the coffee pot, my phone buzzed with a text from Justin. Hey, I stopped by your house, thinking you might be home by now. Are you around tomorrow?

Why don't you come for dinner around seven? I typed out. The Italian in me always wanted to make sure the entire world was well nourished. Ever since his wife left him, Justin ate fast food or soup straight from the can. It made me ill when I thought about it.

I placed the phone on top of Gabby's dorm-size fridge and dumped the contents of the coffee urn into her sink. As I started to clean the inside, she appeared, purse over her shoulders. "Leave it to soak. I'll take care of it on Monday. Let's get out of here—I'm beat." She handed me the plate of cannoli.

"Why don't you take those home?" I suggested. Only six remained.

She shrugged. "I guess. Lou can eat them when he comes by tomorrow. If I'm feeling up to company by then."

I grabbed my purse. "Everything will be fine. Maybe you can call Preston up in a couple of days and try to smooth things over."

"Maybe." Gabby flicked the lights off and then locked and shut the door behind us. "But for now, all I want to do is go home, watch some television, and drown my sorrows in another glass of wine. Or five."

When I opened my eyes the next morning, Luigi's face was the first thing I saw. Lying on Dylan's pillow, he'd been gently tapping my face with his paw until I awakened.

"Okay, I know," I mumbled and turned over to check the clock on my nightstand. It read six o'clock on the dot. "Ugh. You're brutal, big guy." I stumbled to my feet, and he waited in the doorway as I grabbed my robe from the bottom of the bed.

We went downstairs together, and Luigi rubbed against my legs as I filled his dish with fresh water and star-shaped kitty crunchies. I toyed with the idea of going back to bed but knew that I wouldn't sleep. Lazy Sundays slumbering until noon were a thing of the past. Since Dylan's death I'd had a terrible time sleeping.

After I fixed my coffee, I looked around for my phone, but it was nowhere in sight. That was strange. I checked my purse but had no luck there either. I thought back to the previous evening and the last time I'd used it. Yes, I'd texted Justin back. I groaned out loud. I must have forgotten it in Gabby's back room. Shoot. I wasn't a big fan of social media but had recently created a Facebook page for the restaurant and a website. Plus, what if my interviewee needed to cancel? I also didn't know if Justin was coming over tonight for certain. I'd have to go over to the bookstore to retrieve it. With a sigh, I headed upstairs to shower.

When I emerged, it was almost seven o'clock. I got

dressed in jeans and a short-sleeved V-neck black sweater. I brushed my dark hair, mumbling when I found a couple of new grays, and then drew it back into a ponytail. I always wore it like that when I went to the restaurant. Perhaps I should look more business-like for my interviews, but it was Sunday and I wanted to be casual. It wasn't practical for a chef to get dressed up to work in a kitchen, so why put on airs for the interview?

I waited until eight o'clock before I called Gabby on my landline. As suspected, her cell rang three times and went to voicemail. I redialed the number, and she picked up after the second ring, sounding groggy and disoriented. "What?"

"Someone had a rough night," I teased. "Too much wine? Or did Lou stop by after his shift?"

"No, he's supposed to come over later," she murmured, as a crash sounded simultaneously in the background. Gabby swore under her breath. "I knocked over the rest of the bottle. At least there wasn't much left. What time is it? Wait, what day is it?"

Jeez Louise. She was in rougher shape than I'd thought. "Sorry to call so early. I left my phone at the bookstore last night and need to grab it. Can you let me in?"

"*Now?* Really, Tess," she moaned into the receiver. "Why don't you just run me over with your car while you're at it? That would be less painful."

This clearly wasn't one of her better days. "Okay, how about I stop over for your key and I'll go in myself? I'll need your alarm code, too."

"I didn't set the alarm last night. There's something wrong with the stupid thing. I've got a technician coming tomorrow to fix it. Can I leave the key on the porch for you? I need to go back to bed. I feel like death warmed over."

"Well, I guess, but you shouldn't leave it where—"

"Don't worry, Mom, it'll be fine. I'll put the key in an envelope in the mail slot." A small jingling noise could be heard on the other end of the line. "I'm getting it off my key ring right now." She paused. "Huh. That's weird."

"What?" I stuffed my feet into sneakers while I waited.

"The bookstore key isn't here."

"Are you sure?" She had a separate fob for the store but kept it on the same ring as her others. It was easily distinguishable by a clock face and the words printed on it, *So Many Books, So Little Time.*

"Maybe it separated from the rest," she sighed. "Oh well, I've got an extra one in my kitchen drawer you can use."

"I hope no one picked it up."

"What does it matter?" she asked. "I don't keep money in the register overnight, and when Preston spreads the word, my store will go belly-up anyway."

Preston and his posse, namely Daphne, had done quite a number on my cousin last night. "Come on. That's not like you. Stop the pessimistic attitude. The glass is always half full, not empty, remember."

She gave a low giggle. "That was my problem last night. Every time my glass was empty, I'd fill it halfway again."

I rolled my eyes toward the ceiling "How about I stop over with some minestrone after my interviews?"

"Yum, my favorite. No appetite right now, but maybe I could force myself to eat some later. You're not having dinner for the family tonight, are you?"

"Since our mothers are out of town, no, but you're welcome to join Justin and me. I'm making pasta with Bolognese."

Gabby yawned into the phone. "No thanks. I plan to sleep and then read before Lou comes over."

"Okay, rest up and we'll talk later."

"That's the best suggestion I've heard all morning," she murmured and clicked off.

I grabbed my purse, patted Luigi on the head, told him I'd be back soon, and locked up. Gabby had bought a small house in town shortly after Dylan and I moved into ours. If the bookstore went under, she'd be forced to move back in with Aunt Mona. And Gabby would rather die than let that happen.

Within five minutes I pulled up in front of her cute beige cottage. It had been built in the 1970s but only had one previous owner and was in very good condition. An old-fashioned swing hung on the generous screened front porch. In the summertime Gabby loaded it with pillows. She claimed it was her favorite reading spot on days off.

The key was where she'd promised, inside an envelope in the mail slot with my name on it. I peered in the window to thank her, but the blinds were all drawn and the house dark. No doubt that Gabby had gone back to sleep. Well, she was entitled.

As I drove to Once Upon a Book, I rolled the window down to take a moment to appreciate the beautiful spring day in my hometown. The temperature was already in the mid-fifties and our weather might finally be turning the corner.

Cobbled streets and brownstones were plentiful. Harvest

Park Avenue ran through the center of town, where both my restaurant and Gabby's bookstore were located. There was about a quarter of a mile radius between the two. A dozen or so shops peppered the road on either side of the main attraction—a beautiful park, rich in lush greenery during the summer.

The park was already starting to come to life, and in a week or two colorful tulips would be blooming, followed by my favorite flower, lilacs. The flowers were one of the things I loved most about spring. In the fall, grounds people would set out pumpkins for the annual festival. A sparkling tree light display would finish out the year for Christmas.

My first Christmas without Dylan had been a quiet affair, and except for the cookies I baked every year for friends, family, and various townspeople, I hadn't put in much of an effort. No one expected me to, and my family was even surprised that I'd volunteered to cook dinner, but it had helped me to cope with the day.

All the firsts had been extremely difficult for me—Dylan's birthday, Christmas, and our sixth anniversary last Valentine's Day. My mother told me it would get easier over time, and I clung to that aspiration.

The town looked deserted at this early hour. I pulled around to the back of the shop and into the alley, wishing that Java Time was open. A cup of Archie's dark roast would hit the spot right now. All the main necessities in life were located on the same side of Harvest Park Avenue—the Meat and Greet where I'd stop every week for spareribs and rump roast to make my braciole, Java Time, Carlita's bakery, and Gabby's bookstore.

On the other side of the park was Spice and Nice, where I bought my weekly supply of herbs and seasonings, which included fresh oregano, basil, and garlic. Next was The Flower Girl, an exotic floral shop where I'd already placed orders for bud vases and carnations for opening night. Grab and Go Grocery and Suit Yourself, a men's clothing store that Dylan had liked to frequent, rounded out the street.

I inserted the key into Gabby's back door, and the knob turned easily. The coffee urn was still in the sink where she'd instructed me to leave it last night. My phone was lying on top of the fridge, and the screen was loaded with text messages. My mother had asked how the signing went. *Oh boy.* There was one from Justin responding to my previous text, saying he'd stop over for dinner tonight.

Another message told me that my menus wouldn't arrive until Tuesday. Great. The last one was from the woman I was supposed to interview yesterday. She apologized for not showing up and said that she'd changed her mind about the job. Jeez, thanks a lot. Couldn't she have told me that *before* the interview?

I placed the phone in my jeans pocket and was about to leave when I noticed a single cannolo lying on the floor next to the door to the main room. We hadn't dropped any last night, or at least I didn't think so. Puzzled, I bent down to pick it up and realized immediately that this wasn't my cannoli. The filling was chocolate as opposed to my vanilla. This made no sense. What was going on?

Slowly I opened the door and proceeded into the store. It was quiet and still, with shadows cast from the sunshine outside. Uneasiness knotted the bottom of my stomach as I walked from aisle to aisle.

"Hello?" I called out. "Is someone here?"

There was no answer. At the end of the aisle labeled Romance, I spotted another cannolo. This one wasn't mine either.

Someone had clearly been enjoying a midnight snack at Gabby's expense. Had they found her key and entered the place after we left? Was anything stolen? Gabby couldn't afford any more losses right now.

Maybe I should call Gino. What if someone was still hiding here? I started to dial 911, and kept my finger hovered over the call button. Maybe there wasn't anyone in the store, but something was definitely wrong. When I reached the aisle labeled Mystery, several books were scattered on the floor. Another pastry was in the middle of them and, next to it, a hand. An unmoving, lifeless hand.

I let out a small whimper and clutched the end of the aisle to steady myself. *Oh no. Please Lord, no.* With dread, I forced myself to peer around the corner and look down at the floor.

Staring back up at me were the dull, lifeless eyes of Daphne Daniels.

FOUR

MY BLOOD RAN COLD AS I stared at Daphne's face. "Oh God." I forced my trembling knees down onto the floor and felt for a pulse in her wrist. Nothing. Those enormous brown eyes kept staring at me. Tears crept into mine as I searched for a pulse in her neck. Again, nothing. Despite the overcoat she wore, Daphne's body was ice cold. I knew she had to be dead.

In desperation I looked around, but it was a futile, almost laughable effort. There was no one here to help me. With a sob, I pressed "Call" on my phone and a woman's voice immediately came on the line. "911, what is your emergency?"

"Please send an ambulance—right away! There's a woman here. Oh, God. I'm sure she's dead."

"Slow down, ma'am," the operator said calmly. "What is the address?"

My mind had gone blank, and I had to stop and think for a moment. "Once Upon a Book—uh—23 Harvest Park Avenue. Please hurry!"

"All right, ma'am. What happened? Do you know this woman?"

"Her name is Daphne Daniels. I have no idea how she got inside." I had watched Gabby turn the lock on the door myself. "It belongs to my cousin." Poor Gabby. Things had gone from bad to full-fledged disaster for Once Upon a Book's future.

The operator interrupted my thoughts. "The EMTs are on their way. Stay on the phone with me until they arrive. Does she have a pulse?"

"No, and she's ice cold. She must be dead." My hands shook badly. How had this happened? Upon closer inspection, I noticed that Daphne's face was swollen. Dread settled on my chest like a heavy boulder. As I listened to the operator, I wondered what exactly had happened to her.

"Is anyone else there with you?" The operator inquired.

The woman was only doing her job, but I was about ready to go into full panic mode. Plus, I wanted to get her off the phone so I could call Gino. No matter where

I turned, there was no escape from those empty eyes of Daphne's. "I need to call my cousin—he's a cop—"

"Stay on the phone with me, ma'am," she said in a quiet but firm voice. "An officer will be arriving shortly. What is your name?"

"Tessa—Tessa Esposito."

"Do you see any other signs of distress? Does she look like she fell? Are there visible bruises?"

My heart raced as if I'd just run a marathon. I felt violently ill. Dylan's face appeared before me in a foggy haze, and I must have whimpered out loud because the operator's voice sounded alarmed. "Ma'am, are you all right?" she asked.

A siren wailed in the distance, and I sent up a silent prayer of thanks. I managed to get to my feet and held on to a bookshelf to steady myself. Vehicles with flashing lights pulled up next to the curb. "They're here," I managed to say. "I need to let them in. Thank you."

"All right, ma'am. Take care of yourself." The operator clicked off.

I walked on shaky, unsteady legs toward the door. When I opened it, the two male EMTs were poised to knock it down. "Where's the woman in need of medical assistance?" asked a tall man with bleached blond hair.

She's not ill, she's dead. "Three aisles down," I managed to say as they rushed past me with a gurney. I glanced out into the street and saw Gino's unmarked sedan behind their van. Thank God. Then I noticed a crowd of people starting to gather across the road. Great. This was all we needed. I walked over to where the men were trying to revive Daphne.

"Allergic reaction?" the first EMT said to his partner, a shorter man who sported a goatee.

"Possibly." He shook his head ruefully. "I'm not getting anything. From the looks of it, she's been dead several hours. We need the coroner."

So that was it. Daphne was really gone.

A hand settled on my shoulder from behind, and I almost jumped ten feet in the air. Gino was standing there, his jaw set in a determined manner. "Tess," he said. "What exactly happened here?"

"She—I—uh..." Tears welled in my eyes and ran down my cheeks. "I found her like that. She was already dead. I have to call Gabs—"

Gino pulled me to his side and spoke gently. "Slow down and stand back so you're not in their way." He addressed the man with the goatee. "What do you think, Jay?"

Jay frowned at my cousin. "I can't say for sure, but it looks like anaphylactic shock to me." He studied Daphne's face, which was ghostly white, except for the redness on her cheeks and around her mouth. "See the swelling? She's been dead at least nine or ten hours." He placed a sheet over her head. "Our job's done here, but we'll wait out front for the coroner to arrive."

"Thanks for getting here so quickly," Gino said.

"Gabby," I croaked out, and looked around for my phone. It was still in my hand. "I have to call her."

"Calm down." Gino wrapped an arm around my shoulders and walked me into the Employees Only room. "I phoned her as soon as I heard the call come in. She freaked and thought something had happened to you." He stared at me grimly. "So did I."

I wiped at my eyes with a paper towel. "I don't understand. How did Daphne even get inside? I watched Gabby lock up last night."

"Was that Daphne Daniels?" Gino asked. "The one who always gave Gabby a hard time in school?"

I nodded. "She was here at the book signing last night. She is—*was*—Preston Rigotta's publicist. We didn't even know until she showed up."

Gino grimaced. "That must have gone over well with my sister. And what are you doing here on a Sunday? The store is closed."

"Everyone was gone when Gabby and I locked up last night. I stopped over at her house this morning to get the key because I left my phone here. Gabby's store key was missing from her ring, so she gave me an extra one. Daphne must have found the other key and used it to get back inside."

Gino leaned against the table and studied me. He was commanding, with classic Italian looks—dark wavy hair, dark brown eyes, and an olive complexion. He'd been a detective on the Harvest Park police force for the past six years and was excellent at his job. Even though he drove his younger sister crazy, it was obvious how much he adored her and vice versa.

Gino always wore a guarded expression when performing his job, and it carried over into his personal life at times. His "cop face," Gabby called it. At this moment, his real feelings were exposed, and he lifted troubled eyes to meet mine. "This isn't going to look good for her," he said softly.

"What are you talking about?"

He answered my question with another. "How did she and Daphne get along last night?"

"Nothing has changed," I said. "Daphne was rude and conceited and fawned all over the author like a schoolgirl. When Lou stopped by later, and she found out he was Gabby's boyfriend, she started flirting with him as well."

Gino narrowed his eyes. "How did my sister respond? Oh wait, don't tell me. Did she throw a tray of cannoli at her?"

"Don't be like that," I said reproachfully. "Gabs put up with a lot of crap last night and went out of her way to avoid trouble. She spilled wine on Daphne, but it was an accident." *Okay, maybe not.* "The signing was a big deal to her."

"What exactly did she put up with?" Gino asked.

My temper flared when I thought back to Gabby's treatment. "Preston Rigotta, the author, acted like she was his servant, and Daphne tormented her all evening. For the record, Gabby isn't the only one who disliked Daphne."

Gino folded his arms across his broad chest. "Please go on. I'd like to hear more."

"Is this a formal statement? Should I get ready for a

trip to the police station?" I couldn't believe I'd have to go through an inquisition again. Shortly after Dylan died, Gino had been the one to tell me that his death in a car crash had not been accidental. I'd made more than my fair share of trips to the police station.

"Don't get sarcastic with me, cuz." Gino gave me a sour look. "I know you've been down this road before and don't like it any better than you do. But since you are the one that found Daphne, yes, you'll have to come in for a formal statement. It won't take long—"

"Tess?" Gabby's voice, panic stricken, called from the alley. She started to bang on the door, and I hurried over to open it. Her dark eyes were wide with fright as she hugged me. "Thank God you're all right! What happened? Who's hurt? Did it happen inside the store?"

Gino's mouth was grim. "Sis, you should sit down." He grabbed Gabby by the arm, but she shook him off. Her eyes were bloodshot, her hair messy, and her skin a sickly pallor. I hoped Gino didn't realize she was hung over.

"Don't treat me like I'm five, Gino," she snapped. "Tell me what happened. Someone got hurt in my store." She turned to me. "Did you let a customer in?"

"Of course not," I assured her and then looked over

at Gino expectantly, but he made no attempt to continue. Thanks a lot. It was probably better to just spit it out. "I found Daphne Daniels lying in one of the aisles when I got here. She's been dead for several hours."

Gabby put a hand to her mouth and staggered backward. Gino reached out to help steady her as a strangled cry broke from between her lips. "No way. How did she die? And how did she get in here?"

I shrugged. "Maybe she found your key last night."

"That doesn't make any sense," Gabby said. "Why would she come back here? Preston's books had all sold out. There was no reason for her to be here. Did she leave something behind?"

A police officer I hadn't seen before tapped on the door and motioned to Gino. "Sorry to interrupt, Detective Mancusi, but can I have a word with you?"

Gino pressed his lips together and nodded. "Excuse me for a second, ladies." He and the officer walked into the Self-Help aisle where they continued speaking in hushed voices so we couldn't hear.

Gabby and I followed them into the store, and she immediately sank into the chair Preston had used for his signing last night. The pillows were still there. "Why? Why did this happen? Couldn't she have picked somewhere else to die?"

"Gabs!" I was horrified by her choice of words.

She shot me a sheepish look. "Sorry, that came out wrong. Look, I know we never liked each other, and I'm sorry she's dead. But if anyone finds out that she died *here*, I might as well shut the doors forever."

I glanced up front. The other policeman was still stationed by the front door, and the crowd outside seemed to have thickened behind him. "Uh, Gabs, I hate to say it, but I don't think we're going to be able to keep this under wraps."

Gino walked over to us. He was holding a plastic bag with two cannoli inside, the ones I'd spotted on the floor. He held the bag out to me. "It looks like Daphne was eating these when she died, or shortly before. You made them, right?"

I shook my head. "Not these. Mine had vanilla filling, not chocolate. There were only six left, and Gabby took them home with her."

A muscle worked at his jawbone. "Are you sure?"

"They're still at my house, if you need them for evidence, detective," Gabby said snidely.

"Of course I'm sure." He was making me nervous. "I'd know my own cannoli. You're scaring me. Do you think that's what killed her?"

Gino watched his sister closely. "Possibly. From the looks of her she had an allergic reaction to something, and food is usually the culprit."

I swallowed hard. "She ate several of my cannoli during the night and was fine."

Gabby placed her hands on her hips. "What are you saying? Do you think someone deliberately killed Daphne by adding something to the cannoli?"

He held up a hand. "Whoa. I don't know anything yet. Toxicology tests will take a while to come back. In the meantime, we'll have the cannoli analyzed to see what we might find inside. Look, Gabs, I know you guys didn't get along in high school—"

She shot him the evil eye. "Gino, that was twelve years ago. Give me a little credit. Sure, I couldn't stand her, but for God's sake! I don't carry grudges around in my back pocket. Do you really think I could have harmed her?"

"I never said that," Gino replied, his eyes darting around the store, as if he was afraid someone had overheard. "What I want to know is, did she argue with anyone else last night? How did she get along with Preston's fans?"

Gabby groaned. "I need coffee. Anyone else?" We followed her back into the Employees Only room and she filled the pot with water.

"Daphne herself didn't have many fans," I admitted. "I overheard Preston and his wife arguing about her. Sylvia implied that he was having an affair with Daphne."

Gino's jaw dropped. "Are you sure about this?"

"What?" Gabby shrieked as she spooned coffee into the machine. "Why didn't you tell me?"

"Because I didn't want to upset you during the signing," I said. "I was going to tell you tonight."

She gritted her teeth in annoyance and pressed the "On" button for the coffeemaker. "I was already upset when I saw her manhandling Lou."

"That's when you threw the wine at her," Gino volunteered.

"No!" she said angrily. "Stop trying to make me out to be the bad guy here. Preston immediately sprang to her defense and said my behavior was deplorable. Then he swore he'd never do another signing in my store. I couldn't believe he stuck up for her. Tess is right. They must have been having an affair."

Gino cursed under his breath. "Do you have anything else to add, Tess?"

I hesitated for a second too long. My face must have given me away because they both looked at me in alarm. Shoot. I hated to bring Lorenzo into this, but Gino needed to know what I'd heard. "During the signing I went back to my house to grab a tray of cannoli I'd forgotten. When I returned, I used the back door. Daphne was in the alley, talking with someone."

Gabby sucked in a sharp breath. "Lorenzo Garcia."

"How did you know?"

"Carlita's son?" Gino asked. "Why was he there? No offense, but he doesn't strike me as the bookish type."

Gabby looked nervously from Gino to me. "I was waiting on a customer when I saw Lorenzo come in. I thought it was a little strange, because I'd never seen him in here before. When I finally got a chance to run into the back room and found Tess waiting in the alley, I remembered that I hadn't seen him leave. So I kind of put two and two together when you said someone was with Daphne. I wasn't aware they knew each other let alone that they might be—involved."

"Sounds like Daphne made a few enemies last night," Gino remarked. "I don't like to speak ill of the dead, but apparently not much has changed since high school. What happened after that?"

Gabby looked at me. "Guess this is where you come in."

"They were arguing," I said tersely. "She called him a loser, and he accused her of only being interested in Preston and his money. Daphne told him they'd had some fun, but it was over with now."

"They said this right in front of you?" Gino asked, amazed.

My face heated. "Ah, no. They didn't know I was there. I heard them talking so I—"

"Wait, let me guess. You thought you'd eavesdrop." Gino grunted and shook his head. "Why am I not surprised?"

Gabby bit into her lower lip. "Do you think he did it? Maybe Lorenzo came back to meet Daphne."

"I don't think he harmed her," I said quickly. "Plus, we don't even know yet if someone intentionally killed Daphne."

"Right." Gabby poured coffee into three cups and handed one to Gino and me. "Maybe she had an accident."

Gino frowned as he sipped his drink. "Doubtful. If I have to wager a guess, I'd say that she had a reaction to the cannoli and died. What's in cannoli that could have caused her to become ill?"

"No idea. Maybe she was allergic to dairy?" I suggested. "But she was eating them all night, so that doesn't make sense."

Gabby grabbed her brother's arm. "You have to keep this quiet, Gino. If anyone finds out she died here, my store is ruined!"

He looked at her sympathetically. "I'll do what I can, Gabs, but there's a crowd outside and they're about to see a body go past them. It's already out of my hands." He took us each by an arm. "You're going to have to come down to the station and give a full statement."

"But you already questioned us," Gabby protested. "Isn't that enough?"

"You're both related to me," Gino explained. "Another officer will need to take it from here. And then my boss is going to pull me aside and tell me I'm off the case."

"No way!" Gabby narrowed her eyes. "Because you're my brother."

He nodded. "Exactly. Warner is strictly by the book. There's no chance he'll let me work this."

"What about Lou?" Gabby asked.

Gino pursed his lips. "Doubtful. Everyone at the station knows you two are dating. Let's get the statements over with, but there's something else I need to tell you."

A sick feeling swept through me. "We're suspects in Daphne's death, aren't we?"

"What?" Gabby exclaimed.

"You were both here last night." Gino pointed a finger at me. "You made cannoli, and even though the ones we found aren't yours, we don't know where they came from. Plus, it's Gabby's store and people saw her fighting with Daphne. You each have a history with her."

"I can't believe this is happening," Gabby moaned.

Gino pinched the bridge of his nose between his thumb and forefinger. "Look, I know it sounds crazy, but what I think doesn't count. So, to answer your question, Tessa, yes. For now, you're both suspects in Daphne's murder."

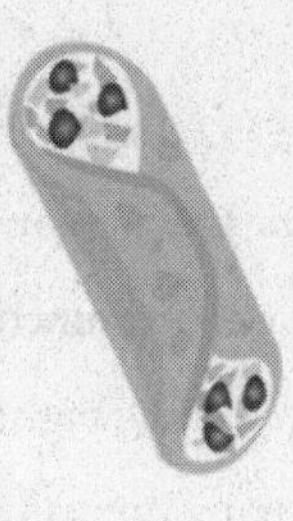

FIVE

THIS WAS NEW TERRITORY FOR ME. I'd never been a murder suspect before, but had almost been the victim a few months back when someone had tried to kill me during my hunt for Dylan's murderer. So far, neither role held much appeal.

Gabby's situation was far worse than mine. As Gino mentioned, people had witnessed the argument between her and Daphne. Preston had defended his publicist, and I was certain that he wouldn't lend Gabby any support. Unless the killer was found immediately, her business was sure to suffer.

After Gabby was questioned, Gino led me into the interrogation room where a burly man was sitting cross-legged behind a small square table. With horror, I noticed that both the table and chairs were bolted to the floor. I turned back to look at Gino, who nodded and gave me an encouraging smile.

The man stood when we came in. He was taller than Gino's six-foot stature with broad shoulders like a football player, short, cropped auburn hair, and a well-trimmed beard that slimmed his face. But it was his eyes that caught my immediate attention. They were a piercing metallic blue that seemed to look right through me.

"Tess, this is Detective Padraic McDermott," Gino said. "He's new to our town. Paddy, my cousin Tessa Esposito."

I extended a hand. "Nice to meet you."

He nodded curtly at me, and then his eyes shifted to Gino. "Mancusi, I'll take it from here."

The detective's tone was cool and abrupt. I turned to Gino, expecting him to say something, *anything*. Gino certainly was allowed to stay in the room with me. Or was he? Maybe the fact that we were related automatically forfeited that right.

Gino patted me on the shoulder. "I'll be right outside, Tess."

My stomach sank as I watched him leave. The detective eyed me sharply while he sat back down and thumbed through a file. A wave of anxiety passed over me. Sure, policemen weren't supposed to be fuzzy and warm, but this guy's demeanor was colder than a New York icicle in January.

Paddy nodded to a chair. "Please sit down, Mrs. Esposito." He gestured to a digital video recorder on a shelf next to him. "I'll be recording this conversation, of course."

This guy was making me feel like a common criminal. "Where are you from, Mr. McDermott?" I asked, my attempt to make small talk.

He looked up from the file he was studying and frowned. "It's *Detective*, Mrs. Esposito. I worked at the Brooklyn PD before coming here."

"How do you like our town?" Harvest Park was a picturesque place, especially this time of year when everything was starting to come alive again after the winter. Buds were blooming, grass growing, and the park itself turning a lush green and smelling of honeysuckle.

Paddy's eyes met mine, and the expression in them unnerved me. "Sorry to say, I'm not really a fan. Too much gossip and everyone minding each other's business in small towns like this. Guess there must be nothing else to do around here." He grunted in exasperation.

His words stung like a wasp. How could anyone dislike Harvest Park? Sure, people were inquisitive here, but mostly out of genuine concern for one another.

I was about to reply when he cut me off. "You were the one who found Miss Daniels?"

"That's right." I nodded.

"Did you try to perform CPR on her?"

"No, I called 911 right away. It was obvious to me that she was already dead."

He looked at the report. "And there were books and food scattered near her body?"

"Yes," I said. "Cannoli."

He made a face. "I hate those pastries. Too sugary for my taste."

You should try one. Maybe it would help sweeten you up.

"So, what did you put in the cannoli?"

My head shook from side to side. "I didn't make them."

He examined my face closely. "Your cousin stated that you made cannoli for her book signing."

"Yes, but not the ones found next to Daphne's body."

"I see." The doubt was evident in his tone.

I struggled to control my temper. "There's no reason for me to lie about it. I made cannoli with vanilla filling, and the ones by Daphne were chocolate. You can ask anyone who was at the signing last night."

He clicked the ballpoint pen in his hand several times,

as if trying to process a thought. "The background check on you says that you're a trained chef. I'm sure it would be easy enough for you to make more than one batch."

I didn't like what he was implying. "I already told you that I didn't make the cannoli. Did Gabby tell you that she took the rest of mine home?"

"She did," Paddy agreed. "But since she's your cousin she may be saying that to protect you."

If this man wanted to get under my skin, he was certainly doing a good job. "I had no reason to kill Daphne. Why, I haven't even seen her in years."

A slight smile tugged at the corners of his mouth. "Daphne and Gabby had an argument that was witnessed by several people. Your cousin said that she hoped she never saw her again. No offense, but I've asked around and heard that the two of you are as close as sisters. I'm sure you'd both have each other's back."

"You do know that Gabby is Gino's sister, right?" This man's arrogance amazed me.

He continued to click the pen obnoxiously until I was tempted to shove it up his nose. "I do. And that doesn't make one iota of difference." He leaned forward on his arms, putting his face near mine. "*Anyone* is capable of murder, Mrs. Esposito. Your cousin disliked Miss Daniels so much that she threw a cup of wine on her and ruined her dress."

"It was an accident," I snapped, then closed my eyes and counted to ten in my head. This wouldn't do. I was letting this guy get to me, and that would solve nothing. One false move and he'd probably lock me up and throw away the key. Paddy was trying to get a rise out of me, and I wouldn't give him the satisfaction. "Sorry, I didn't mean to be rude."

He ignored my comment. "When was the last time you saw Miss Daniels?"

"Right after the wine landed on her dress. She became angry and stormed out of the bookstore."

Paddy wrote something down. "And you didn't see her again later last night?"

"No, sir."

"Not even when you returned to the bookstore with your cousin?"

Heat rose in my face. Was the detective trying to set me up? "No, because I never returned to the bookstore until this morning."

Paddy crossed his left foot over his right knee and sat

back in the chair. "What were you doing there on a Sunday morning?"

"I left my phone in the back room. Gabby gave me a spare key and I let myself in."

"Because she was too drunk to let you in herself? Is it possible your cousin went on a late-night drinking binge, drove to the store to meet Daphne, and doesn't remember?"

"No!" I exploded, forgetting my earlier resolve not to let him make me upset. "That's ridiculous!"

To my surprise, Paddy rose from the chair and indicated for me to do the same. "I think I have everything I need for now, Mrs. Esposito. I'll be in touch if I want more information. Have a nice day."

"My cousin had nothing to do with her death. Someone met Daphne at the store last night—they brought cannoli and—"

He waved a hand at me dismissively. "That's all."

While I watched him, Paddy opened the door for me. In shock, I forced my feet to move forward. Maybe he had everything he needed, but *I* didn't. I gritted my teeth in exasperation. Who the heck did this guy think he was? He'd practically accused both Gabby and me of murdering

Daphne in cold blood. I almost let the door slam behind me but caught it in the nick of time.

Gabby sat on the wooden bench near the front counter. Gino stood next to her, paper cup of coffee in hand. "How did it go?"

I looked at him in astonishment. "How did it go? That guy is a first-class jerk!"

"More like a lowdown snake," Gabby said angrily. "He thinks I killed Daphne!"

"Keep your voices down," Gino muttered under his breath.

Gabby stood and put her face next to her brother's. "Are you going to let him abuse your family like that? He had no right! Why he even—"

Gino's face turned a crimson color. He put the coffee cup in the trash, grabbed Gabby's arm, and dragged her outside the station, with me following. Once we were in the lot, he turned on her, his eyes blazing.

"You need to knock it off," he said quietly. "I know Paddy seems a bit on the rough side, but that's just the way he is."

She shot him a look of amazement. "A bit? Was he a criminal prosecutor in a previous life? Because he would have made a great one."

"He was a jerk to you, too," I pointed out to Gino. "You've been a detective here for almost six years. You don't need to take that kind of treatment from the likes of him."

"You two don't know anything about my situation," Gino said. "Paddy's a former New York City detective. He's seen it all. Major drug busts, prostitution rings, homicides on a daily basis. We're lucky to have someone with his experience here."

Gabby's eyebrows shot up. "You've got to be kidding."

Gino shook his head. "Smalls towns like Harvest Park are dying to have a detective like Paddy on their force, with his knowledge and contacts. It's just a shame that he doesn't want to be here."

I tried to hold back a snort but didn't quite make it. "That was obvious. He basically said that we had nothing better to do but sit around and gossip all day."

Gino's mouth twitched at the corners. "You have to understand. Sure, he's a bit rude and abrasive. Most big-city cops are. But he's been doing this for more than twenty years and has a heck of a lot more experience than me."

"So, why's he here if he doesn't want to be?" I asked.

Gino glanced around the lot, as if worried someone might hear. "You can't go repeating this, okay? Paddy was fired from the force. He has family in Albany, so when he heard about the opening in Harvest Park, he applied. We know he might decide to leave at any time, but Warner wants to keep him here as long as possible."

"What did he do?" Gabby asked. "Assault a suspect? Gee, what are the chances?"

Gino grunted in exasperation. "No, pain in my butt. Colleagues of his were involved in tampering with evidence. He knew about it but wasn't directly involved himself. He has a legal obligation to report such things. When questioned, he decided to retire and the department agreed not to charge him. After six months he came back to the force. It's been done before."

Gabby's eyes were shining. "What were they tampering with?"

"None of your business," Gino retorted. "I already told you more than you should know. Look. No one's going to charge you guys with anything. It would have to be over my dead body first. If Paddy comes looking for you again, just humor him, okay? It will make my life easier too, trust me."

He ruffled Gabby's hair and then turned and went back inside. With resignation, we got into my car and I drove back to the bookstore where she'd left hers. Thankfully the earlier crowd had dispersed.

"My brother the wimp," Gabby said furiously. "I never thought I'd see the day."

"Let it go," I replied wearily. "He's got a wife and kids to think about. He can't afford to rock the boat, no matter how long he's been there."

"But it's ridiculous," Gabby fumed. "Paddy is focused on us, not the real culprit. At this rate, he'll never find the killer. All we need is for it to get out that you and I had something to do with the murder. Then we'll both be hanging *going-out-of-business* signs."

My doors hadn't even opened yet. I'd never heard of a business that had closed before its first day. Maybe I'd be setting some new type of record. Despite everything, I tried to think positive. "Want to hang out with me? I have an interview in an hour."

"No thanks," Gabby sighed as she let herself out of my car. "If anyone needs me, I'll be in bed with the covers pulled up over my head."

I mulled over the morning's events while I sipped a cup of coffee in Anything's Pastable's kitchen. It had started to rain a little while ago, and I listened to its comforting sound on the roof. Still frustrated, I closed my eyes for a few seconds. The restaurant's opening had taken a backseat to becoming a suspect in a murder. Things weren't looking good for either Gabby or me right now. Gabby was furious that her brother couldn't work the case and felt like he'd betrayed her. Deep down I suspected she knew it wasn't his fault but needed to blow off steam—and Gino was an easy target.

As the day wore on, things proceeded to go downhill. My first interview at one o'clock had arrived fifteen minutes late and immediately wanted to know what kind of health benefits were available. Since my staff was under twenty people, I wasn't obligated to provide medical insurance, plus there was no way I could afford it at this point. When I'd explained there was none available, she'd gotten up and left without another word.

I carried my coffee back to the table where I'd been conducting my interviews. In the downtime I'd put together a list of things to get done before opening night. The permits and fire inspections had all concluded last week. I was still waiting on the menus, and the new sink in the bathroom was dripping, but that could be put off if necessary. Yesterday I'd hired a linen service, so that was one thing to cross off my list. I was in the process of obtaining more vendors for food deliveries and figured that I'd probably have to order produce three times a week, and meat at least twice.

Then there was the matter of the restaurant's taxes. Dylan had been an accountant by trade, so that would have been ideal. There were plenty of people he'd worked with whom I could consult, but he hadn't left the company on good terms and I was reluctant to hire one of his former coworkers. Gabby had used Dylan for Once Upon a Book before, but I'd forgotten to ask her who had done the store's taxes for the past year. I made a note to check when she was in a better frame of mind.

The search for qualified help was starting to depress me. I'd never dreamed it would be so difficult to find people who were both eager and willing to work. My stomach twisted. What if the three waitresses I'd hired didn't show up on opening night? I prayed that my last interviewee today would work out. Heck, I hoped she at least *showed* up.

I glanced down at the application in my hands, the result of an ad I'd placed online last week. Stephanie Beaudry was only a year younger than me, but her name wasn't familiar. For work experience she'd listed two years of waitressing at the Golden Spoon Diner in Delaware until last November. Her address was 29 Summer Place, a five-minute walk to my restaurant.

My phone buzzed with a text, and I stared at the screen. It was from Vince. Will you be at the restaurant today?

My fingers flew over the keyboard. I'm here now. What's up?

His response came promptly. How about a private tour? I'd love to see what you've done lately.

Sure. I'll be here for a while.

Vince had been in New York City for the past couple of days. He'd lived there at one time and owned a gourmet restaurant until it closed last year, through no fault of his own. It was always fun to chat with him about my vision for the place because he was one of a few people I knew who understood the business, plus he'd given me several useful tips.

We'd gotten off to a bit of a rocky start last fall when I'd been employed at Slice. Vince had occasionally helped out in the kitchen as a favor to the man who'd been renting the building from him at the time. A sous chef himself, he didn't seem interested in pursuing cooking full time. He had no other job, at least not one that I knew of, and I couldn't help but wonder how he spent his days. Did he have an unlimited pile of cash at his disposal? Vince never held his hand out for the rent money, but I was careful to always pay on time.

The private tour part made me uneasy. Sure, Vince was interested in the restaurant, but there was a time when he'd also been interested in me as well. He'd backed off from asking me out again after learning I was widowed but still made several visits to the restaurant each month, just to ask how things were going. Last month, he'd run into Gabby and me at Java Time and joined us for a cappuccino. He'd been polite, interesting, and charming as all get-out. Every woman who'd come into the shop while we were there had ogled him, some more discreetly than others.

I didn't have time to worry about giving Vince a tour right now. There were bigger concerns—like the fact that I'd found a dead body earlier today, and the new detective in town was breathing down my neck. Daphne's face kept appearing before my eyes. Suddenly, another thought occurred to me. Had Daphne been alone when she died? Was she lured there by someone else, or had she gone willingly to meet her killer? I tried to think who might hate

Daphne enough to want to kill her. The Rigotta women, for starters. Lorenzo. Was there someone else in the picture who hadn't been at the signing? What if—

"Mrs. Esposito?" A woman with short, curly auburn hair was standing in front of me. She gave me a shy, hesitant smile.

Startled, I jumped up from the seat and managed to knock my cup of coffee all over the cover of my planner. I hadn't even heard her come in. "Excuse me, I'm a bit distracted today."

The woman was quicker than me. She produced some napkins from her purse and started to blot the table while I ran out to the kitchen for a dish towel, then removed the tablecloth. "Please excuse me."

She examined my face closely. "Are you okay? You acted like you'd seen a ghost."

Or a corpse. There was no way I'd tell a potential employee about what had happened earlier, but the truth was that Daphne's death had affected me more than I'd imagined. "Fine, thanks. Too much caffeine. Are you Stephanie?"

She nodded and held out her hand. "It's very nice to meet you, Mrs. Esposito."

"Please call me Tessa." I picked up my coffee-scented

planner, thankful I'd bought a leather instead of cloth one, and gestured to a table near the fireplace. "Let's sit over here."

She took off her jacket and hung it on the back of the chair while I studied her. Stephanie was tall with a medium build, dressed in black slacks and a purple blouse. A dusting of freckles dotted her cheeks and upturned nose. Deep-set green eyes waited for further instruction as she sat down in the chair across from me. There was a girl-next-door quality to Stephanie that made her seem wholesome, and when she smiled it lit up the entire room.

I tried not to get my hopes up, but it was difficult. I had not checked references yet, because why bother if she hadn't shown for the interview? "Can I get you something to drink?"

"No thanks." She looked around the room in pleasure. "Wow. I've never been in here before, but my neighbor told me this used to be a dive pizza joint." Color rose in her neck. "Sorry. That sounded insulting. Sometimes I don't think before I speak."

I laughed. "That's okay. I didn't own the place when it was a pizza parlor."

Her cherry-colored lips parted into a winsome smile. "Alice, my neighbor, said that you'd done a lot of renovations. It's the talk of the town. I think the place is amazing."

"Thank you." I would never tire of hearing that. I glanced down at the application in front of me. "So, you waited tables for two years at the Golden Spoon Diner. How long have you lived in Harvest Park?"

"I moved here last December. I've been working at Pie Carumba since then."

Pie Carumba sold mouthwatering pies and cakes and had a small breakfast menu. They'd been a bit of stiff competition for Carlita lately. "Oh, I know the owner, Greg Dennison. He's a nice guy."

Stephanie nodded. "He is, but I'd prefer to work in a restaurant, not a bakery. If it's as a waitress that's fine, but I do have some training in the kitchen, too."

My eyebrows lifted. *Be still my heart.* This was exactly what I had been looking for—someone who might be able to help me create simple side dishes and do some hosting or waitressing if needed. "What type of training?"

"I went to culinary school, but I had to drop out after a couple of months," Stephanie explained. "My mother became terminally ill while I was there, so I quit and went back home to take care of her. She died three months later, and I've never regretted the decision."

My heart went out to her. "I'm so sorry. Did you

ever think about going back? Or decide you wanted to do something else?" I didn't want to pry, but she was easy to talk to and I found her candor refreshing. Most of the other applicants I'd interviewed hadn't been as forthcoming. Hope bloomed in my chest. *Please, please don't ask for an insane amount of money.*

Stephanie shifted in her seat. "I thought about it, but the timing wasn't right anymore. A year after she died, I got married and then immediately got pregnant with my daughter." She hesitated for a moment. "My husband didn't like the idea of me working. He was a bit controlling and when he started to become abusive last year, I left him."

"I'm sorry to hear that." An uncomfortable silence fell between us. This was an extremely personal subject that I didn't feel was any of my business, unless she wanted to pursue it further. "How old is your daughter?"

Stephanie's face brightened. "Zoe's five. I know this job would require nights, of course, and that's fine. I live in a duplex, and the woman on the other side has a daughter the same age and has already told me she'll watch Zoe. *If* I get the job, of course."

"The restaurant will be closed on Sundays and Mondays," I explained. "I plan to give everyone at least a thirty-hour work week, except for a couple of waitresses who have asked for less. For this position, I'd prefer someone to work four days with extended hours, say one to ten, or something like that. Closer to forty hours. It would be a little of everything—some light cooking and serving if we're shorthanded. The cooking wouldn't be too complicated and under my complete direction. I freeze many items ahead of time, such as pasta and my tomato sauce."

She looked impressed. "You make your own pasta? Not all restaurants do that."

"I like my food to be authentic."

"That's amazing. Alice told me that you were a trained chef. To have the opportunity to learn more from you would be a dream come true." Her expression sobered. "She said that your husband had died recently. I'm so sorry for your loss."

"Thank you," I said politely and quickly changed the subject. I explained what the job would pay and to my relief, Stephanie seemed fine with it.

"That's more than I make at the pie shop," she said. "Plus, a four-day work week would be fantastic." She nodded toward the application in front of me. "You have my references—well, if you're thinking about offering me the job, of course. I didn't mean to assume."

Oh, I was definitely thinking about it. "Yes, I do plan to call them."

She beamed. "Awesome. Is there any way I can see the kitchen before I leave?"

A girl after my own heart. "Of course you can." I rose from the table, and she followed me to my pride and joy. Sure, I was proud of the entire restaurant, but a chef's true passion was her kitchen.

"There used to be a pizza oven in this spot," I told her, pointing to the right. "A contractor built extra shelving and counter space in its place." I gestured to the other side of the room. "He also installed a pantry next to the fridge, and the stove is new." I had a love affair with my new gas stove—a ten-burner, Southbend stainless-steel piece of art with two standard ovens. It cooked everything to perfection and was an absolute delight to use.

"This is gorgeous," Stephanie said in awe as she ran her finger over the light-blue Formica countertops. "I hope I get the job." Then she blushed. "Maybe I'm not supposed to say things like that, but it would be terrific to work with you. I know I'd learn so much. What's better than doing something you love, and getting paid for it? Do you know what I mean?"

"Totally." Even though I'd been cooking since the age of ten, I still had to pinch myself at times that this was finally happening to me.

"Pardon me, ladies. I hope I'm not interrupting anything."

We both looked up. Vince Falducci was leaning against the doorway, a broad smile on his handsome face and a silver gift-wrapped box in his hand. He gave a slight bow. "Hail to the chef."

"Welcome back. I didn't even hear you come in." Vince had a key to the restaurant, and this wasn't the first time he'd shown up unannounced. It was still his building so he could do whatever he wanted, and he always did.

"That's because I move like a cat." He ran a hand through his curly, dark hair, which always looked slightly mussed. Stephanie's tongue was practically hanging out of her mouth as she watched him. *Oh brother.*

"This is Stephanie Beaudry. Stephanie, my landlord, Vince Falducci."

Stephanie recovered from her daze in time to give him

a full-fledged smile, which he returned. She held out her hand. "It's very nice to meet you."

"Likewise." Vince brushed his fingers against hers. The scruff around his mouth was more pronounced than usual, and when he smiled, his sensual lips parted, displaying perfect white teeth that glowed against his bronzed skin.

"I can wait in the other room until you're done," he told me. "I didn't realize you had company."

"That's all right. I've been interviewing Stephanie for a job." I turned to her, but she seemed to have forgotten me. "Stephanie, I have everything I need, unless you have further questions."

"Huh? Oh, sorry." She forced her eyes away from Vince's face and back to mine, her cheeks tinged with pink. "Um, when do you think you'll be making a decision by?"

I considered. "As soon as possible. The restaurant opens in less than a week. I'd say by tomorrow or Tuesday at the latest, depending when I hear back from the rest of the candidates." God, I was such a liar. Who was I kidding? Stephanie was my *only* serious candidate. How I prayed that her references would check out.

"Greg wouldn't mind if I had to give him less than a week's notice. He knew that I was coming here for an interview. I wanted to make you aware, in case that's a factor in your decision." Stephanie's eyes held a pleading look.

"Sounds good. Thanks for coming, and I'll be in touch soon."

"Bye," she said shyly, and then her face colored as she waved to Vince. He nodded casually while I bit into my lower lip, attempting to hide my smile. Vince was another Lorenzo type who attracted women like magnets.

After we heard the front door close, Vince placed the package on the counter in front of me. "Here you go. A little housewarm—er, I mean, a little restaurant-warming present."

"That was thoughtful, but you didn't have to do anything."

"I know," he teased and removed his leather jacket. Vince was wearing a short-sleeved, form-fitting navy T-shirt that displayed a prominent tattoo of a scorpion on his well-developed left bicep. "But you're going to love it."

I tore off the paper. Inside the rectangular shaped box was a custom-made cutting board. The background was red with white letters that read "Anything's Pastable When Tessa's in Charge."

I laughed out loud. "This is great! I'll hang it in here for inspiration. Thank you."

He smiled and leaned across the counter, his eyes dark and warm like fresh coffee beans in the morning. "You're welcome."

Vince seemed to be deep in thought as he watched me emptying the dishwasher. "Something wrong?" I asked.

His eyebrows rose, causing the scar above his left one to become more pronounced. "Not at all."

Then it dawned on me. "You're looking for the rent money." It wasn't due for a couple more days, but I had it ready.

Vince shook his head. "I'm not worried about that. I'm actually worried about you. Your car is always here."

Jeez, was he spying on me now? I barked out a laugh. "Well, that's usually the way it is when you own a restaurant. I'm sure you remember. You practically live there."

Vince ran a hand over his chin. "True. But this place hasn't even opened yet, and from what I saw of the main room, everything looks ready to go. It's almost like you're inventing work to do here."

I carried the plaque over to my office door. "Maybe I'll hang it here. What do you think?" I was purposefully avoiding his question, and he knew it. I wasn't going to admit it, but Vince was right. Except for a few minor details, everything was done, but I needed to keep busy. Some days were better than others, but I wasn't quite there yet.

When I turned around, Vince was standing there, arms folded across his muscular chest, watching me carefully. "What?" I asked.

His expression told me that I wasn't fooling him, but he merely said, "You're right—that's a great spot. Let me grab some nails and I'll hang it for you."

SIX

FOUR HOURS LATER, I HAD RETURNED to my happy place. I stirred the stainless-steel pan with carbonara, inhaling the rich and tantalizing scent. A pot of drained pappardelle stood on the counter next to it. I tossed the pasta into the pan of sauce. The carbonara coated the wide noodle strips to perfection and absorbed the sauce nicely.

My house smelled heavenly. I'd been fortunate to find *guanciale* from a specialty store about forty miles away and arranged for them to ship it directly to the restaurant, although I'd been warned they might stop carrying it soon. I could always get the meat directly from Italy, but that was an added expense I hoped to avoid. When I tasted the sauce, though, I knew that was irrelevant. Guanciale added so much more flavor than pancetta, and the fat from the pig's jowl made it tender and tastier.

As I continued to mix the sauce and pasta together, I reflected on all that had transpired earlier today. Gabby had filled me in on the latest when I'd stopped over with her minestrone. A few customers had tried calling her to ask what happened, but she'd chosen not to respond. I'd invited her for dinner again, but she'd refused. Lou had been called into work this evening, and I hated for her to be alone. Liza would be back at the store tomorrow, ready to work, and I hoped that Gabby had already told her about Daphne's death.

A knock sounded as I placed piping-hot garlic bread from my oven onto the table. Luigi trotted over expectantly and stood by the door, waiting. Justin, tall and athletic looking, with windblown, dark wavy hair, greeted me when I opened the door, a bottle of merlot in his hand. A broad smile broke out on his face when he saw me, and he stepped inside to give me a hug. "Hey, Tess."

"It's so good to see you." I gave him a squeeze and then took the wine from his outstretched hand as he stooped down to pet Luigi. When he stared up at me again, I was startled to see how much thinner his face was. He was still handsome in a rugged sort of way, but the fine cheekbones were compounded by a brittle look, most likely caused by too much responsibility and too little sleep. His smoky-gray bluish eyes were still the same, though, and they brightened when I smiled at him. "Is everything okay with you?"

"It will be." Justin stood up and wrapped an arm around my shoulders as we walked into the dining room together. He set the wine down on the table.

I wasn't sure what his comment meant. "Did you walk here?" He only lived a block away, and I hadn't seen his truck in the driveway.

He nodded. "Yeah. I needed the air."

Luigi rubbed against his legs. "Looks like someone missed me." Justin laughed and petted Luigi again, then scratched him behind the ears. "How's the big guy? Did you take care of everything while I was away?"

"Like a boss. Wine or beer?" I called from the kitchen.

"I'll take a beer for now, thanks."

I grabbed one from the fridge and set it on my breakfast counter, which he was now standing beside. "Back at work already?"

He sipped his drink and nodded. "Last night." Justin was a firefighter at the local station, an occupation that made me proud and terrified for his safety every day. As far as I knew, he'd never wanted to be anything else.

"How's your mom?"

Justin leaned over the counter, watching as I fussed with the salad. "She's okay. Every day is a little better than the one before. It's going to be tough for her—getting used to life without the man she's loved for so many years."

I said nothing. When I turned to offer him a glass, his eyes were stricken. "Oh God, Tess. I'm sorry. That was insensitive of me."

"It's okay." I picked up the cheese I'd grated earlier. There was something masked behind his eyes that bothered me. "Is there something else bugging you?"

Justin heaved a long sigh. "She's been talking about me moving back home."

"To California?" My heart sank into the pit of my stomach.

He nodded. "I can't do it, Tess. Katie will be back home in a year when she finishes college. I told Mom she can come to New York and live with me, but she hates the cold." His eyes regarded me solemnly. "And I don't want to leave here."

I didn't want him to leave either but refrained from saying so. It would only make things more difficult for him, and that wasn't my intention. Plus, I still had to relay the story of what had happened to Daphne before he heard it from someone else. Justin didn't need to worry about me on top of everything else. He had enough to deal with.

While I carried the pasta and cheese to the table, Justin brought the salad. Careful not to look at him, I said, "You have to do what's best for you and your family. I'm sure any fire department would be thrilled to have you."

"Thanks, Tess." Justin's eyes widened as he unfolded his linen napkin and gazed at the food. "Oh, wow. You made carbonara? This looks fantastic." He helped himself to a large portion while I brought a glass of wine to the table for myself. "So, tell me what's been happening while I've been gone. The restaurant opens what—next week?"

"In six days. You should stop by so I can give you a tour."

Justin took a bite and let out a groan. "This is amazing. You have no idea how good it feels to be back. What else is new in Harvest Park?"

"Well, now that you mention it…" I relayed the details of the signing last night and finding Daphne's body.

Justin's fork clattered against the china plate. "Tess, this is unreal. First you almost get yourself killed looking into Dylan's death last year, and now you find a dead body in Gabby's bookstore?"

I took a long sip of wine, and then another. “Yeah, I know. It’s like we have some kind of death hex on our heads. Poor Gabby.”

“Actually, I was thinking *poor you*. I mean, to find someone like that is a horrifying experience to go through.” Pain flickered in his eyes. “It’s something you never forget. God knows I’ve seen my share, and it doesn’t get easier. If anything, it becomes more difficult.”

I waited to see if he’d go on, but he didn’t. Justin usually refrained from lengthy conversations about his work, and I knew why. He saw devastating events all the time—lives and homes lost on a daily basis. When he managed to save someone, he’d modestly reply that he was only doing his job. Still, it had to weigh heavily on him. “You know that you can always talk to me about anything,” I said.

“I do know,” he said, “and hope you feel the same way.”

“Of course.” We lapsed into companionable silence for a few minutes while Justin continued to eat with considerable relish, as if he hadn’t seen a decent meal in days. My heart soared with happiness. Nothing pleased me more than to watch someone enjoy a meal that I had prepared. That’s what cooking was all about for me.

Justin reached for another piece of garlic bread and

eyed me sharply as I poured myself a second glass of wine. "You're not going to get drunk again, are you? I remember a night not too long again when you could barely stand."

I winced at the memory, and then we both laughed. "What a mess I was that night, huh? No, I don't plan on a repeat performance. Between the restaurant about to open and finding Daphne, I'm a bit on edge today."

"Yeah, that's understandable."

"There's something else bothering you. Do you want to talk—"

Justin's phone beeped, and he glanced apologetically at me as he drew it out of his pocket. "Sorry, Tess. It could be work."

"No worries. Go right ahead." I brought my glass to my lips as a loud pounding commenced at the front door. I stared at Justin, but he seemed distracted by the text message he'd received. So much for our quiet dinner. I went to answer the knock with Luigi at my heels. Another banging sounded before I could reach it.

"Tess?" Gabby's voice filtered through the door. "I need you!"

What now? I unlocked the door, and Gabby collapsed into my arms. "What's wrong? Are you sick?"

"Coffee," she croaked and made her way through the vestibule and past the dining area. She cocked her head at me when she caught sight of Justin, who was typing out a message on his phone. "Sorry," she said sheepishly. "I forgot you had company."

Justin looked up and gave her a quick nod. "Hey, Gabs. How's everything?"

"Welcome home. Nice to see you," Gabby said. When I came back to the table with her coffee, she pulled me down into the chair next to hers and immediately downed half her beverage.

"What's going on? Is this about Daphne?"

She stared at me grimly. "You and I are mentioned in the online version of the *Harvest Park Press* tonight. I told Gino about it, but he doesn't think Paddy gave our names to the newspaper. I for one am not so convinced."

"Paddy's a detective. Why would he do something like that?"

"Because he's a *jerk*!" In frustration, Gabby pounded her fist on the table. Startled, Justin looked up from his phone, and her face turned the color of raspberries. "Sorry."

"It must have been someone else," I insisted. "The media was probably at your store after I found Daphne's body."

Gabby sniffed. "Gino said that reporters constantly hang around the police station, trying to dig up dirt. But I wouldn't put anything past that creep. He's convinced that you or I have something to do with Daphne's death. He's like a bloodhound sniffing out a bone."

It felt like Paddy had a personal vendetta against us. "Do you have any more good news to share?"

She gulped her coffee. "Since my relationship with Lou is part of Harvest Park's grapevine, he's not allowed to work the case either." Gabby looked like she was about to cry. "And because Daphne died in my store I can't reopen until the police give the say-so, and with the big brute detective in charge, that's *never* going to happen." She wrapped her trembling hands around the mug to steady them.

"Oh, Gabs. He can't intentionally keep you out of there. I'm sure Gino will do something."

Gabby shot me a disbelieving look. "Gino said he'll speak to his boss, but if you ask me, everyone is walking on eggshells around the new kid in town. They don't want to rock the boat and lose the big-city detective wonder. The word is out that Preston's publicist died in my store. People know Daphne, and I have a history and not a good one. I even had to shut down Once Upon a Book's Facebook page because people were posting hateful messages. Let's face it, I'm ruined." She put her head in her hands as if it ached.

"No, you're not. We'll figure out who did this, don't worry." But I knew firsthand that word of mouth was vital to a business, especially new ones like mine and Gabby's. I'd been accused of serving Daphne the deadly dessert, and on top of everything else now I had to contemplate the unpleasant gossip about me and my new restaurant at Harvest Park's dinner tables tonight.

She pushed the empty mug toward me. "May I please have another? I'll take it black this time."

"Of course you can." I rose and looked over at Justin, who was texting again on his phone and seemed oblivious to our entire conversation. Maybe his mother was sending him pleas to return home. If it had been a work-related call, he would have already left.

As I refilled Gabby's mug, Justin came into the kitchen with his windbreaker on. "Tess, I'm sorry, but something's come up and I have to leave."

"Oh, no. Is it work?" Maybe I had been wrong. Justin's job was always unpredictable. He'd once confided to me that he believed his demanding career had led to his ex-wife Natalie sleeping around on him. In my book, though, there was no excuse for what she'd done. When he'd served Natalie with divorce papers, she'd walked away from the house they'd owned and not even offered him a dime. Justin was so anxious to get on with his life that he hadn't pursued the matter.

Justin hesitated. "No. It's something else."

I placed the mug in front of Gabby and walked with him to the front door. "Your mom? Is she okay?"

He nodded. "I'll call you later, okay?" He turned and gave Gabby a wave. "Good seeing you, Gabs."

"Yeah, you too." She sighed into her mug.

Justin gave me a quick peck on the cheek. "Thanks for dinner. It was amazing." His troubled eyes searched mine for a second, and then a smile flickered across his face. "And so are you."

Before I could say anything further, Justin let himself out the front door. I waited as he jogged up the street, never glancing back once. What was going on?

When Justin had turned the corner and was out of sight, I closed the front door and went back into the dining room. I gathered up his empty plate, glass and beer can while Gabby watched me. "Why'd he take off so soon? Was it because of me? Sorry I'm such a downer."

"It isn't you." I knew Justin well, and his behavior had been different tonight. I suspected there was something besides his father's death bothering him. "He's not the same Justin that he was before he went away."

Gabby looked puzzled. "What do you mean?"

"He's distracted. Something else is going on."

Another knock sounded on my front door, and Gabby held up a hand. "You go ahead, I'll grab it. Maybe he forgot something."

When I returned from the kitchen, Gabby was sitting at the table with Gino beside her. "Hey, Tess. Sorry to interrupt your dinner," he said.

The look on his face told me this wasn't a social call. "Would you like some carbonara? I have plenty."

"No, thanks. Lucy made pot roast tonight. And she didn't burn it for once." Gino gave a wry smile. He loved to tease his wife about her cooking mishaps, but most of them weren't Lucy's fault. She was too busy chasing their six-year-old twins and never had a spare moment to herself.

Gino stared from me to Gabby. "I suppose Gabs has told you about the bookstore being closed, and the so-called leak in town."

"And let's not forget Detective Paddy McJerk who

wants Tess and me to wind up behind iron bars," Gabby scoffed.

Gino pressed his lips together tightly. "He's not going to arrest you. Paddy is just doing things the way he knows. I told you not to take it personally."

Incredulous, Gabby stared at him. "How am I supposed to take it then?"

"Paddy didn't cause the leak," Gino insisted. "There were reporters sniffing around the station earlier. It happens all the time. There is such a thing as freedom of the press, you know."

"Well, remind me of that when I can't pay my mortgage and have to move in with you and Lucy," Gabby retorted. "Because there's no way I'm living with Mom again."

I sat down on the other side of Gabby. "Are the toxicology tests back yet on Daphne?"

"No." Gino folded his hands on the table. "It could take a few weeks. But the testing on the cannoli was completed."

"I knew it," Gabby groaned. "She was poisoned. And everyone will think that I did it."

"What was wrong with them?" I asked fearfully.

"First off, a Gucci handbag was found in Gabby's

dumpster out back," Gino said. "It belonged to Daphne. There was an unused EpiPen inside."

"So, she did have an allergy," I mused.

Gino nodded. "Her father confirmed that it was a severe one, to shellfish."

Gabby looked at him like he had corn growing out of his ears. "What's that have to do with the cannoli she ate?"

"Let me finish," Gino said. "We found shrimp powder in the cannoli. Is that a common ingredient used to make them?"

"No, of course not," I said.

His mouth formed a thin, hard line. "I didn't think so. Then this was no accidental death. Someone wanted Daphne dead, and they got their wish."

SEVEN

GABBY PUSHED ASIDE HER MUG AND reached for the wine bottle. "I don't know how much more of this I can take."

Gino snatched the bottle out of her reach. "That didn't exactly help you last night, sis. A couple of customers mentioned that they saw you throw wine at Daphne."

"But I told you that I didn't!" She shrieked so loud that I was tempted to cover my ears. "Instead of lecturing me, why don't you try to help me?"

The lines in his forehead deepened. "If Sergeant Warner finds out I'm working this case against his direct order, I could lose my job, Gabs."

She closed her eyes. "Well, I might as well put up the going-out-of-business sign tomorrow."

"Don't talk like that," I chided her, trying to make sense of the situation. "Someone obviously knew about Daphne's allergy and hoped she'd eat the cannoli. They must have taken her purse away, so she had no chance to use her EpiPen. They brought the tray of cannoli in special for her. That clears Gabby, right? We left the store together."

Gabby opened her eyes and looked at me hopefully. "Besides, I didn't know about her allergy. I hadn't seen her in years before last night."

"Daphne's allergy wasn't exactly a secret," Gino said. "Preston was interviewed for the *New York Times* last month and asked about his favorite food. He said that it was scallops. He then went on to mention how he'd ordered the dish when out with his publicist for dinner one night and had to send it back because the smell of the seafood made her ill."

What great timing. Anyone who had seen that article would have known about Daphne's allergy. "So, if Preston knew, the rest of his family probably did, too, and the chances were excellent that Lorenzo was aware of it as well."

Gabby snorted. "From what you overheard, Tess, the chances are excellent that Daphne and Lorenzo were doing other things besides sharing a fish fry dinner."

"That's a delicate way of putting it," Gino mused. "What I'd like to know is, wouldn't someone notice that the taste was off in the cannoli? Fish and chocolate don't usually go well together, at least not in my book."

"Not if it was ground finely, which I suspect it was."

Uneasiness swept through me. Lorenzo worked in his mother's bakery. If he'd wanted to kill Daphne and put the blame on someone else, he knew enough about the pastry to make it work. Then again, it wouldn't be difficult for anyone, even Sylvia Rigotta, whose cooking skills barely rivaled Luigi's. "Maybe the killer found Gabby's key and lured Daphne there."

Gabby tried to snatch the wine back from Gino, but he was having none of it. She folded her arms on the table and sunk her head into them. "This makes me sick. Why would someone want to do this to me?"

Gino shrugged. "It might just be bad luck on your part. Is there someone who had a grudge against you and Daphne? Or maybe Tessa?"

I stabbed a finger into my chest. "You think someone is framing me?"

"Maybe someone hoped this would affect your restaurant opening." His eyes grew as dark as the sky outside. "Was there an individual who asked for a job at Anything's Pastable and you refused to hire them?"

I burst out laughing. "Don't I wish. Do you know what a tough time I've had finding capable help on what I'm paying?"

He spoke gently. "Tess, could there be another skeleton lurking in Dylan's closet that we don't know about?"

"Gino!" Gabby gasped. "How can you say such a thing? Hasn't she been through enough already?"

"It's okay," I said quietly. "I wondered the same thing, but no, I honestly don't believe it has to do with me or Dylan." There was no way I could go through that again. All the secrets he'd kept had devastated me. "How are we supposed to get to the bottom of this if you and Lou can't work the case?"

Gino cocked an eyebrow at me. "What's this *we* stuff? Don't even think of interfering."

Gabby straightened up with a definitive air. "Remember, Tess was the one to discover who murdered Dylan. Perhaps you've forgotten that important detail."

She was giving me way too much credit. "Yes, maybe a split second before I had a gun held to my head. And I don't deserve all the credit. You and Gino helped, too."

"No, I haven't forgotten." Gino pressed his lips together tightly. "Tess did a great job putting the pieces together. But she was reckless and almost got herself killed in the process. And ahem—someone else as well."

Gabby tossed her head. "I have no idea what you're talking about."

Gino was right. Once I had discovered Dylan's death was no accident, I'd been driven to find the killer at any cost, even if it meant losing my own life as well. Grief had consumed me, and I wasn't thinking straight. The worst part was that it had almost cost Gabby her life. I hadn't seen that coming until it was almost too late. But this time we were both suspects, so what else was there for us to do? I wasn't going to sit back and watch someone destroy our livelihoods. "Come on. What harm would it do if Gabby and I did a little snooping?"

Gino eyed the bottle of wine longingly. "You don't think Harvest Park's Police Department is smart enough to figure it out for themselves?"

"You know that isn't true." Why did he always have to be so stubborn? Because it was a family trait, and all three of us were guilty of it. "Of course the police know what they're doing."

"Even Paddy McJerk," Gabby commented. "He's a creep but nobody's fool."

I went on. "No one is personally invested in this like Gabby or me. The news about Daphne has already leaked out, and that will mean people staying away from her store." I hesitated before continuing. "If that happens, she may have to shut down."

My cousin's lower lip quivered as she voiced my unspoken thoughts. "It may affect Anything's Pastable's grand opening, too. Once word gets out that Daphne died from the cannoli—"

"No one's going to find that out," Gino said quickly. "People know she died at the bookstore but that's all."

"Right," Gabby mocked. "It's not like Harvest Park townspeople are busybodies or anything." She mimicked our local news anchor. "'The publicist for bestselling author Preston Rigotta, whom the bookstore owner hated, died of suspicious circumstances in the store after it had closed to the public for the night.' Gee, that makes me look like a peach, doesn't it?"

I spoke quietly. "All I'm suggesting is that Gabby and I talk to Preston and his family. Or maybe go down to the television studio and have a chat with Sylvia. I'll pretend that I need some cooking tips from her, or something."

Gabby looked at me in disbelief. "You're a trained chef, while she's an overpaid, glorified phony. Why would she believe that?"

"Why wouldn't she?" The woman had an ego larger than life and would probably eat it right up.

"Please, Gino." Gabby turned pleading eyes on her brother. "I can't sit around and do nothing while I wait for my store to close."

Gino's stern expression softened as he reached down to give his sister's hair an affectionate tousle. "A few questions with Sylvia, and that's all." He turned to me. "You're pretty close with Carlita, right?"

Uh oh. I had a feeling about what was coming next. "I guess. Why?"

"I don't know Lorenzo well," Gino confessed. "Paddy doesn't know Carlita or her family at all, and I have a feeling he won't get much out of them. I told him about the exchange you overheard between Lorenzo and Daphne, so he will be questioning him. Maybe it wouldn't hurt for you to have a little chat with Lorenzo and Carlita. She trusts you."

Great. I did not want to talk to Lorenzo about his relationship with Daphne, especially with Carlita overhearing.

She'd probably go into cardiac arrest. "I'm not sure I would be comfortable with that."

"Please, Tess," Gabby begged. "Without Gino or Lou working the case, what else can we do? You're my last hope. What if Paddy botches everything up?"

Gino stiffened at her words. "He's not going to botch it up. What do you think, he's a clown from the circus? I simply thought it would be a good idea since Carlita is fond of Tessa. They might open up a bit more to her."

"Carlita's not an idiot, Gino," Gabby scoffed. "She must know that Lorenzo's a ladies' man. I've heard there are nights when he doesn't come home at all."

I squirmed in discomfort. "I don't want to know the details of Lorenzo's love life." How would Carlita react if she knew that Lorenzo had been sleeping with Daphne and was now a murder suspect because of it? Not well, I suspected. Maybe deep down she knew what her son was doing at night, but Carlita preferred to look through rose-colored glasses where her children were concerned. To her, the world was filled with sweet things like buttercream icing, vanilla, and chocolate chips, all the ingredients to soothe. It was similar to me and my tomato sauce.

"All right," Gino said. "A few questions, and that's it."

Gabby slung an arm around my shoulders "Tessa and I make a great team."

Gino placed his hands on his hips. "Some team. More like a head-throbbing migraine for the police department. Let me know what you find out. Just between us, Lou and I will discreetly be doing some checking on our own when we can. We expect Daphne's autopsy report back in the next day or two. The toxicology tests will take longer."

Gabby made a *tsk-tsk* sound. "You could get in trouble for this, big brother," she said. "Poking around where you're not supposed to."

"I know what I'm doing. Unlike some people." He gave her a kiss on the forehead. "You're a proverbial pain in the butt most days, Gabs, but you're also my only sister." He turned and bussed my cheek. "And you're okay, too."

Gabby watched in surprise as Gino let himself out the front door. "I'll be darned. Guess Harvest Park's top detective is human after all."

I began to clear the table. "He's only concerned about us." It was rare for Gino to show his sensitive side on the job. He was a great guy, but he spent so much time in work mode that he found it difficult to show emotion. Lucy and I had discussed it, but after eight years of marriage she knew what to expect from him and never complained. They complemented each other perfectly.

Gabby stood and yawned. "I need to sleep. What time should we talk to Sylvia tomorrow?"

"I have a couple of vendors stopping by to see me in the afternoon, and I need to call your accountant. What was his name again?"

"Barney Wingate. Yeah, he's cool. I'll give you his number."

"Plus, I have to contact Stephanie's references, and if they check out, I'm offering her the job. I thought I'd spend the morning making pasta but can easily move that to the afternoon. I'll pick you up at ten o'clock."

She twisted a strand of hair around her finger. "Hmm. Preston mentioned that Sylvia tapes her show until eleven every morning. How about ten thirty?"

"That's fine." I placed the leftover carbonara in the fridge. "But I need to be back at the restaurant by one. If Once Upon a Book is still closed, you can hang out with me for the afternoon." I didn't want her to be alone but was careful not to say so. Gabby was fiercely independent. "Want to learn how to prepare homemade pasta? You could make Lou a great meal."

"Thanks, Tess, but Lou knows not to expect anything from me in that department." Her eyes twinkled and revealed the Gabby that I knew and loved, not the recent anxiety-laden one. "But I'm always happy to be your personal taste tester."

When I honked the horn the next morning, Gabby immediately stuck her head out the door and raised a finger, indicating she'd be another minute. I yawned and stared up at the gloomy gray clouds overhead that threatened to burst and soak the ground at any second.

I was already in a foul mood that threatened to last all day. Per usual, I hadn't slept well, but this time I'd dreamed of finding Daphne's body. It used to be Dylan I dreamed about every night, which had been painful, but at least then I didn't wake up screaming.

I'd already been to the restaurant, and my excitement about the menu delivery arriving a day early was doused like water on a fire when I spotted major errors. The menus were supposed to be maroon with gold trim. Instead, the restaurant's name was embossed in large gold lettering on a blue cover, identifying it as

"Anything's Pasteable." No, paste wasn't on the menu and never would be.

The distributor had apologized and promised new ones would ship by Wednesday. He assured me they'd be there in time for opening night, but I was getting nervous.

I stared down at the text I'd received from Justin earlier this morning. *Sorry I had to run last night. How about I make you dinner tonight? Even chefs need an evening off, right?*

My heart ached for Justin and everything he'd been through—first Natalie's deception, the horrific day-to-day details of his job, and now the guilt over leaving his newly widowed mother. Like Gino, even though he was trained to deal with life-and-death situations, no one could always be immune to them. I wanted to be there for him, like he'd been there for me since Dylan died, but for some reason, he was not opening up.

I had to laugh at the dinner invite. Justin had once made me breakfast, and another time he had burned grilled cheese sandwiches to the point where he almost needed his firehose. *Sounds interesting, lol. I'll probably be at the restaurant until eight or so. What works for you?*

Hi response came within seconds. That's fine. Come over whenever you get done. I'll be home all night.

See you then, I typed back.

Gabby ran down the driveway in her yellow slicker and jumped into the seat next to me. As soon as her seat belt was in place, I backed the car out of the driveway. "Any news about the store?"

She popped a breath mint into her mouth. "Lou just called, which is why I asked you to wait. He said the autopsy report was back and he wants to discuss it with us. Anyhow, the good news is that I should be able to reopen this afternoon."

"That's awesome." Maybe things were looking up.

She grunted. "Well, it would be, but I doubt I'll get any customers. Everyone knows what's happened, and although people in this town are polite, deep down they'll think I'm responsible. Archie called this morning and said that Daphne's death was the topic of conversation in his shop while everyone was sipping their lattes. I really hate this. One of the local busybodies even asked Archie for dirt because they know he's chummy with us, but he told them he didn't know anything."

"Arch is as loyal as a dog. Thank goodness he's in

our corner. Now stop worrying. We'll get to the bottom of this."

Gabby gave me a feeble smile. "I knew I could count on your help."

"And I promise you, no dangerous situations this time. Gino's right. I'll never forgive myself for almost getting you killed last fall."

She held up a hand. "Whoa. Forget what my brother said. I wanted to be involved in the hunt for Dylan's killer. There's nothing I wouldn't do for you. I hope you know that."

A lump the size of a mountain formed in my throat. Gabby was the sister I'd never had, and I thanked my lucky stars for her every day. "Ditto."

"So, what's the plan? Come on, fill me in."

I turned into the television-studio parking lot. "We're going to feel Sylvia out a bit. I'll talk about cooking and see if it can lead to Daphne's death."

Gabby stared at me thoughtfully. "She had the biggest motive if her husband was truly having an affair with Daphne. Plus she bakes—or pretends to. She could have slipped the shrimp powder into the cannoli."

I slammed the car door and hit the remote to lock it. "That's exactly what I was thinking too."

News Channel 11's studio was in the heart of Albany, only a few blocks from where Dylan had previously worked. When I'd won the State Fair's competition with my tomato sauce, I'd been interviewed on their morning news program. I knew there were two studios inside—one for the kitchen where Sylvia taped her show and the other where the six and eleven o'clock news were filmed.

The young woman stationed behind the receptionist counter looked like she was barely out of her teens. Her expression was bored as she listened to someone on the office line while studying her iPhone. The name plate on the counter identified her as Liz.

"Yes. I'll tell him you called." Liz placed the phone back in its cradle and muttered, "Again." She stared up at us expectantly. "May I help you?"

"Hi, is Sylvia Rigotta still here?"

Liz glanced down at her iPhone again, which I noticed displayed her Instagram page. "Yes, she's wrapping up her show for the day. Is she expecting you?"

"Yes," Gabby said quickly. I nudged her but she ignored me. "Tell her it's about her husband."

She glanced at Gabby with suspicious eyes. "And you are…?"

Gabby's cheeks reddened. "My name is Gabby Mancusi."

"Hang on a second." Liz heaved herself out of the leather swivel chair, her stilettos clacking against the linoleum as she walked toward a door marked PRIVATE—TAPING IN PROGRESS and closed it softly behind her.

"Are you nuts?" I whispered. "Why didn't you let me handle it?"

Gabby jutted her chin out in defiance. "My name will get her out here quickly. Mark my words."

She was right. The door swung open a few seconds later. Sylvia stormed toward us, her blue eyes cold as ice cubes when they focused on Gabby. Without further thought, I jumped in front of my cousin, a vain attempt to protect her from the woman's wrath.

"What in God's name are you doing here?" Sylvia thrust a finger into my face. "Liz, call the police! These women should be arrested for murder."

EIGHT

"THIS IS ALL A MISTAKE," I said in my most reassuring tone. "We didn't kill anyone. Gabby only wanted to apologize to you and your husband."

"I did?" Gabby whispered before I reached over to pinch her hand. "Ouch. I mean, yes, I did."

When I stepped aside, Gabby immediately lowered her head to the floor and spoke in a timid voice like a naughty five-year-old. "I'm really sorry about what happened."

An acting career was definitely not in Gabby's future.

Sylvia stared at her in disbelief. "You're a liar. Why did you kill that poor, innocent girl? Preston said that you were jealous of her."

She didn't know I'd overheard her conversation with Preston at the signing, unless Willow had told her. Did Sylvia really think Gabby and I hadn't noticed her dislike of

Daphne? She'd almost jumped for joy when Gabby spilled the wine on her. What was she trying to pull? We needed to tread lightly, and I was afraid my somewhat brazen cousin might come out with a smart-mouthed remark at any moment.

"Sylvia—may I call you Sylvia?" I gave her what I hoped was a starstruck smile. She glared at me and didn't answer. "The truth is that Gabby hoped you'd deliver a message to Preston on her behalf. He was so upset the other night that she's afraid he won't give her bookstore a good recommendation on social media. But that's only part of the reason why we're here, though."

Gabby cast Bambi-like eyes upon me, as if I was her last hope.

"When I found out Gabby was coming here, I asked to tag along." I stared at the floor, as if embarrassed. "You see, I'm a huge fan of your show and always wanted to—" I broke off.

"Yes?" Sylvia's voice bristled with impatience.

Nausea rumbled in my stomach. I hated groveling, even if it was pretend. Unlike Gabby, I was never dazzled by celebrities. Okay, if I'd ever gotten the chance to meet Julia Child, that might have been different. In truth, I had disliked Sylvia from the start. Anyone who pretended to have cooking skills was an insult to chefs everywhere.

"I can't believe I'm asking this." No lie there. "Do you think that I could be a guest on your show sometime? It would be great exposure for my restaurant."

Her loud, haughty laughter filled the room. Yes, she hadn't disappointed. I'd expected nothing less from her.

"Really?" Sylvia was clearly amused. "You can't be serious. Do you think that just *anyone* can be on my show? Sorry, darling. Once you have some *real* cooking experience, come back and see me."

I bit into my lower lip so hard that I tasted blood. Again, I told myself to ignore this woman. Gabby's livelihood and mine were at stake and that was all that mattered right now.

"That's okay. I expected you to say no." I tried to act like she'd crushed my last dream and then pulled a small pad from my purse. "Could I at least have your autograph?"

Sylvia gave me a condescending smile, momentarily forgetting her indignation. "Well, of course. Anything for a fan." She scrawled her name across the page in illegible fashion and handed it back to me. Her haughty attitude had replaced her blustering ire, and I sensed her guard was down.

"Thank you so much. Again, we're both sorry the signing ended so badly. It's so awful how Daphne died."

As I'd hoped, Sylvia took the bait. She glanced around the room, but Liz was on the phone and paying no attention to us. "Preston heard that she might have been poisoned."

"Really?" I tried to convey surprise in my response.

"They say from the cannoli." Sylvia watched me carefully for my reaction.

"That's impossible." I was annoyed that someone had already told Preston how Daphne had died. It must have been Paddy, since he was the only one who knew.

Sylvia's eyes glittered with triumph, as if she'd gotten Final Jeopardy right. "So, are they certain it was your desserts that made her ill?"

"How well did you know Daphne?" I asked, sidestepping her question. "Did she have a lot of friends? A boyfriend, maybe?"

"How would I know? She was Preston's employee and nothing more." Sylvia placed special emphasis on the last two words.

"Of course. But we'd love to find out who is responsible, since it's affecting Gabby's business." In an attempt to gauge her reaction, I went a little further. "I only asked because, hey, it's always the boyfriend, right?"

"Daphne was employed by Preston for four months?" Gabby asked.

"I believe so." Sylvia made a big deal out of checking her watch. "His former publicist took another job outside of the publishing industry, so he decided to find one on his own." She stopped to draw a deep breath. "But that—woman—lied to Preston. She said she had experience in marketing and had done this type of work before, but it quickly became obvious she was bluffing to get the job."

"Why did he hire her then?" Gabby wanted to know.

Sylvia's nostrils flared. "He felt sorry for her. She told him her father was ill, and they were drowning in medical bills."

That would be easy enough to check out. From what I could recall, Daphne's parents had divorced years ago, and she'd had no contact with her mother. Preston obviously had another reason for hiring Daphne, but I wasn't about to suggest it in front of his wife. "I heard one of Preston's fans mention last night that Daphne—" With a gasp, I brought a hand to my mouth. "Oh, forgive me. I shouldn't be spreading rumors."

Gabby was on to me. "Tess, how many times have I told you to stop doing that?" She shook her head at Sylvia. "She's so addicted to gossip."

I nodded meekly. "Thanks for talking to us, but we've taken up enough of your time."

Sylvia's eyes widened. "Hold on. You heard what?"

She was so predictable. "Well, I overheard one woman mention to her friend that Daphne was openly flirting with Preston."

She gave a toss of her head. "Preston and I have been married almost twenty-five years. Trust is the basis for a marriage. Without it, you have nothing."

Yes, I knew all about the trust factor. It had reared its ugly head after Dylan's death. "You're very lucky."

"Thank goodness Preston saw through Daphne's act," Gabby said wisely. "If a man ever cheated on me, I'd take him right to the cleaners. But I'm sure you're much nicer than me."

Sylvia's deep, throaty laughed filled the room. "Oh, my dear. No man's going to make me look like a fool. It would be the last thing that he ever did."

We mumbled a hasty goodbye and left the television station in a hurry. Sylvia might be a pretentious phony, but there was something dangerous lurking underneath that carefully made up face of hers.

"What do you think?" Gabby asked as we drove away.

"She has a motive," I said. "If Preston was sleeping with Daphne like she accused him, there you go. She may have been jealous and decided to do away with her."

Gabby made a face. "To think that I idolized the man. He seemed so nice when we first corresponded through email, and I was thrilled to pieces by his interest. What a fool I was."

"You do realize that it could have been Willow emailing you?" I asked. "Preston said she took care of his website. Correspondence too, I'm guessing."

"True, but you don't think about all that stuff when it concerns one of your idols." Gabby heaved a sigh. "I'm never going to get all sappy about an author again. Well, except for Stephen King," she added hastily.

"Do you want to come back to the restaurant with me?" I asked.

She stared down at her phone screen and typed out a message. "Might as well. I'll tell Lou to stop over and let us know what he's found out. Give me your theory, Nancy Drew. Who do you think laced the cannoli with shrimp powder?"

I took a left down Harvest Park Avenue. "Anyone could have brought the cannoli in when they met Daphne. Who knows? And they might have told her I made them." That was a disturbing thought. "This was someone Daphne trusted or, at the very least, knew well enough to come back and meet at your store."

"It could be someone we haven't even considered yet," Gabby pointed out.

This was entirely possible. "Did Gino check your security camera footage?"

She nodded. "Not Gino personally, but one of the other officers did. Gino said they didn't come up with anything after hours. Besides, there's only one camera out in front of the building. Daphne and whoever brought the cannoli must have used the back door. My key works in both doors, remember."

"You need to get those locks changed as soon as possible," I reminded her.

"I know," Gabby said darkly. "More money down the drain, thank you very much."

We pulled in front of the restaurant. After unlocking the door and deactivating the alarm, I stopped to adjust one of the tablecloths in the dining room, while Gabby proceeded into the kitchen. She let out a sudden giggle. "Looks like someone has an admirer."

"What are you talking about?" I went into the kitchen and on top of the counter stood a large crystal vase full of pink roses. There was an envelope next to them with my name on it, and my pulse quickened. Next to lilacs, roses were my favorite flower. I immediately thought of Dylan, who'd sent me pink roses on our fifth anniversary—our last one together. The memory squeezed at my heart so tightly that I found it difficult to breathe for a moment.

Before I could react, Gabby grabbed the card off the counter. She waved it at me teasingly. "Can I open it?"

"No!" I laughed. "My name is on it."

"Oh, come on," she pleaded. "I'm dying to know who they're from."

Her expression was so cute that I relented. "Oh, fine. Go ahead, if it makes you happy. My mother probably sent them. Maybe Vince was here to let the delivery man in."

Gabby was already reading the card. "Vince didn't let anyone in, Tess. They're from the Italian Stallion himself."

My jaw almost hit the floor. "Let me see that." But she was telling the truth. I read the card to myself: *Congratulations on doing the Im-Pastable! Vince.*

Gabby gave me a teasing grin. "My, my. I'll bet that he doesn't send flowers to all of his tenants."

"I'm his *only* tenant." At least I thought so. "We have a good time talking about cooking. The flowers are just a nice gesture on his part." I went to the sink to wash my hands.

She gave me a thumbs-up. "Right. I'm just saying, the guy obviously has more on his mind than your tomato sauce and rent checks."

I lifted mixing bowls out of the overhead cabinet. "It's a good thing not everyone thinks the way you do." Gabby watched as I poured semolina flour into a bowl, added eggs and salt, then dug my hands into the mixture. An immediate sense of calm washed over me as I formed the dough into a ball. Cooking was so relaxing for my mind—cheap therapy at its best.

Lou's voice interrupted my solace. "Gabs, where are you?" he called.

"In the kitchen, babe." Gabby winked at me. "Lou will never hear that phrase out of my mouth again. He knows that I can't even boil water, but thank goodness he doesn't seem to care." She called out to him again. "Go through the dining area. Door on the right."

Since it was only the three of us, Lou leaned down to

kiss her and then nodded at me. "Hi, Tessa. Gee, I haven't been in here since Slice closed. You've done a great job."

"Thanks." The comment warmed me from head to toe.

"I can still open the store back up soon, right?" Gabby's face had become pinched tight with worry. "Why do I get the feeling something else has happened?"

Lou frowned. "I'm trying to keep my ears and eyes open, since I'm not supposed to be working this case. Frankly, I don't have much more leverage than Gino. I can't take statements or gather evidence because of our relationship, but Paddy has passed some information on to me."

"That's hard to believe," Gabby remarked.

Lou suppressed a smile. "He even let me have a look at Daphne's autopsy report. We won't have toxicology results back for a while, but as suspected, Daphne died from something she ate."

A light switch clicked on in my brain. "The cannoli were analyzed, right?"

He nodded. "Didn't Gino tell you they found shrimp powder in them and that Daphne had an allergy to seafood?"

"Yes, he did. Sorry, what I actually meant to say—is it possible to get me a list of all the ingredients in the cannoli?"

"That shouldn't be a problem." Lou arched a blond brow at me. "Why, what are you thinking?"

"I'm not sure," I confessed. "But there's always a chance that one of the ingredients, besides the shrimp powder, might tell us something. That's the beauty with a recipe. The ingredients all have their own hidden secrets."

Gabby clutched his arm. "Come on. I know there's something else going on. I'm an expert at reading cop faces, remember."

Lou's mouth tightened into a thin line. "The autopsy revealed more than we expected."

Gabby and I exchanged glances. "Such as?" she asked. "Was Daphne doing drugs? Or sick with some type of illness?"

"No, nothing like that."

Impatience seeped into Gabby's face. "For heaven's sake, don't keep us in suspense. What else did you find out?"

Lou's expression was grim. "Daphne was four months pregnant."

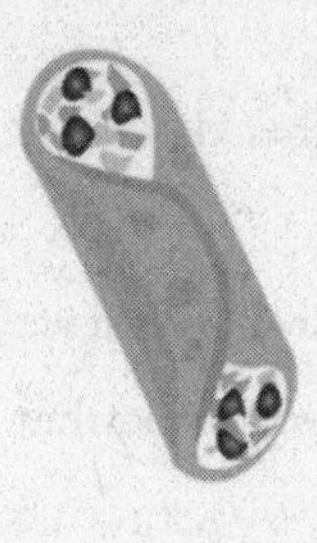
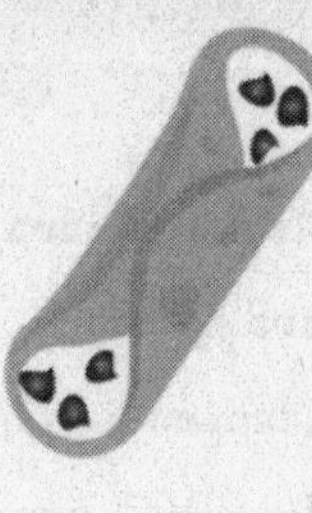

NINE

GABBY GASPED OUT LOUD. "Are you sure?"

Lou nodded solemnly. "Autopsies don't lie, Gabs."

This was a new twist I hadn't been suspecting. Was the baby Lorenzo's? Preston's? Or maybe someone else's? I tried not to be judgmental, but Daphne had a reputation for promiscuity that dated back to high school. If sleeping with half of the varsity football team came with any accolades, Daphne would have been first in class.

Gabby's mind must have been working the same way as mine. "Is there any way to determine who the father was?" she asked.

"Not unless you can get him to take a blood test or obtain DNA from him," Lou replied. "We just can't go around asking random guys to take one."

"I'll bet the baby was Preston's," Gabby mused.

"Daphne would have done anything to sink her claws into him and his money."

I tapped my fingers against the metal bowl. "But if we got the father to willingly submit to a test, you could find out if it was his baby, right?"

Lou regarded me with suspicion. "Yes, but why are you asking? Gino said he wanted you to ask Carlita a few questions, not conduct an inquisition."

I hesitated. Lou was a great guy, but he was still a cop. Gabby and I had to be careful about the details we gave him. Even though Lou had a calmer demeanor than Gino, he'd still be upset if he knew what we were up to. "Oh, I'm only grasping at straws, that's all."

Lou's phone beeped, and he stared down at the screen. "I have to go." He gave Gabby a swift kiss. "I'll call and let you know when the store can be reopened. It should be within the hour, but I need confirmation. Good seeing you, Tessa."

"You too." Gabby walked him to the front door, while I made another ball of dough. One was probably enough, but I enjoyed my kneading time. The dough would have to sit for a little while before I could cut it and feed it through my pasta machine. Pasta making was a long process that might seem tedious to some, but I loved every minute of it.

The clock on the wall read twelve thirty. I was behind schedule, but it couldn't be helped. I hadn't even had a chance to check Stephanie's references yet. The cobwebs in my brain started to clear, and I closed my eyes, getting into a rhythm. My mind began to relax.

"Tess." Gabby spoke quietly.

"Hmm?" I opened my eyes in surprise. I hadn't even heard her come back in the room.

She grinned. "It's like you're in a different world when you're cooking. A peaceful expression comes over your face. I was afraid to disturb you."

"It's my happy place. I'm sure yours is inhaling the scent of a brand-new box of books."

Gabby pondered this for a moment. "I never thought about it like that before, but yeah, you're right. We all have different passions. My newest one is discovering who left Daphne Daniels to die in my store."

Someone had known about Daphne's allergy and was most likely in the same room with her when she went into anaphylactic shock. Had they just stood there, watching her die? Did they know about the baby? "I have a little time before the vendors are due to come by. Why don't we stop over at Sweet Treats and see if Lorenzo is there? Maybe we can talk to him while Carlita isn't around."

"She's always around," Gabby remarked. "The bakery is her home away from home."

My mind went back to the alley that night. "After I witnessed the argument between Lorenzo and Daphne, he told me to forget I'd seen him there."

Gabby's eyes almost bugged out of her head. "What do you think he meant by that?"

I shrugged. "Sounds to me like they were seeing each other on the sly. Lorenzo still lives at home, so how was he getting cozy with Daphne? Carlita would never permit anything like that under her roof. Daphne said she lived in Saratoga, so I'm guessing they must have always spent time together at her place."

Gabby snickered. "'Spent time together.' That's being polite. Lorenzo might be a mama's boy, but he does what he wants. Lou and I have seen him at On the Rocks having beers with plenty of women before. He's twenty-six, Tess, and I don't think he has a curfew."

"No, I guess not." I dusted two bowls with semolina flour, placed a ball of dough in each one, then covered both and set them aside. "All right, let's go. The dough needs to rest for a while anyway." I hung my apron on one of the brass hooks on the wall. "We'll see if Lorenzo's at the bakery. If he is, maybe you could distract Carlita so I can talk to him privately."

After I'd washed my hands, we locked the door and took off in my car. "Do you want to come back here afterward?"

"Might as well, at least until Lou calls to say my store is all set." Her expression was glum. "Tess, I don't know what I'll do if I have to close the store. This has been my dream since I was a little girl."

"I remember. You were always reading Nancy Drew, while I only wanted to play dress-up with Barbie. You made me play bookstore with you, and I hated being the customer."

She laughed. "I know you understand what it's like. To want something so badly in this world that you'll do almost anything to get it."

I patted her hand. "Yes, I do, but you have to trust that everything will work out. Maybe you'll even get more customers than before. This is terrible to say, but tragic events sometimes end up drawing more of a crowd."

Gabby looked at me hopefully. "Do you really think so?"

No, but I wanted her to stay optimistic. "Sure." As far as I was concerned, a positive attitude was half the battle. In the meantime, Gabby might get some curious looky-loos, but I doubted they'd be buying books.

We drove in silence to Sweet Treats, and Gabby gazed forlornly at her store on the way by. "It looks so lonely," she sighed.

I parked a few spots down from the bakery, hoping that Carlita's roving eyes wouldn't see us approach.

"What should I say to her?" Gabby asked. "And where will you be?"

"I'll go around back and knock on the kitchen door. You pretend that you're having another signing or something, and you want to buy the cookies from her this time. Ask Carlita what kind she thinks would be best."

She gave me a look of disbelief. "Um, *hello.* Carlita knows that you did the cannoli for Preston's signing because she sulked and turned up her nose at me afterward. She's going to wonder why you're not making them."

"Tell her I'm too busy with the restaurant then. Jeez, Gabs, make up something." I was nervous and not looking forward to asking Lorenzo about his relationship with Daphne, or if he knew about the baby.

"All right, I'll try." She swung herself out of the car and walked down the sidewalk to the main entrance, while I scurried around back. The door was locked, as I'd expected. There was a good likelihood that Giuseppe, Lorenzo's father and Carlita's husband, was in the kitchen as well, but it was a chance I had to take. I rapped softly on the door and waited. Nothing. I rapped again.

The door swung open, and I found myself face to face with Lorenzo, wearing a white bib apron dusted with flour. He looked at me in surprise. "Hi, Tessa. What are you doing here?"

I stole a glance around the kitchen. It appeared that Lorenzo was alone. A bun-pan rack stood next to the oven, loaded with different types of recently baked cookies. There was a two-tier cake frosted with vanilla buttercream standing on the prep table. It read "Happy Birth" in green icing. I must have caught Lorenzo mid-sentence. "Can I talk to you for a second?"

He glanced uneasily over his shoulder toward the swinging doors that led to the storefront. "Um, it's not really a good time. I'm working."

"It will only take a minute."

His eyes remained focused on the door, and I knew what he was thinking. Lorenzo was afraid Carlita might overhear our conversation. Her voice rang out loudly from the other side of the wall, and Lorenzo froze at the sound. He swallowed nervously, his Adam's apple bobbing up and down. "All right, I guess."

Lorenzo's dark, thick hair was contained underneath a baseball cap he wore backward on his head. He stuffed his hands into the bib apron's pockets. "What do you want to talk to me about?" His tone had changed to one of annoyance.

I watched him carefully. "You heard about what happened to Daphne."

He shifted from one foot to another and wouldn't look at me. "Yeah. The service is the day after tomorrow. I wanted to go, but it's private."

Just say it, Tess. "Does your mother know you were dating?"

Lorenzo's ominous eyes regarded me in brooding silence for a moment. "No, she doesn't. I'm an adult, remember. My mother doesn't call every shot in my life."

I blinked. This was not the polite, carefree Lorenzo

I remembered. Was he grieving or could it be something else? Guilt? "Her death wasn't an accident, Lorenzo. Do you know who wanted to kill her?"

"Do you?" he shot back. "I heard Daphne had a reaction to something she ate at the signing. She was allergic to shellfish. Maybe you had a reason to kill her."

Gabby's giggle sounded from the other side of the wall, loud and forced. *Great.* Carlita would see through her act in a second, so I needed to move fast. "You know that's not true. I only want to find out what happened. Did you see Daphne again after the signing?"

He shook his head vigorously. "No. She made it clear that we were done. You heard her."

"Did she—" I hated to bring up the pregnancy. What if he didn't know about it? Maybe Daphne hadn't planned to go through with it. Then again, she was four months along, so chances were good that she was planning to keep the baby.

He watched me curiously. "What were you going to say?"

"Did Daphne happen to tell you anything else that night? If she was seeing someone besides you, or if her life had recently changed?"

Lorenzo's lips curled into a sneer. "Wasn't it obvious to you? Because it was to me. She was only using me until someone better came along. I was in love with her." He let out a ragged breath. "I thought we might have a future together. But all she was interested in was—how to do I put this delicately? Being friends with benefits."

"Lorenzo?" Carlita called out. "Who is in there with you?"

Oh, crap. The color drained from Lorenzo's face as I hurried toward the back door, but it was too late. Carlita pushed through the swinging doors and stood there, hands stationed on her broad hips, eyeing us both sharply.

"Theresa." Like my mother, she always called me by my given name. "What do you need?"

In her mid-fifties, Carlita was Spanish while her husband Giuseppe was 100 percent Italian. Carlita spoke both languages and English fluently. She was about my five-foot, four-inch height, although heavier, with sharp dark eyes that missed nothing.

I struggled to think of an excuse. "I was asking Lorenzo if he knew the ingredients that went into your cannoli." Boy, did that sound lame to my own ears.

Doubt registered in Carlita's eyes. She glanced over

her shoulder at Gabby who stood behind her, a distressed look on her face. "Aha. You two put nothing past Carlita."

"Mama, it's not like that," Lorenzo protested.

Carlita beamed at me. "Theresa, tell the truth. Why do you see Lorenzo? You want to date him?"

Oh. My. God. This was worse than I had imagined. "No, Carlita, I don't."

Carlita nudged Gabby in the side and cocked her eyebrow at me. "You have your cousin keep me busy while you come and get cozy with Lorenzo." She clucked her tongue like a chicken. "No, no. It too soon for you to date anyone. Your husband just died!"

My cheeks burned at her accusation. "Carlita, I can assure you that I'm *not* dating Lorenzo."

"Tell her the truth, Tess," Gabby suggested. "There's no way around it."

"What is it?" Carlita demanded.

Lorenzo's face fell. I waited, giving him a chance to speak up first, but he remained mute and looked at me expectantly. Did Lorenzo expect me to answer for him? Resigned, I blew out a sigh. "I overheard Lorenzo talking to Daphne the other night. They were having a bit of a disagreement."

"The girl who died at Gabby's store?" Carlita's mouth hardened as she addressed her son. "You knew her?"

Lorenzo's eyes shot daggers at me. "Yes, I knew her. We went out a few times."

Carlita mumbled something under her breath in Italian, and then went over and grabbed Lorenzo's ear as I winced.

"Mama!" He tried to shake her off. "Stop it!"

"Why did you not tell me?" she demanded.

His mouth set in a stubborn streak. "Because it was my business."

That was the wrong thing to say to a Spanish mother of six. Carlita's mouth exploded in a stream of Italian—no, some might have been Spanish—but every other word was punctuated by a shriek.

"Are you crazy, my boy?" She turned to me with panic-stricken eyes. "The police—they think Lorenzo did this?"

I tried to sidestep the question. "I can't say for sure."

"Baloney!" she huffed. "You know." She wagged a finger at Gabby's face. "Your brother, he tell you that Lorenzo is in trouble?"

Gabby shook her head. "Tessa overheard Daphne and Lorenzo arguing outside my store."

Carlita took off her apron and whacked Lorenzo over the head with it. "How many times I tell you?" she shrieked. "Work hard, get married to a nice Italian or Spanish girl. Have some babies. That Daphne always had a bad reputation, and now someone kill her. You going to ruin your life." She sat down on a nearby stool and began to cry as she flung her apron over her head.

"I didn't hurt her!" Lorenzo insisted, but the look he shot in my direction unnerved me. He acted like he was hiding something. Did he know she was pregnant?

Carlita defiantly squared her shoulders against me, as if I'd suddenly become the enemy. "Lorenzo, he would not do such a thing. They cannot arrest him."

"I'm sure the police will want to question him, but that's no big deal, Carlita," I said gently. "Gabby and I were questioned as well."

Carlita's face paled. "There is something else. I know there is. You tell me now, Theresa."

Dang, she was good. I glanced at Lorenzo, but he merely shrugged. "Maybe I shouldn't be the one to say this, but I happen to care about both of you."

"Just spill it," Lorenzo said sharply.

Carlita came over and whacked him on the head with

her apron again. "You shush up and listen. Tell us, Theresa. *Now.*"

I swallowed hard. "Daphne was four months pregnant."

The room was so quiet that you could have heard a chocolate chip drop. It was difficult to say who looked more shocked, Lorenzo or his mother. Carlita stood stock still for a moment and then started to sway from side to side, as if about to collapse. Gabby and I both jumped forward to grab her before she fell to the floor.

She began to sob in my arms. "Oh, my God. She was going to have a baby. This is bad. Very bad."

I looked over Carlita's head at Lorenzo, who was motionless. "You didn't know?" I asked him.

Lorenzo appeared dazed as he shook his head. "She never said a word. Was it—mine?"

Carlita let out a low moan and looked like she might faint. Gabby helped her sit back down, rolled her eyes at me, then glanced at the door. Yes, I wanted to get out of here as badly as she did.

"They don't know yet. That's why I wanted to talk to you. If you'd be willing to take a blood test, you'll know for certain if it was your baby—" I hesitated, "or someone else's."

Carlita wiped at her eyes with a tissue. "It cannot be his. That girl, she was always promiscuous. I remember—"

"Mama!" Lorenzo's face was suffused with anger. "Stop it. I didn't kill her, and I don't have to take a test if I don't want to."

"You *will* take the test," she snapped back. "If you don't, it look like you try to hide something." She turned to me. "Who else knows—about pregnancy?"

"I can't say for sure," I admitted. "The police and at least Daphne's family must have been told."

Lorenzo slammed his apron on the counter. "That does it. I've had enough. I need to get some air." The look of contempt he shot me sent a shiver down my spine. "And all of you need to stay out of my life."

Carlita shouted after her son—in Spanish this time. Lorenzo ignored her and slammed the door in response, the sound reverberating in my head.

Carlita wiped at her eyes again. "He is no killer."

I didn't answer because in truth, I wasn't sure. Gabby had once told me that "no one was exempt" when it came to a murder, and I believed it. She gazed at me quizzically now, as if she'd guessed what I was thinking.

Carlita twisted her hands so tightly together that I was

afraid she might wring them off. "Is there something else?" I asked.

"I—no. Nothing." She swallowed hard, as if trying to force back words.

I laid a hand on her shoulder. "Carlita, we're not the police. You can trust us."

Her eyes swam with tears. "I am afraid for Lorenzo. When the police find out what else he has done—" She sobbed into her hands. "They may arrest him—again."

TEN

A SICK SENSATION SWEPT OVER ME. "Carlita," I said slowly, "are you trying to say that Lorenzo has a record?"

Carlita inhaled several gulps of air before she spoke, her head still in her hands. "*Si*. He was arrested a few years ago." Her head jerked up. "But it was not his fault."

Gabby and I exchanged glances. "What was he arrested for?" I asked.

"He was only twenty at the time," she began. "Lorenzo make friends with some other boys. They do not live in Harvest Park. I told him they were no good, to stay away, but Lorenzo—he no listen." Carlita's face hardened like stone. "They told him they play a joke on a friend. They take his television and then bring back later. Lorenzo stay in the car. When they come out they have all these expensive electronics—the Play Stations, televisions, computers. They yell at Lorenzo to drive the car—drive it fast."

"Oh, no," I murmured.

Carlita nodded in misery. "Oh *yes*. The police chase them and arrest everyone. Lorenzo try to tell them that he did not know—he would never rob anyone. He call up Giuseppe and me at three o'clock in the morning! We go down to the police station and bring bail money."

Gabby's brow furrowed. "Did Gino arrest them?"

She shook her head. "I ask for your brother, but he was not working. Take two weeks off when Lucy have the twins."

"He must have known about it, though," I murmured. Gino had never mentioned Lorenzo's arrest to me, but then again, why would he? Gino was a detective for goodness' sake. He didn't kiss and tell, and it was none of my business anyway.

Carlita gulped. "We hire very good attorney, and he get Lorenzo off on community service. But people in this town, they like to talk. Many treat Lorenzo different after that. I know he a bit lazy, but he is no killer. He would not hurt Daphne or any other woman."

"Talk to him, Carlita," I suggested. "Please try to convince him to take the test. He'd want to know if the baby had been his, wouldn't he?"

"But what if it *was* his baby?" Tears ran down her cheeks. "Maybe they would put him in jail. They would think that is why he kill her."

Would Daphne have told Lorenzo that she was carrying his child? Or did her silence mean that the baby was Preston's?

"Theresa, help me," Carlita implored. "You must find out who killed Daphne. I trust you. This will destroy Lorenzo's life. Please."

How could I refuse her? "We'll do what we can," I said slowly.

"This is affecting us too, Carlita," Gabby announced. "The detective in charge of the case is looking at both Tess and me as suspects."

"Baloney," she declared. "I know all about that man—Patty something? He think he still in the big city. We are bunch of hicks to him."

I struggled to keep a straight face, even though I agreed with her sentiment.

"It is true," she insisted. "He come in bakery for bread last week. I try to talk to him. Ask about his wife, kids. He tell me he is divorced, no kids."

"Gee, it's difficult to imagine why a woman wouldn't

want to stay married to him," Gabby murmured. "Must be that soft, endearing side."

Carlita sniffed. "I tell him, you stick with me, I find you nice Harvest Park lady. Lots of pretty ones at the Catholic church. He start to laugh, then say he no go to church. Say God is punishing him by sending him to our town. Then he say it like purgatory here." Shock registered on her heart-shaped face. "So blasphemous."

"Yeah, he's a keeper," Gabby agreed.

The bells chimed from the storefront, announcing that Carlita had a customer. She rose to her feet and wiped her eyes. "I must go now. You girls take care of everything, okay?" With that, she pushed through the swinging doors with her usual determination.

Our job was done here, so to speak. Gabby and I drove back to the restaurant in silence. When we were back in the kitchen, she leaned over the counter, watching with interest as I cut up each ball of the sitting dough into six parts and fed them through my pasta machine. "Why do you have to put each piece through the machine eight times? I'd go crazy with boredom."

"It has to be smooth and not sticky," I told her, "otherwise the pasta won't be the right texture. And it's not boring—the process helps me to think." Homemade pasta was so much fresher and tastier than store-bought and totally worth the time spent. The thought of people eating and enjoying my food on opening night filled me with anticipation and joy.

"What are you smiling at?" Gabby asked.

"Was I smiling? Sorry, I won't do it again."

"Don't be a wise guy. Do you think Lorenzo could have killed her?"

I fed the sheet of dough through the machine one more time and then cut the flat piece into long, even strips of noodles. "I don't know."

She looked at me, startled. "Tess!"

"Well, I don't!" I wiped my hands on a dish towel. "Don't get me wrong. I hate the idea that Lorenzo could be a killer. It would devastate Carlita. But we both know what people are capable of when they've been wronged. Daphne was pregnant, and someone may have killed her because of it."

"Don't forget the Rigottas," Gabby put in. "Maybe Sylvia poisoned the cannoli and got her doting daughter to help. Before Saturday, I would rather have cut off my tongue before saying this, but Preston's a suspect, too. If it was his baby and Daphne told him, that would ruin his squeaky-clean image and his book sales."

"Who else might have a motive?" I finished cutting the pasta into slices and placed it in freezer bags.

"Maybe her father knows of someone. I mean, no offense, but there had to be other people that she made miserable—besides me, that is." Gabby's phone buzzed, and she glanced at the screen. "Hey. Check this out. Lou said he got word from the higher-ups that I can reopen the store! He also sent the list of ingredients used in the cannoli and asked me to pass them along to you. Hang on, I'll forward the message."

My phone pinged a second later. I washed my hands and then scrolled through the items listed. They were standard ingredients. Salt. Granulated sugar. Confectioners' sugar. Vegetable oil. Wine, a fairly common ingredient for the shells. I read on. Cinnamon. Shrimp powder—aka, the deadly addition. Several more were listed, since both filling and shells were in the mix. At the bottom of the list were two words that gave me new hope. "Ah. Very interesting."

"What?" Gabby looked up from studying the list on her phone. "Yeah, I know. Shrimp powder. But how will that lead us to her killer? You can buy it anywhere."

"Not the shrimp powder. Look at the last item."

Gabby squinted down at her phone. "It says Valrhona chocolate. That's quite a tongue twister. I've never heard of it."

"No reason you should have," I said. "Most people don't know of it, unless you're a baker. I used it a few times when I worked at Magnifico's Restaurant. It's difficult to find and expensive." A tingle of excitement ran through me. This was the break I'd hoped for. "If we can find the store that sells the chocolate, it might help us track down who bought it."

"I'm betting on Sylvia. It would fit," Gabby declared.

I hurried into my office, which branched off from the kitchen. "We can't be positive, though. Come on."

Gabby followed me into the eight-by-ten-foot room. I hadn't altered much from the original decor. Gabby had given me a name plate for my desk that read *"The Chef Is In."* I also had a swivel chair and metal file cabinet. When I had more time and money, I'd do a makeover. The room served its purpose for now, and I preferred doing interviews in the dining area anyway. It was more personable.

I sat down in front of my desktop computer and wiggled the mouse for the screen to light up. Gabby fingered the pile of receipts in the basket on the corner of my desk. “Dang, Tess. Are these all bills from vendors?”

“Unfortunately, yes.” I let out a small sigh. “Also, the sign man, plumber, coffee company, linen service, you name it.” I'd have to sell out every night for the first month to break even. I opened Google and typed in “Valrhona.” Within seconds, I had my answer. “Here we go.”

Gabby peered over my shoulder. “Gourmet Goodies is the closest store. Fifty miles away? No problem. I'll drive. We'll be there in twenty minutes.”

“Very funny. How about we go over tomorrow morning? Can you break away from the store?”

She snorted. “Please. Liza will be there, and even if she wasn't, I don't think it would be a problem. Something tells me that people aren't going to come running when they hear it's reopened.” Gabby hoisted her purse over her shoulder. “Speaking of which, I'd better get over there. Just for giggles, you know.”

“Do you want me to drive you?”

She shook her head. “Nah, it's not that far. Besides, I need the air.”

I walked with her to the front door. “Call me later, and I'll pick you up.”

"Thanks, but Lou's coming to get me. He's taking me to dinner tonight. At least I have something to look forward to. What about you?"

"I'm going to hang out with Justin for a while. We didn't get much of a chance to talk last night."

Gabby frowned. "That's my fault for interrupting."

"No, it's not. I didn't mean to sound accusatory. Now go to your beloved books. I know they've missed you. Then go out and have a great time with your boyfriend, okay? I'll stop by for you about ten o'clock tomorrow morning. My staff is coming for a quick meeting in the afternoon, and I have some orders to place, so the rest of the day is pretty full."

She gave me a somber look. "It's the way you like it. Once the restaurant opens, you'll be busier than ever. Hey, that's a good thing, right?" She waved and then disappeared around the corner.

When she was out of sight, I shut the kitchen door and started to clean up. After making sure that the room was spotless, I made a few phone calls to check on Stephanie's references. They all gave her glowing reviews. What a relief. I immediately dialed the cell number she'd left me but got her voicemail.

"Hi, Stephanie, it's Tessa Esposito. Could you give me

a call when you have a minute?" I recited my number and then clicked off, praying she hadn't found another job in the meantime. I had no way of knowing if she had interviewed with others, or not. I wasn't the only restaurant in Harvest Park, although I would have preferred to be.

I made a few other calls, then decided to go home. It was six o'clock and my stomach rumbled with hunger. I'd grab a quick shower and then drive over to Justin's. He wasn't expecting me until eight but said to come over anytime.

Luigi met me at the bottom of the stairs, blinking in the evaporating sunlight as if I'd interrupted his afternoon slumber. When I reached down to pet him, he turned up his tail at me and hurried back upstairs. I followed. "What's this, bud? The cold shoulder?"

He leaped onto my bed and settled himself on Dylan's pillow. It was his favorite place to sleep, and his purrs comforted me throughout the night.

"Hey." I scratched Luigi behind the ears, and he rewarded me with a little squeak. "I know I haven't been around much lately. When I get back tonight, we'll watch some television together. Okay?"

Luigi shut his eyes, and sounds resembling a V8

engine filled the room. I took that as a good sign and went into the bathroom to shower.

I changed into jeans and a black-and-white polka-dotted shirt my mother had bought me for Christmas. As I applied a coat of mascara to my lashes, my dark eyes stared back at me. There were faint circles of weariness underneath them. I'd had a difficult time sleeping since Dylan's death, but now I had to worry about being a suspect in a murder case as well.

After blow-drying my hair, I started to pull it back into a ponytail but decided to leave it loose around my shoulders. I added a shiny pink coat of lip balm and was ready to leave. I gave Luigi a hug, grabbed my keys, and locked up the house. When I sat down in the driver's seat, the clock on my dashboard read seven o'clock. I hoped that Justin would open up to me tonight. Plus, it would help take my mind off everything else happening in my own life.

As I turned down Justin's road, a woman emerged from his front door. Surprised by this unexpected person, I drove past his house and down a side street. I made a U-turn and proceeded slowly back up the road, stopping a couple of houses away. Justin was standing on the front porch in jeans and a striped blue-and-white Oxford talking to the mystery woman. The weather had turned cool, and the hood of her pink sweatshirt was pulled over her head, shielding her face from my view. The jeans on her slim figure and sweatshirt gave no clue as to who she was. She kept touching Justin on the arm, and he didn't move away. She must have been doing all the talking, because his mouth didn't move as he watched her.

After a minute, Justin spoke briefly, and then he nodded. A dusky pink twilight had settled, forming a picturesque background behind the two.

The woman reached out and put her arms around Justin. He didn't move. She ran down the porch steps, turned and waved to him, then let herself into a red convertible. He watched as it pulled out of his driveway, hands thrust deep into his jeans pockets until her car was out of sight.

When Justin finally went inside, I moved the car down the street past his house, praying he wouldn't look out a window and see me. I took a left onto the next street and pulled into my own driveway.

I didn't know what to do. Should I go over to his house for dinner as planned? Would he still want company?

My watch read seven fifteen. Justin wasn't expecting

me for at least forty-five minutes. I needed something to settle my stomach. Carlita's bakery was closed for the night, but Java Time was still open. Archie had amazing cinnamon rolls, and one of those would hit the spot right now.

Once Upon a Bookstore's lights were off when I passed. I found a parking spot in front of Java Time, locked my car, and went inside.

The place was deserted. The delicious, inviting scents of cinnamon and chocolate wafted through the air, which soothed me. There were a few tables, and a solitary booth in the back. The entire shop was cozy, with dark wood veneer walls and a pine beam ceiling overhead. Framed photographs of the shop over the years decorated the comfortable space, with other memorable pictures of Archie's deceased wife, Ella, and their kids. Archie's shop was the longest-running business in Harvest Park and a staple in our community.

Archie was sweeping the floor and glanced up when the door opened. He gave me a megawatt smile that caused his large jowls to droop in the process. Archie's persona was similar to that of a bartender—serving up specialty drinks while being a sympathetic listener with no judgment. He preferred to hear about you instead of talking about himself.

Next to the dark roast, my personal favorite was his peppermint hot chocolate with homemade whipped cream—a treat only served during the holidays. Archie's kids were grown and had moved out of state, except for one son, Jake, who also worked in the shop. Customers had become Archie's extended family over the years.

Archie stuck the broom in a corner, took off his Giants cap, and scratched the top of his balding head thoughtfully. "Well now, this is a nice surprise. I never see you in here this late. How's everything going with the restaurant, honey?"

"It's coming along." I smiled at him fondly. Archie had been a dear friend since I was a child and was like a father figure, especially since my own had died.

"What can I get you?" He moved behind the counter and washed his hands in the sink.

I studied the contents of the case intently. "No cinnamon rolls left?"

"I'm fresh out, but I've got some good-looking croissants leftover from Carlita's bakery. Or do you want your usual dark roast?"

"No, I'm afraid it will keep me up. I haven't been sleeping well lately."

He nodded in understanding. "I went through that after Ella died, too. For a long time. Some days it felt like it was never going to end. But it will get better, honey. Trust me."

"I hope so."

Archie winked. "I know what you'd really like. A cup of my peppermint hot chocolate."

My jaw dropped. "I'd love one. But it's not in season."

He chuckled. "Wrong. I always have a little on hand for special customers. You need to keep it a secret, though."

"You're the best." I placed a five-dollar bill on the counter and stared at the pastries again. Next to the croissants a few of Carlita's chocolate crème doughnuts remained in the display case. "Since when did you start carrying baked goods from Sweet Treats?"

Archie placed my drink in front of me. "Carlita asked me if I would. Seems her business has dropped off a bit lately, and she thought that if people had easier access it might drive sales back up. I told Carlita maybe she ought to think about extending her hours until six o'clock every evening instead of five. She might get more traffic from people on their way home from work." He leaned over the counter. "Now tell me what's really bothering you."

Where to start? "You know me too well. The grand opening is making me nervous. I need it to be a success, but with everything that's happened at Gabby's bookstore and the fact that I made desserts for—well, you know the deal. The new detective in town is taking a hard look at us."

He stroked his white whiskers thoughtfully. "It's a lousy rap for you both. Does Gino have any idea who killed her?" Since Daphne, Gabby, and I had gone to school together, Archie knew who she was. His coffee shop had been a favorite hangout for many of us back then. While our lives had changed considerably over the years, Archie's shop had remained a constant.

I took a long sip of my drink, letting the rich chocolate roll over my tongue. "Oh, so good. I've missed this." There was no reason to keep information from Archie about the murder. He could be trusted, and like me, he had Gabby's best interest at heart. "Gino's not allowed to work the case because of his relationship with Gabby. Daphne had a shellfish allergy, and they found shrimp powder in the cannoli."

Archie's caterpillar-like white eyebrows rose in alarm. "The cannoli *you* made?"

"No. That's the strange part. When Gabby and I locked up, the cannoli weren't in the store. We took the extras home with us. Whoever met Daphne there must have brought their own cannoli with them. They may have—watched her die." How horrible was that? To stand and watch her struggle, while making sure that her EpiPen was out of reach. Maybe Daphne had even begged for it. I shivered. "The way I figure, someone at the signing saw her devouring my cannoli and knew about her allergy. And they hoped to either pin it on me or Gabby."

Archie frowned. "Sounds like you're on the right track. I remember Daphne coming in here for coffee when you ladies were in high school. She was a pretty little thing but always so uppity. Had a new boyfriend every week, too, if I remember right."

Oh, if Archie had only known the half of it.

He pursed his lips together. "I haven't seen her father for a long time but believe he still lives in town somewhere. I know that he's been in poor health. To her credit, I did hear that Daphne always took good care of her dad."

"Really?" This surprised me, but it was nice to know Daphne had been human after all.

Archie went on. "As a matter of fact, I saw her in here about a week before the book signing. I tried to ask her how he was, but she pretended she didn't know me."

That sounded more like the Daphne I'd known. Archie would give you the shirt off his back, and it annoyed me she'd behaved that way toward him. "Was she alone?"

Archie hesitated. "Ah, no. She was with a man."

"It was Lorenzo, wasn't it?"

Archie's mouth dropped open in surprise, and he looked slightly disappointed. Like Carlita, he enjoyed being the first one in town to deliver the news. "That's right. What made you think of him?"

I took another sip of my drink. "Because he's a suspect in her murder. They were involved, Arch."

"Yeah, I guessed that," he said grimly. "Lorenzo kissed her as soon as she sat down and she acted upset about it. Then Daphne stared around the room, as if afraid someone had seen them. After a couple of minutes, she got up and left, and he looked like he'd lost his best friend." Archie shook his head. "That kid never had much sense. Don't get me wrong. I think the world of Carlita and her family—but that one, he's always been a problem."

"Lorenzo's not a bad person," I protested. "Sure, he likes to have a good time, and the women flock around him. He's not overly interested in working for a living, either."

"That's only the start." Archie placed his hands flat on the counter's surface. "This has to stay between the two of us, okay?"

Uh-oh. Hairs rose on the back of my neck. "You're scaring me. What else do you know?"

Archie leaned over the counter. "Look, I don't think Lorenzo's a terrible person and want to believe that he was telling the truth, but I can't be sure. Maybe he's changed, but the kid did have some serious issues once upon a time."

I didn't like the sound of this. "Why, what else has he done?"

Archie's jaw tightened. "Lorenzo had quite an angry streak back in high school. He's the same age as my Jake, remember? He was a hothead—always picking fights with other kids, skipping classes, and smoking cigarettes on school property. One time, Jake spotted him and a few of his friends joyriding through the school's baseball field late at night. They did some serious damage to the field, and their parents ended up footing the bill for repairs. He's given Carlita and Giuseppe a lot of headaches over the years."

"I had no idea he'd been in so much trouble."

"No reason you would," Archie said simply. "I believe you and Dylan had just gotten married when this all went down. Besides, Carlita and the other parents hoped to keep it under wraps. That was back when I was serving on the town board. A lot of people wanted those kids to do community service or spend a month in jail, but they got off with a slap on the wrist and a small fine."

"Well, he was a kid. People make mistakes, and you learn from them." Why did I insist on defending Lorenzo? I didn't know him that well, and my own suspicions were already present. But Carlita had asked me to help him. Her children were everything to her, and I didn't want to see her hurt.

I threw my cup in the trash. "Thanks for the hot chocolate. I need to get going. I'm meeting Justin for dinner."

Archie looked surprised. "Really? I didn't even know he was back in town until about an hour ago."

"Justin was here?"

"No, but his ex-wife was. She said she was on her way to see him. Natalie, right? Beautiful lady. I never saw much of her when they were married, but she seemed friendly enough tonight. We chatted for a bit."

My stomach twisted at his words. So, it had been Natalie I'd seen Justin with. Why was she back, after all this time? "What was she was going to see him about?"

"No idea. Natalie only said that there was something she needed to take care of, and that she regretted not doing it long ago." Archie studied my face. "Everything all right? You look a little pale."

"No, I'm fine. It's been a rough couple of days, that's all." My chest tightened when I remembered Natalie putting her arms around Justin. Hadn't she caused him enough pain? One thing was for certain—Natalie was back because she clearly wanted something, and I suspected it was Justin. "Thanks again for the hot chocolate. It was amazing."

He winked. "Anytime. Have a good night, honey. Sleep well."

ELEVEN

AS I DROVE TOWARD JUSTIN'S HOUSE, my thoughts wandered back to Natalie. As far as I knew, Justin and Natalie hadn't been in touch since their divorce over a year ago. An avid skier, she'd moved to Vermont with her boyfriend—the man with whom she'd had an affair. Was this why Justin had been so distracted at dinner the other night?

There had been a time when Justin, Natalie, Dylan, and I had gotten together almost every weekend, or whenever Justin's work schedule allowed. Natalie and I were on friendly enough terms, but our relationship was nothing like our husbands' rapport. Dylan had never cared for Natalie and told me so several times. Perhaps that had put me on my guard as well. Dylan felt Natalie took advantage of Justin—that she was too spoiled and pampered. When Justin broke the news that he'd caught her cheating with another man, Dylan had been livid. He'd told his friend that he was better off without her, and Justin had not taken the advice well. It was the only time I remembered them not speaking for a given amount of time.

Justin's house was a small white ranch that Natalie had left him to pay for after she'd breezed out of town with her boyfriend. Questions crowded my brain. Did she think she could just waltz in and get back together with him, as if nothing had ever happened? Hadn't she messed with his head enough? And lastly, why was I starting to obsess about this? I had no claim to Justin. Besides, I'd told him that I wasn't ready for a relationship—with anyone.

Loving someone often came with the risks of disappointment and heartache. I'd experienced both. Once upon a time, I thought Dylan and I had the perfect marriage. After he died, I'd discovered some terrible secrets he'd kept from me and dishonest things he'd done, which had led to his murder. In his own mind, he'd felt justified in doing them, but that still didn't make it right. However, Dylan always had my best interest at heart and was never unfaithful to me. That was the one thing I couldn't have handled.

When I finally parked and rang the bell, a smell of burned meat permeated the air. My mood boosted, and I bit into my lower lip to keep from laughing. Justin opened the door immediately, a potholder in one hand and a can of air freshener in the other.

"Uh, there's been a little change of plans," he said, looking sheepish. "I called and ordered a pizza."

I walked into the kitchen and stared at the blackened mess in the loaf pan on top of the stove. Justin had several windows open, but the smell was still strong, and I coughed. "What was it?"

He gave me a wry smile. "Meat loaf."

I burst out laughing, and after a few seconds Justin joined me. "This is silly. I would have been happy to make dinner." I waved a hand at the acrid air. "Plus, I would have enjoyed it. Something tells me you didn't have a great time creating this—masterpiece."

"No, I hate to cook. But I wanted to treat you to a night off." He got down two mismatched glasses from the cupboard next to the stove. Justin wasn't much of a housekeeper, but then again he was rarely home. There were dirty dishes in the sink, and when Justin opened the fridge to grab a bottle of wine, only condiments and beer decorated the shelves. It was much like the inside of the dorm fridge he and Dylan had shared many years ago. "Would you like a glass of wine?"

"Half a glass, please."

He poured some Chianti for me, filled his glass, and then drank most of it in one gulp. Something in his demeanor was off, and I wondered if it had to do with Natalie's earlier visit. "What did you do on your day off?"

He shook his head and poured himself more wine. "Nothing special. I spent some time making dinner—not that you can tell now. And I watched television. It was nice to have a day to myself and not have to think."

"We all need that occasionally. You work too hard. How *is* work, by the way? I'll bet they're glad to have you back."

A shadow passed over his face. "There's good days and there's bad days. The good days are when you're able to save lives." His grayish-blue eyes became stricken. "It was horrible to get the news about Dad back in February, but I wasn't that sorry to leave my job for a while. I was burned out. No pun intended." He smiled ruefully.

"Everyone has to have a break at some point," I said. "You're an amazing fireman." He'd received several awards and recognition during the eight years he'd served in the department. "Are you thinking about a new career?" Frankly, I couldn't picture it.

He gave me a wistful smile. "I honestly can't imagine doing anything else. Probably like you can't imagine not cooking. It's always been my dream to be a fireman, since I was five years old. But this isn't all shiny red fire trucks and cute spotted dogs. The work is stressful, intense, and I always have to have my wits about me. We're talking about people's lives here, and I can't afford to screw up." He paused and drew a deep breath. "But it's also difficult to have any type of life for myself some days and not fair to those who are close to me. Does that make sense?"

"Of course." He sounded guilt ridden, and I wasn't sure why.

"Tess," Justin said quietly, "there's something I need to tell you."

I hated it when people used that expression. Sure, I always tried to be optimistic, but that phrase usually meant something bad would follow. I had a suspicion as to what was coming. "It's about Natalie, isn't it?"

He stared at me, thunderstruck. "How'd you know?"

"I was at Java Time earlier. Archie said that he saw her tonight." I left out the part about spying them together on the front porch.

He rubbed a hand over the stubble on his chin. "I

forgot. Nothing is a secret in this town." His tone was matter-of-fact, as if it didn't really bother him, and then he lapsed into silence.

"What did she want?" I asked with interest.

Justin blew out a long breath and stared down at the table. "She asked me if we could get back together."

Yes, I'd suspected as much, but it was still a surprise. "I see."

He looked into my eyes. "Do you? Because I don't. I've never been so confused in my entire life."

"If you still love her," I said slowly and carefully, "then the decision is easy."

"I did love Natalie once. I wouldn't have married her if I didn't." He hesitated for a moment and then poured himself another glass of wine. "I don't know. My life feels like it's spiraling out of control these days. Natalie kept begging me for another chance. She said she was lonely during our marriage, and that I was always working. She said that she turned to another man out of fear for me."

"What?" This statement made no sense.

Justin smiled wryly. "Yeah. She said she worried that one night I wouldn't come home to her."

I said nothing. Justin didn't need my judgment, but

Natalie's excuse sounded bogus. Justin had always been a workaholic, and she knew what she was getting into when she married him. I suspected he felt guilty for not being around much while he tried to work his way up the ladder. Dylan and I had talked about it a few times, and he felt that Justin indulged her every whim because of the guilt. Still, I couldn't come right out and tell Justin what I thought. This was his life and his decision to make, not mine.

We both stood there with our drinks in companionable silence, lost in our own heads. The doorbell rang, and Justin went to answer it. He came back a minute later with a pizza box that he laid on the stove and grabbed two plates from the cupboard. Half of the pizza was plain, and the other side covered with sausage and peppers. He smiled sheepishly as he handed me a slice of plain. "Yours is ten times better than this."

I bit into the slice. The pizza was hot, flavorful, and gooey. "It tastes pretty good to me. Mine isn't the best in the world."

"It has to be in the top ten," he insisted as we sat down at the table. Justin opened a beer and held it out in question to me, but I shook my head. He was drinking more than usual—another sign that he was upset. "Enough heavy talk.

Tell me about Anything's Pastable. Is everything ready to go? I've requested the night off from work, but you know that something might come up."

I did know. There was always a chance Justin would be called in if a fire broke out and more hands were needed. He'd been ready to resign from the station back in February if they hadn't granted his leave of absence. Fortunately, the fire department had agreed because they knew they couldn't afford to lose him permanently.

"There've been challenges I didn't expect," I admitted. "More repairs than I'd planned on, and additional expenses. I think everything is finally under control, and my staff's almost in place. I'm waiting to hear back from one woman I interviewed the other day. There are always going to be unexpected things that come up, but I can handle it."

He smiled into my eyes with genuine affection. "You definitely can. I'm so proud of you, Tess. Dylan would have been, too."

"Thanks." No matter what happened between Justin and me, we'd always have a bond because of Dylan. Personally, I didn't know if true love was in the cards for me again. Maybe you were only allowed one per lifetime. Besides, I wasn't sure if I could ever love anyone as much as Dylan.

I reached for another slice of pizza. The sauce, cheese, and spices blended together perfectly. I had to remember to put more oregano in mine.

Justin broke into my thoughts. "By the way, I forgot to thank you for taking care of the house while I was away."

"It was no trouble. You would have done the same thing if I needed it. Which reminds me, I still have your house key." I wiped my hands on a napkin and went over to the front door where I'd hung my purse on a hook. As I reached inside, I happened to glance out the front window and spotted a BMW that looked like Sylvia Rigotta's on the opposite side of the road, under a street light. Startled, I opened the front door. The car roared to life and zoomed past Justin's house. The windows were tinted so I couldn't see the driver, but I did glimpse the vanity plate—*SpiceItUp.* A cold, clammy sensation ran through me. Sylvia was following me. But why?

I left Justin's about a half hour later. It had been a long day, and I wanted to try to get some sleep before meeting Gabby tomorrow morning. After that, I needed to experiment with some new dishes at the restaurant. As I got into the car, my phone buzzed. *Gabby.*

"Hey." She sounded depressed. "Want to stop over for a girls' night?"

I glanced at the clock. It was nine fifteen. "What happened to Lou? Is your date over already?"

"He got called into work." She sighed. "Cops. What can I tell you? You can't live with them, and you can't live without them."

Her comment made me want to laugh, but I stopped myself in time. Someone desperately needed some cheering up tonight. "Did Lou give you any new details about Daphne's murder?"

"No. Like Gino, he only said that the autopsy was expected back tomorrow." Her tone became indignant. "Of course, it depends on whether good old Paddy is willing to share any details. So, will you come over?"

I really wanted my bed but hated to disappoint her. "Okay, I'll swing by for a little while but no wine for me. I already had a glass."

"That's okay, I can think of something even better. I just thawed out a cheesecake." She chuckled into the phone. "Hey, I know the frozen ones from the supermarket aren't as terrific as the ones you make from scratch—"

"That sounds pretty good to me. I'm on my way."

I pulled into her driveway about five minutes later, after glancing in my rearview mirror repeatedly along the way and scanning the street to make sure no one was around. The idea of Sylvia Rigotta lurking in the darkness, following my every move, was not a pleasant one.

Gabby was waiting at the door. "What's wrong?"

I told her about seeing Sylvia's car at Justin's and she gasped. "She was following you? Did you call my brother?"

"I left Gino a voicemail but haven't heard back yet. I'm guessing he'll say there's nothing the police can do. It's not like she threatened me or anything."

Gabby shook her head in disgust. "Once Detective Paddy McJerk finds out, he'll look for a way to blame you instead. Mark my words."

"Let's not talk about him tonight," I suggested and flopped down onto her couch with a yawn. Gabby went into the kitchen and returned a minute later with the cheesecake, two plates, napkins, and silverware that she set on her rustic coffee table. Despite the pizza I'd eaten, I was still hungry. "Looks good."

Gabby sliced two huge pieces, handed me one on a glass plate, and then clicked the remote to a rerun of *The Office*. "I need to laugh tonight."

We settled ourselves against the overstuffed pillows of her couch positioned in front of the slider window. Gabby reached up behind us to draw the curtains partway and then began to eat. "Okay, I don't think it's completely thawed, but it still tastes good."

"No complaints here." I took a bite and then wiped my mouth with a napkin. "Let's see, that makes pizza, hot chocolate, wine, and now cheesecake, and that's only for tonight."

"Sounds like a reasonable diet to me." Gabby scraped her fork against the plate and moaned with satisfaction. "I think I'm going to need another piece."

I took another large bite. "Hey, do you have any whipped cream?"

She grinned. "That's like asking if I have wine." Gabby rose from the couch and walked into her adjoining kitchen. I moved over to her spot on the couch to grab a pillow, as a loud crash sounded behind me. Gabby let out a shriek while I dove under the coffee table, sending the cheesecake and Gabby's glass of wine flying. From my position on the floor, I turned around to see a large, round hole in her window.

"Oh, my God!" she screamed and hurried to my side. "Are you hurt?"

I shook my head and shakily raised myself up on my elbows. "What the heck was that?"

Gabby ran to the front door and flung it open, peering out into the darkness. "Maybe a prank? There's a family down the street with six kids who I swear have no curfew. They're always lurking around on the street till all hours." She shut the door and came back over to me. "At least it's not a bullet hole." Gabby went into the kitchen and came back with a towel to blot the wine. She then pressed a button on her phone. "I'm going to see if Lou can swing by."

On my hands and knees, I peered underneath the easy chair across from the couch and spotted a large rock, about six inches wide. A piece of paper was attached to it, held in place by a rubber band. My heart knocked against the wall of my chest as I held a napkin in my hand and gingerly picked up the rock.

"Babe, it's me. Call me back as soon as possible. It's important." Gabby clicked off and then sank down on her knees next to me. "A rock? What's that attached to it?"

"My guess is a note of some kind." My hands shook as I opened the paper with the napkin, careful not to touch it in case of fingerprints. The paper turned out to be a piece of personal stationery. "This wasn't a prank done by kids."

Gabby stared over my shoulder at the words printed in black marker, "BACK OFF OR DIE." On top of the paper, in raised gold letters, were an *S* and *R*, intertwined. Fear registered in her dark eyes as they met mine.

"Looks like Sylvia's had a busy night," she whispered.

TWELVE

"OKAY, DON'T KEEP ME IN SUSPENSE, Gabs. What happened after I left last night?" It was ten o'clock on Tuesday morning, and we were headed down the Thruway in the direction of Gourmet Goodies. I'd gone home shortly after Lou had arrived the evening before. Gabby had refused the offer to stay at my house.

Gabby yawned and leaned her head back against the seat. She looked tired. "Lou got someone to fill in for him and stayed on the couch all night. He didn't want me to be alone."

"That was sweet. Did they bring Sylvia in for questioning?" I asked.

She shook her head. "He said he'd pass the information along to Paddy, but there was no proof that the stationery belonged to Sylvia. Blah blah. I told him about her following you, but he said Paddy was handling it. I got annoyed with him and went upstairs to bed."

"I wonder how Paddy *does* plan to handle it."

Gabby's lips formed into a pout. "Exactly. Sure, there's no proof that she was following you, but why else would she be on Justin's street? If you'd been outside her house, I bet Paddy wouldn't hesitate to slap a pair of handcuffs on your wrists."

"What did Gino say when you told him?"

Gabby stared out the window. "I didn't tell him—yet."

I almost veered off the road. "What? Why the heck not?"

She jutted her chin out in defiance. "Because he'll just say the same thing that Lou did. It won't do any good."

"Lou will tell him then."

Gabby folded her arms across her chest. "I don't care. Lou's out of town the next two days for a friend's wedding. He won't speak to Gino until he gets back. Let him find out then. I can do without another 'Let Paddy handle it' from him." She mimicked her brother's tone.

I struggled not to roll my eyes. "For heaven's sake. You're being ridiculous. This isn't Gino's fault."

"Gino doesn't understand that my business is about to

go up in flames. I don't need another lecture from him to stay out of police business. Someone obviously feels threatened by our snooping, so maybe we're on to something."

"He needs to know. Does Lou have the rock?"

She nodded. "He took it for evidence. Maybe I'll tell Gino about it before Lou gets back."

"Right." Gabby wasn't fooling me. I knew that tone and doubted she'd follow through. It was difficult to say who was more stubborn, her or Gino.

She gritted her teeth in annoyance. "Mr. Big City Detective will probably say that I planted the rock to get myself off the hook. He makes me sick."

"Gabs, calm down."

She went on. "And if he goes to the Rigottas', I wouldn't put it past Preston to say we harassed his wife at the television station."

"If Preston's smart, he'll keep his mouth shut. He's a suspect as well. I wish somehow we could get him to submit to a blood test." My mind was spinning like a hamster wheel. "Do you think Willow would talk to us? If we could get her alone, I mean."

"I doubt it," Gabby said. "They've got her trained like a dog. It's always *yes, Daddy; no, Mommy. Whatever you say.*

Jeez, can you imagine living like that?" Her face twisted into a frown. "She's totally devoted to both of them."

"Willow could have killed Daphne to save her parents' marriage," I said, thinking out loud. "She might have known about the baby and wanted to stop Daphne from making trouble."

"And then we have Lorenzo, who has a history of making trouble," Gabby said. "If he knew Daphne was cheating on him, he may have plotted to kill her. Maybe he lied to us and did know about the baby. That could have pushed him over the edge. Lorenzo might have brought over cannoli from his mother's bakery and put the shrimp powder inside. He knew about Daphne's allergy."

I pulled my car into the near empty parking lot adjacent to a small gray brick building. A square metal sign on the side read *Gourmet Goodies. Est. 2005.* "Come on. Let's see if we can find out anything about the chocolate that will help."

A delicious variety of spicy smells drifted toward us when we opened the emporium door. There were aisles of exotic seasonings, coffees from different countries, and a small delicatessen case in the back.

A man in his early twenties was behind the counter. He looked up and smiled at us. "Help you with something?"

"Yes, I'm looking for a certain type of baking chocolate," I said. "It's called Valrhona. Do you know where I'd find it?"

His forehead creased in concentration. "Never heard of it, but then again, I've only been working here a few weeks." He waved down a woman with shoulder-length gray hair who had emerged from a nearby door that read *Office*. "Penelope, can you help these ladies find Valrhona chocolate?"

Penelope beamed at us. "Of course. Right this way." She led us down aisle five and pointed at the bottom shelf. There were five bars of the chocolate in a display box.

I gulped when I saw the price—forty dollars apiece. It was more than I'd remembered. "Thank you. Do you sell a lot of this?"

"Don't I wish." Penelope leaned down to examine the packages. "Oh, my. Looks like we did sell one. I had six in stock last time I checked. It must have been last week when I had my root canal, because I would have remembered that sale."

Gabby and I exchanged a glance. "This is going to

sound strange," I said, "but is there any way you can track down who bought it?"

Suspicion clouded Penelope's eyes. "What's this all about? Don't you want to purchase the chocolate?"

"Of course." No, I wasn't interested in purchasing the chocolate, but it looked like I didn't have much choice. I supposed I could use it in the restaurant. As my grandmother used to say, there was no great loss without some small gain. A *very* small one. "You see, I'm in an upcoming baking competition," I lied.

"She owns a restaurant," Gabby said with an unmistakable note of pride in her voice.

The woman scanned me up and down. "Well, that's nice, but what does it have to do with tracking down who bought the chocolate?"

I looked around the store and crooked my finger, indicating for Penelope to come closer. "We were all given specific ingredients to use, and mine was Valrhona chocolate. I don't trust my competition, though. I think they're planning to use it, too. Since your store is the closest, I thought I'd try to learn if the other contestants have already been here."

"They may have purchased it online," Penelope pointed out.

Shoot. I hadn't even thought about that. Why did she have to throw a wrench in my plans? "Sure, that's possible," I said smoothly, "but all of the contestants' mail is being tracked." *Where the heck did I get such a stupid idea?* There was no way she'd fall for this bull.

Penelope studied me for a long moment. "I've heard some of those contestant rules can be pretty brutal. What's the contest?"

"The Harvest Park Bake-Off," Gabby replied before I could stop her.

Penelope cocked her head to one side. "I've never heard of that competition. Is it new?"

There was a bake-off held during Harvest Park's annual Apple Festival in the fall, but I didn't want to give this woman too many details. What if whoever had bought the chocolate came in again, and she mentioned us to them? "I only need to find out who bought the chocolate. I believe there should be complete honesty in competitions. It's always the best policy, right?" What a joke after the lies I'd been telling lately.

My heart sank as Penelope shook her head. "I wasn't here when it was purchased, so I'm afraid I can't help you."

It was time to pull out the big guns. I picked up the

display box with the chocolate and smiled pleasantly. "But you *could* check your computer system to see if you have the person's name on file, right? Or maybe a credit card slip? I'd be so grateful and more than happy to buy *all* the chocolate, for your trouble."

"This way no one else will have a chance to cheat again," Gabby added.

Dollar signs appeared in Penelope's eyes. "Well, I don't normally do this, but okay. It may take me a little while to find the transaction, since I can't be positive it was bought the day I was out. If they paid with cash you're out of luck, I'm afraid."

I was also out two hundred dollars but refrained from saying so. The three of us proceeded to the register where Penelope herself rang us out. Gabby handed me a fifty. "It's all I have, Tess."

"No worries." I pushed the bill back at her. "I'll use it in the restaurant."

"What will you make with the chocolate? Can you share any details of your recipe for the contest?" Penelope asked with interest as I wrote my first name only and cell phone number on a piece of paper. I thought about giving her a business card but wasn't sure that was wise.

Gabby looked horrified at the suggestion. "But she can't. It's top secret. She didn't even tell me and I'm her best friend."

"I can't take a chance on being disqualified," I murmured.

"Oh, yes. Of course." Penelope took the paper from me. "Do keep in mind that the chocolate is wonderful for many baking dishes, especially cannoli. It brings out the flavor of the mascarpone filling."

"Really?" I tried to act surprised. "Thanks for the tip."

Penelope handed me my receipt. "I'll try to call you this afternoon, with the name only. No other information will be included."

"That's all I need. Thank you."

Penelope's cell phone buzzed, and we took the opportunity to exit the store. Gabby glanced meekly at me as we got into my car. "Tess, I'm sorry. You're trying to help me and all it's doing is costing you money."

"I already told you, it's fine. I'll use these at the restaurant."

"What now?" she asked. "Do you have some free time before you go back to the restaurant?"

I didn't, but Gabby's face looked so hopeful that I

couldn't bear to squash whatever she had in mind. "A little. My staff is coming in this afternoon for a quick meeting, and a repairman to fix the sign. I may make more sauce, too."

She winked. "What are you stressed about now?"

I laughed. My tomato sauce was a running joke between those who knew me best. It had a calming effect on me and was therapeutic in some ways. After Dylan's death, I'd filled so many ziplock bags full of it that I'd contemplated buying a second freezer. No, I didn't need more sauce, but I did want to think about the entire Daphne puzzle. Something was missing. "What did you have in mind?"

She was scrolling through Facebook on her phone. "I was right. Today's the day. Preston has a book signing in Buffalo. That's four hours away."

I immediately understood. "Are you suggesting we go to Preston's house and snoop through his kitchen to find the chocolate?"

Gabby grinned wickedly. "Why, Tess, I thought you'd never ask."

THIRTEEN

"WHAT ABOUT WILLOW?" I ASKED. "And Sylvia?"

Gabby checked her watch. "It's not even noon yet, so we don't have to worry about them. Sylvia's still at the television station and Willow will be with Preston. He doesn't have a publicist anymore, remember, so she'll accompany him to the signing."

I exited off the Thruway and in the direction of Saratoga. "How are we going to do this if no one is home? Are you suggesting we break in?"

She gave a little excited giggle. "This is going to be such fun. And no, the housekeeper will let us in. She should remember me. I know where the kitchens are because Preston gave me a tour of the house."

"Kitchens? They have more than one?"

She nodded. "Willow has her own private quarters

upstairs. It's like one of those mother-in-law apartment setups."

"Is she in college?" I asked.

She shook her head. "Not anymore. Willow has an associate degree in web design and, like I told you, takes care of his website but I'm guessing she has no choice in the matter. I've heard that she's very sheltered, especially since she's an only child."

"I'm an only child, and I wasn't sheltered," I reminded her.

"You don't count," Gabby said. "In Italian families, it doesn't matter whether there's one kid or ten. Everyone gets suffocated equally."

She had a point. "I wish we could get Willow alone to see what she has to say."

Gabby sighed. "She strikes me as one of those who aren't supposed to speak unless spoken to types. She's devoted to her parents. You saw her and Sylvia at the signing. They were thick as thieves."

"Well, it's worth a shot. Let's get this over with. Where do they live?"

Gabby bounced in her seat. "Awesome! Stay on the Northway until you hit Exit 15."

I glanced at the clock but said nothing. If our visit was brief, I could drop Gabby off and make it to the restaurant just in time for my staff meeting. My phone buzzed, and I pressed the Bluetooth on the steering wheel. "Hello?"

"Hello, Tessa? This is Stephanie Beaudry. Sorry it's taken me so long to call you back. My daughter had to get stitches last night. She fell at the playground."

"Oh, no. Is she okay?"

"Zoe's fine," Stephanie replied. "Five stitches in her forehead and she just missed hitting her eye. Kids. They always keep you moving. What did you want to talk to me about?"

Call it intuition, but I was confident this was going to work out perfectly for the both of us. "I'd like to offer you a position at Anything's Pastable as my assistant."

She gasped. "Oh, my God! Thank you so much. I promise that I won't let you down. When would you like me to start?"

Exit 15 was approaching. "The restaurant opens Saturday. I know it's short notice, so if you need to give Greg another week or two, I understand." I'd have to find a way to manage on opening night without her. Maybe Gabby would still be willing to help.

"No, he'll be fine with it," said Stephanie. "Trust me, there's other employees who are dying to get their hands on my hours."

"Wonderful. Is there any chance you could come in for a quick meeting this afternoon? The rest of my staff will be there, and it would give you all a chance to get acquainted."

"No problem. Zoe can stay with my neighbor." Stephanie giggled and sounded like a little kid herself. "I am so excited, Tessa. I can't thank you enough."

"I'll see you at two o'clock." I disconnected and might have done a happy dance if I hadn't been driving. "My staff is all in place now," I told Gabby, "except for maybe one more part-time waitress or waiter."

Gabby clapped her hands. "You rock, girl. Take a left here on to McChesney Avenue. This is their street."

I glanced around the neighborhood in awe. Saratoga, whose name derived from a Native American word, was a historical town filled with lovely attractions. The most popular was their famous racetrack, which operated during the summer. There were several wealthy homes located in the town that belonged to local celebrities.

"It's the second mansion on the right," Gabby said.

I turned into a private driveway covered with crushed

marble. My jaw dropped as I stared up at the impressive Victorian mansion. It appeared to be from the nineteenth century, but was incredibly well preserved. The lawn had been manicured to perfection and was dotted with rose and azalea bushes. A large, bronze bust of Preston stared ominously at us from beside a stone water fountain. The bust was magnificent and garish at the same time. Intricate carved stone surrounded the exterior of the mansion, and colored panes of stained glass decorated every window.

"This is gorgeous."

"It's stunning on the inside, too," Gabby remarked, "but a bit more modern. When the Rigottas bought the place about twenty years ago, they chose not to change much of the exterior. The house is almost too nice to live in."

"Didn't I hear somewhere that he had old family money?" I asked as we climbed the steps of the large wrap-around porch.

Gabby wrapped the brass knocker against the mahogany door. "He inherited a good sum from his parents, but Preston's made his own pile of cash, too. He's had ten best-selling books, and a few even went to number one."

I couldn't help but wonder how many *New York Times*

bestselling authors might be suspected of murdering their publicist whom they also happened to be having an affair with. Chances were, not many. Did Preston lure Daphne back to the bookstore that night? If he knew she was pregnant with his child, he would have been outraged and most likely wanted her out of the way.

A petite woman in her forties wearing a black uniform dress and tights opened the door and gave us both a polite smile. Her nametag identified her at Marta. "May I help you?"

I cleared my throat. "Hi, we were wondering if we could speak to Sylvia, please?"

Marta's smile faded as she glanced from me to Gabby. She had short, dark hair styled in a bob, with hazel eyes that poked out from beneath long, dark lashes. Her bronze skin and an accent similar to Carlita's suggested she was of Spanish descent. Her face seemed familiar, and I assumed she might have been a customer when I worked at Magnifico's Restaurant, a ten-minute drive from Saratoga.

"I'm so sorry," Marta said. "She is not at home right now. Was she expecting you?"

"Yes," I said quickly. "We're friends of hers. Do you think we could wait?"

The woman started to shake her head and then looked more closely at Gabby. "You have been here before."

"Yes, to see Preston," Gabby explained. "He's a friend, too."

Marta pursed her lips together. "Well, I guess it will be all right then. You can wait in the library." She opened the door and allowed us into the foyer. "This way."

We silently followed Marta by the mahogany staircase and down a long, sterile hallway, past a gleaming kitchen that I longed to explore. Marta stopped in front of a room with a stone fireplace that occupied an entire wall. Across from it were several wingback chairs and a cherrywood coffee table. Other walls contained built-in shelves with a vast range of books and genres. Several of them were vintage and probably worth money. Photographs of Preston's novels and the various awards he'd won dominated the paneled walls.

"Wait here," she commanded, and disappeared before we could thank her. A minute later the sound of a vacuum commenced above us.

Gabby made a big deal out of tiptoeing over to the doorway. "I'm going to sneak up the back staircase. Do you want to tackle the kitchen down here, Nancy?"

"This isn't a joke. What if Marta sees you up there?"

She grinned. "I'll tell her I got lost."

"Don't take too long and don't snoop in any other places. This is risky. Just check Willow's kitchen for the chocolate. What if some of the other staff is around? We can't get caught."

"Yes, Miss Drew," Gabby teased. "Good luck." She blew me a dramatic kiss and then peered out into the hallway. In her best sleuthing style, she moved lightly on the terrazzo flooring, leaving me to do my own exploring.

After Gabby disappeared, I checked the hallway for any signs of life. I was grateful I'd worn sneakers and hurried toward the kitchen. It was a cook's dream with an enormous center island, stainless-steel appliances, a double-wall oven, and built-in cabinets that wrapped around the entire room. I started to open cupboards but found only dishes, glassware, and pots and pans. Where were all the ingredients?

A door on the left led to a patio, which had an in-ground pool and Jacuzzi. Preston had certainly done well for himself. A closed door next to the fridge caught my attention. I opened it and found a walk-in pantry.

"What I wouldn't give for a room like this," I whispered

to no one in particular as I hurriedly scanned the shelves. With satisfaction, I noticed several boxes of cake mixes. Sylvia was no Betty Crocker, that was for sure. I wished I'd taken more time to talk to Marta about Sylvia's so-called cooking skills. For some reason, I suspected Marta might be the real success behind *Spice it Up with Sylvia*.

A shiny red-and-black foil package was sticking out behind a store-bought box of yellow cake mix. *Pay dirt.* It was a package of Valrhona chocolate with only half of the baking squares left. I snapped a quick picture of it with my phone.

Now it was time to get the heck out of here. If we got caught, things would turn ugly. A terrifying thought occurred to me. What if the Rigottas had cameras? Why hadn't I thought of this before? I was about to text Gabby to meet me in the study, when I heard a door slam. Panicked, I placed the chocolate back on the shelf, hurried out of the pantry, and shut the door quietly. When I turned around, I almost jumped ten feet in the air.

Standing in front of me, with a startled expression on her face, was Willow Rigotta.

FOURTEEN

WILLOW'S SAPPHIRE EYES WENT WIDE WITH shock. "*You*. You're Gabby's cousin from the book signing. Tessa something. The one who made the cannoli. What are you doing in our pantry? Where's Marta?"

I spoke slowly and methodically, hoping that panic wasn't evident in my voice. "Oh, hi, Willow. I was hoping to see your mother. Marta's upstairs vacuuming." I didn't mention Gabby and prayed Marta wouldn't reappear and mention her either. "How'd your father's signing go today?"

"It was canceled. Daddy had to go to New York City to meet with his agent and a film producer. They're turning his new book into a movie." Her jaw tightened. "But I still don't know why you're in our kitchen."

"I couldn't help checking out your mother's impressive

ingredients. I'm in awe of her talent." My lies were going to catch up with me soon.

"Are you here alone?"

"Of course." If Gabby was found, things would get worse. I hoped she'd overhear our exchange and head for the car. "Your mother keeps a well-stocked pantry."

"That's right. Mother said you were a chef." Willow gave a smug smile. "She must have been jealous of you. She can barely manage to turn on an oven without help."

I was surprised to hear her admit it. "You're not a fan of her show?"

Willow shrugged. "It's all right. Mother gets paid a ridiculous amount of money for doing nothing. She hates to cook. You know how some mothers bake cookies with their kids?"

"Yes." How I yearned to do that someday.

"Not my mother," she said in annoyance. "I made cookies with Marta instead. She's the one who has taken care of me since I was a baby. Mother was always too busy trying to be in the limelight. The high society princess. Wife of a famous author. No time to be a parent. Honestly, I'm not quite sure why she even bothered to have me."

"Why are you telling me this?" It seemed weird that

she'd share all of this intimate information with a stranger. It also sounded like she resented Sylvia.

"Why not? It makes no difference if you or the entire world knows. I'm sick and tired of being their puppet. As soon as I turn twenty-one and get my trust fund, I'm out of here. They're both so self-centered they couldn't care less what happens to me."

"I'm sure that's not true." I wondered if she knew about Daphne's baby and decided to fan the flame a bit. "It's too bad that your parents never had more children. I'm an only child too and would have loved a brother or sister."

"That was never an option," Willow said. "My mother had a hysterectomy right after I was born. She said there were complications with the delivery." To my surprise, she gave a low chuckle. "Maybe deep down she's always resented me for it. Perhaps I should have studied psychology. I'd have a field day between the two of them."

Wow. Bitter much? Boy, had I been wrong. I'd thought Willow wanted to keep her parents together, when in fact all she wanted to do was get away from them. I couldn't resist delving a little further, and knew I was stepping into dangerous territory. "Daphne was only a few years older than you. Did you ever confide in her?"

A look of disgust came over her face. "Are you kidding? I wanted nothing to do with that tramp. All she cared about was getting her filthy hands on my father's money. Money that will one day belong to me."

"Were you jealous of her?" Daphne had been pretty enough to be a model, while Willow was unfortunately lacking in the looks department. Her blue eyes, while striking like her father's, were small and too close together in her well-rounded face. Her nose was flat, and her cheeks bore several acne scars.

Willow's eyes grew and practically bugged out of her head at my comment. "Jealous? Of *her?* Please. She tried to tell me what to do and was always offering stupid suggestions for the website. That was *my* creation, my baby. Not hers."

She suddenly quieted, as if realizing she'd said too much, and then shot me a look of clear contempt. "Look. We all know that it was your cousin who killed Daphne. She was bullied by her in high school and obviously held a grudge all these years. At least that's what my mother and father said. Now I think you ought to—"

A door slammed and Sylvia's voice rang out through the walls. "Willow? Where are you, dear?"

Willow's face paled, and mine must have as well. I should have gotten out of here sooner. Before I even had a chance to react, Sylvia appeared in the doorway behind her daughter.

"What's this?" Sylvia surveyed me with a haughty expression, like I was a speck of dirt on a spotless floor. "What in the world are you doing here?"

She shot me a look so intense it could have melted the skin off my face. Heat burned my cheeks, and for a moment I worried that she'd succeeded.

"Tessa said she wanted to see your kitchen." Willow glanced from me to her mother, her mouth quivering at the corners. She must have been hoping a war would break out.

Sylvia kept her eyes glued to my face as she waved a hand dismissively at her daughter. "Leave us, Willow."

"With pleasure," Willow growled, then turned on her heel and left the room without another word. A moment later her boots could be heard clunking loudly against the wooden stairs.

Sylvia folded her arms across her chest. "Again, I ask, what are you doing here?"

Time to put my acting skills to work. "I came to ask you a favor."

Sylvia stared at me in disbelief. "*You've* come to ask *me* for a favor? *Again?* Where do you get the gall?"

"I know what a wonderful cook and baker you are." It made me physically ill to say the words. "I was hoping you'd reconsider my request for a guest spot on your show. It would do wonders for my restaurant because of your popularity."

She eyed me suspiciously. "I already told you no. This is turning into harassment. I'll call the police to have it stopped."

All I needed was for her to get the former jolly New York City detective on the phone. "Please. I'm such a big fan of yours and my restaurant needs all the help it can get." No lie there.

Sylvia laughed in my face. "Silly girl. That little hole-in-the-wall hasn't got a chance in your bumpkin town. Owning a restaurant isn't for the faint of heart. Why don't you start on a smaller scale, say, with a lemonade stand?"

Anger flickered in my chest. It was doubtful that Sylvia knew anything about working in a restaurant. For one thing, it was hard, exhausting work. You were run off your feet, the kitchen was an inferno, especially during summer months, and even though most customers were pleasant, there was always a disagreeable one who made trouble no matter how hard you tried to please them. Phony Sylvia only knew about the glory.

"Sorry that I wasted your time." I turned to leave the room.

An egotistical smirk spread across her face. "Perhaps you should start worrying more about your time instead of mine, darling. You may not have much left. I wouldn't be surprised if an arrest is made soon."

"Oh, really?" I managed a smile, which wasn't easy, even though years of working in restaurants had taught me patience. "Are you a detective now, too?"

"Don't be a smart mouth with me," she hissed. "Why don't you just admit why you're really here?"

I glared back at her. "And maybe you could explain why you were following me around last night."

Sylvia wrinkled her nose. "What are you talking about?"

"I was visiting a friend about eight-thirty, when I looked out the window and saw your car parked across the street. You must have seen me open the door because you took off right afterward. What were you doing there?"

Footsteps sounded in the hall. A door closed, and we both stopped talking to listen.

"Marta?" Sylvia called loudly. The vacuuming had stopped, but there was no answer. She turned back to me, her cold blue eyes resembling steel. "I don't appreciate your accusation. If you must know, I was at home all night."

I decided to give her the benefit of the doubt. "Perhaps Willow took your car and—"

She gnashed her teeth together and thrust her hand toward the doorway. "How dare you. You're making this all up. Get out of my house and do not come back. It's obvious you're here on a fishing expedition and trying to pin the murder on someone else other than your cousin. Rest assured that I will tell Preston all about your uninvited visit when he returns tonight."

I was tempted to tell her to go right ahead but stopped myself in time. If Preston sought me out, then maybe I could discover what he knew about the baby. Perhaps he'd become so enraged that juicy tidbits would slip out of his mouth.

"It wasn't my intention to offend you," I said calmly. "Don't worry—I'll see myself out. Thanks for your time."

She stared down her nose at me in disgust, as if I'd just suggested that she shop at a discount store. As I walked down the cold, stark white hallway toward the front door, her heels clicked on the expensive flooring behind me, no doubt watching my every move.

When I reached for the knob, Sylvia beat me to it. She jerked the door back and almost struck me in the face with it. "Don't come back," she hissed, "if you value your life."

For a few seconds, I stood on the front porch, frozen into immobility. Sylvia had threatened me, but why? What was she afraid of?

I crossed the road and hurried to my car. As I opened the door, I glanced into the back seat and saw Gabby crouched down on the floor, finger to her lips and a broad smile on her face. I got inside and started the engine. "Thank God. I was afraid Marta caught you snooping."

Once I was far enough away from the Rigotta home, Gabby swung herself into the front seat with minimal effort. "Sounds like you got in enough trouble for the both of us. I overheard your exchange with Willow and figured I ought to head for the car," she said. "I just missed Sylvia coming in the driveway. Have a nice chat with them?"

"Oh, you're hilarious. Good thing she didn't see you because it would have made things worse. I'm sure Marta will fill her in, though."

"No doubt." She hooked her seat belt and stared

expectantly at me. "Well, don't keep me in suspense. What happened?"

I relayed how Willow had caught me coming out of the pantry, and Sylvia had joined her shortly afterward and told me to get out. "You said she was with her father. Preston's signing was canceled."

"I didn't know it was canceled. Am I psychic now?"

"Whatever," I grumbled. "But Sylvia didn't buy my devoted fan act. In fact, she's more ticked off than ever. We could get charged with harassment. At least I found the chocolate, though."

Gabby did a fist pump. "I knew you would. Where is it?"

"I left it behind. I wasn't taking a chance that she'd discover it was missing."

She frowned as we drove onto the Northway. "She can't cook, remember. She'd never know it was missing."

"Marta might. Willow pretty much told me that Marta has done everything in that house, from diaper duty to dinner."

"It doesn't surprise me they'd get two jobs out of Marta for the same amount of pay," Gabby mused. "People with the most money are often the cheapest."

I put my blinker on to switch lanes. "And Willow—well,

she surprised me. I thought she was the devoted daughter, but it turns out that she can't wait to get away from Sylvia and Preston."

"You'd do the same thing if you had them for parents. That entire family is messed up."

"So it was Marta who prepared the cannoli I found next to Daphne. We need to question her."

"But how? Sylvia threatened you. You can't go in their house again."

"You could go and talk to Preston," I suggested. "Tell him how sorry you are about what happened at the signing."

She looked at me like I had just suggested she cook a five-course meal. "You mean grovel at his feet?"

"Do you want to save your store or not?"

She sighed. "All right, I'll do it. For the record, Tess, I never meant to get you involved in all of this. I don't want it to affect Anything's Pastable's opening."

"Everything's going to be fine," I assured her, with more confidence than I felt. "And I think we should speak to Daphne's father. Maybe he can tell us if anyone else had an ax to grind with his daughter."

"That's pretty much a given," she insisted. "But what makes you think he'll talk to us?"

I pulled up in front of the bookstore. "We'll tell him that we're friends of Daphne's."

"He won't believe that. Daphne didn't have any friends." Gabby glanced hopefully inside the store and sighed. "Looks like Liza's alone."

"Keep your chin up," I told her. "Call me if you need anything."

She waved and went inside. I hated to see her so disconsolate and hoped that customers would start showing up soon. I headed back to the restaurant, my mind turning to thoughts of tomato sauce.

The staff meeting lasted for about a half hour and went well. Everyone was pleasant to each other and seemed to share my excitement for the restaurant. After my new employees had left I busied myself for the next few hours setting up a payroll service for the employees, preparing and baking meatballs to freeze, and updating my website. I also spoke with Barney, Gabby's accountant, over the phone. It had started to grow dark when I realized my stomach was rumbling and decided to go home. Some leftover pasta would hit the spot, then a relaxing bath, and I planned to snuggle up with Luigi to watch some television.

The sky overhead was an ominous black, with only

a sliver of the moon appearing behind my row of cypress trees. With an eerie sense of foreboding, I fumbled with the key. As I inserted the correct one into the door, a shadow passed over me. Fear lodged tightly in my throat. I turned the knob just as someone grabbed my arm. In terror, I tried to scream, but a firm hand quickly clamped over my mouth, and I was pushed inside.

Panicked, I struggled against the strong masculine arms that held me in place, and then to my amazement and relief, I was released. Infuriated, I turned to find myself staring into the cold, angry eyes of Preston Rigotta.

"What do you think you're doing? Get out of my house!" I shrieked and grabbed the nearest item I could find, an umbrella from the stand, which I held protectively in front of me.

He sneered, unimpressed with me and my so-called weapon. "Look, you twit. I don't know what your problem is, but stop harassing my family or I'll have you thrown in jail."

I was outraged by his remark. "Who do you think you are? *You* just assaulted *me*! My cousin is a detective, and he'll have you arrested!"

"Get real." Preston's eyes had approached below

freezing temperatures. "It's my word against yours, and I can come up with a much better story." His lips stretched into a malicious grin. "I'm good at making things up, remember."

Luigi was sitting on the arm of the loveseat. His bright green eyes focused intently on Preston as he emitted a loud hiss. I'd never heard Luigi hiss at anyone before, except my mother's two dogs, Parm and Reggie.

Preston stared down at Luigi, as if seeing him for the first time, and promptly took a step backward. "You and that ditzy cousin of yours killed my publicist, and now you're trying to make it look like my family had something to do with it. That simply won't do, Mrs. Esposito." He leaned forward, pressing his face so close to mine that I could smell the stale coffee on his breath. "You don't want to get on my bad side."

"We had nothing to do with her death. We don't even know why she was killed. But I'm guessing you do, especially since you were sleeping with her," I blurted out.

Preston's face tightened in anger as he took a step toward me. *Whoops.* Perhaps that wasn't a smart thing for me to say.

"Why, you nosy little fool," he muttered. "You're going to be sorry for ever crossing me."

Luigi gave a low growl, and then leapt into the air, landing on Preston's back with his claws extended. Preston let out a scream, but before he could grab Luigi the cat jumped off him and ran yowling into the next room.

Preston threw open the front door and turned to face me. "Be sure to keep that cat inside." He gave a low, menacing laugh that sent shivers down my spine. "It would be a shame if anything happened to him."

A half hour later I was sitting on the loveseat, stroking Luigi's head while Gino sat across from me. "You are going to arrest him, right?"

Gino looked tired. "I'll have a talk with him, Tess, but don't expect too much."

"What do you mean? Don't you care that he assaulted me? And he threatened to harm Luigi, too."

A muscle ticked in Gino's well-defined jaw. "Of course I care. How can you even ask me such a thing? I'm beyond pissed that he laid a hand on you. I hate feeling so helpless, especially where my family is involved. You can press charges against him, Tess, but to be honest, they probably won't stick. That guy carries a lot of clout throughout the state, and I'm sure he's got an expensive lawyer on retainer. He'd be out on bail before daybreak and might try to make things worse for you. That goes for your restaurant, too. What if he has his wife say something derogatory about Anything's Pastable on her show?"

Luigi jumped off my lap, and I slumped forward, defeated. "I hate that he's going to get away with this. And he may have already gotten away with murder."

"I can't believe that I'm even asking this," Gino said, "but was Rigotta right? Did you harass him and his family?"

"No!" I cried. "Gabby and I went to the television station to chat with Sylvia. Then Gabby and I stopped over at their house today to—" I couldn't tell him about the incident in the kitchen. He'd be furious.

His expression was stern. "Go on."

"I had a talk with Sylvia and Willow. That's all. Sylvia got upset and asked me to leave, so I did. That was the end of it."

Disbelief clouded Gino's eyes. "*Right*. I know you've conveniently left out something. Now listen to me. Do not, I repeat, *do not* go near that family again. Understand?"

"But—" I protested.

He cut me off. "No buts. Stay away from all of the

Rigottas. That goes for my sister, too. Never mind, I'll call her myself. Preston's on our suspect list, and he knows it. When questioned, he told Paddy that he's afraid people won't buy his precious book because of this unfortunate situation."

"That's all he cares about—sales. Not the fact that Daphne is dead."

"When killers are arrogant like that, they slip up. If he's the one, we'll nab him, Tess." He rose to his feet. "I've got to get home. Would you like to come spend the night at our house? The twins would love it."

That got a smile out of me. "No, thanks. I'll be fine." Luigi sat by the front of the door, his eyes fixed on us. "I've got my alarm system and a guard kitty to protect me."

FIFTEEN

"HELLO, DARLING." MY MOTHER'S VOICE GREETED me warmly. "I got home later than I thought, and when I stopped at Java Time, Archie filled me in on what happened at Gabby's store. How awful! Why didn't she call her mother? How's she doing? Aunt Mona's been trying to reach her, but she hasn't answered."

This came as no surprise. Mona could be a lot for Gabby—anyone really—to handle. My aunt seemed to live in her own little world at times. She and her husband had divorced when their children were still in elementary school. My Uncle Hal had since remarried and was living in California. Aunt Mona was long past caring about it and instead devoted her time to driving her children crazy. She was the opposite of my mother—brass and outspoken, with no filter.

I cradled the phone between my ear and shoulder as I placed a stainless-steel pot on my stove. "Gabby's been busy with the store." Okay, it was a bit of a stretch, as Gabby had only one customer yesterday, but I knew she couldn't deal with her mother right now. I attempted to change the subject. "How was your trip?"

"Wonderful," Mom gushed. "But never mind that now. Are you all set for the grand opening? Do you need me to help with anything?"

I set out the ingredients to make pesto sauce as she jabbered on. I loved my mother dearly, but she'd never understood my passion for cooking. She preferred dining out or getting takeout instead of making dinner herself. To each her own. Her mother, Greta, was the one who had inspired my love of cooking. Maybe these things skipped a generation.

Mom's voice startled me out of my thoughts. "Theresa, are you listening to me?"

"Of course," I lied. "I'm at the restaurant right now, doing a few last-minute things. Yes, all my permits and inspections are in place, repairs are completed, and my staff got to meet each other yesterday. Everyone's excited and looking forward to opening night." What I purposefully avoided telling her was that last evening had only been quiet and peaceful after Preston's visit, and that I'd barely slept.

"You'll be here opening night, right?" Gino had promised to come and bring his family, and Gabby had offered to waitress if needed. Unfortunately, I didn't need her. At least two of the fourteen tables would be filled. My anxiety was increasing daily. The restaurant opened in three days, and I still had no reservations.

The *Harvest Park Press* had called and told me their food critic would be coming the first week to review Anything's Pastable. At least they'd given me a heads-up. I hadn't thought about restaurant reviews yet but knew how important they could be. I tended to wear my heart on my sleeve where my cooking was concerned, and reviewers were not always kind. The preparation of food wasn't always their biggest concern. There were other factors that figured into their write-ups such as pricing, ambiance, and service. Their words could greatly affect the restaurant's success. One more thing to be a wreck about.

"With bells on, dear. Now tell me all about your staff. Do I know any of them? How old are they?" Mom asked.

Like most people in Harvest Park, my mother lived

for gossip. Might as well give her what she wanted. "I have three waitresses so far. Judy Henry, Renee Simons, and Hannah Gordon. They're all part-time and I need at least one more. Renee and Hannah will be done with classes in a couple of weeks, so I may be able to hold off on hiring someone else until fall. I also have a dishwasher working daily three to nine. His name is Andy Brenner."

"That name sounds familiar," she mused. "Is his mother Patrice? There's a Brenner family that's been in Harvest Park for as long as we have."

I packed fresh basil leaves and the other ingredients into my food processor, keeping it on low so I could hear her. "No, Mom. I didn't ask him what his mother's name was. Oh, and I hired an assistant in the kitchen. She'll help seat people if the waitresses are too busy. Her name is Stephanie Beaudry."

"No, I don't know her either." Mom sounded disappointed. "That's not much of a staff. Only six people, including yourself."

"Well, it's all I can afford right now. It will work out." My voice projected more confidence than I felt. If there were no reservations coming in, I would have too much of a staff.

A scratching sound commenced at the back door, and I watched the doorknob turn as my mother jabbered on. Vince stepped into the kitchen, wearing a brown leather jacket and faded blue jeans. He carried a grocery bag in one hand. I held up a hand in greeting.

He shot me a grin. "I knew I'd find you here."

I covered the phone with one hand and whispered, "You'd make a lousy detective. My car's right outside the door."

He laughed while I kept my hand over the phone. All I needed was for my mother to hear him in the background. She'd start making all kinds of assumptions. "Um, Mom, I have to go. Why don't you stop by tomorrow? You haven't seen the new light fixtures, the table setup, or the fireplace that went in. I want you, Gabby, and Mona to come in on Friday to sample some dishes."

"Certainly, dear. Oh, my, so much to catch up on first. There's an Altar Rosary Society meeting tomorrow, and my knitting group is coming here, plus I still must unpack. Yes, Mona's dying to see the place. She hasn't been in there since you took over from Slice. Now don't work too hard. Love you."

"Love you, too." I clicked off and stared with curiosity as Vince emptied his grocery bag. There were two bottles of wine inside. "What's this?" I asked, mystified.

"I thought we should celebrate your grand opening." He stared down at the pan on the stove as I poured the mixture from the food processor into it. "Pesto? Perfect. The sauvignon will go great with it. Where's your corkscrew?"

"The drawer to the left."

After I grabbed two wineglasses from my overhead cupboard I noticed, with shock, the label on the bottles. *Falducci Vineyard, Hamburg, New York.* Was this a possible clue to the mystery man? "You own a vineyard?"

"It's been in my family for many years. But, yeah, I guess you could say that I own it now." Vince poured wine into each glass as I watched him. His movement was fluent and steady, something a great chef should possess, although I'd never seen him prepare anything but pizza. He was always so sure of himself, a trait that I admired in a man. Dylan had had that same regal air about him, but I suspected Vince used it as a cover-up sometimes. He'd been through some rocky times with his restaurant closing. The demise of Slice hadn't been easy on him either, although he hadn't owned the business, only the building.

I was intrigued. "Did you grow up in the Buffalo area? I thought you were born in New York City."

Vince handed me a glass and then clinked his against

mine. "Nope. I moved there after culinary school. My four brothers and I all worked at the vineyard when we were kids. My brother Sergio and I bought the others out a few years back. All the wine for my restaurant in New York City came from the vineyard. Sergio lives close by, so he runs things and I show up whenever I feel like it." He winked.

That sounded about right. Vince always seemed to do exactly as he pleased, and it made me a bit envious. At least the mystery man had finally given me a peek at his secretive life. I took a small sniff of the liquid. "It smells wonderful."

"Come on. Let's toast to Anything's Pastable's future and certain success. I hope to be here on opening night but may need to be in New York City on a business matter. Are you sold out yet?"

I took a small sip from my glass. The wine had a zesty peach flavor that tantalized my taste buds. "Don't I wish. I've been advertising everywhere but no one's called to reserve a table yet."

"They'll come," Vince said as he watched me add grated cheese to the sauce. "People are always last minute about those things, so don't worry. Ah, you need red pepper flakes. The spicier the better. That's what my mother always told me."

I laughed. "Sounds like your mother and I could be good friends."

Vince smiled sadly and leaned against the counter as I shook a spoonful of flakes into the pan. "She died four years ago."

"I'm sorry."

"Me too. She would have liked you. I learned almost everything I know about cooking and wine from her. As a mother of five boys, she was a force to be reckoned with, in and out of the kitchen." A small smile played on his lips. "I was the one my brothers always made fun of because I would rather watch her cook in the kitchen instead of playing cops and robbers outside with them."

"That sounds like my grandmother and me. The hours I spent cooking with her were the happiest ones of my childhood."

A faraway look came into those dark brooding eyes of his, but he forced it away and stared down at the pan again. "So, what's this I hear about a woman dying in your cousin's bookstore?"

I couldn't help but laugh at the abrupt segue. I gave him the condensed version of Daphne's death, and he was shocked. "Wow. After what happened to Dylan last year, I can't believe you're involved in another murder investigation."

"You're not the only one. And I'm not an actual investigator, remember. Gabby and I are trying to find out who's responsible before her place goes under. She's worked so hard and doesn't deserve to see this happen to her."

Vince's gaze locked on mine. "Gabby's lucky to have you in her corner."

I shrugged. "She'd do the same for me."

His jaw tightened. "It must be nice to have family and friends who are ready to go to war for you. Other than my mother, I wouldn't know anything about that."

I waited for him to go on, but he didn't. Vince had given me a peek at his life today, but there was so much more I didn't know and maybe never would. He was definitely not an open book.

He continued to watch me. The pesto was ready, but I continued to stir, even though it wasn't needed. The process kept my mind occupied and off Vince's dark eyes, which observed my every move. The room grew warm, and sweat gathered on my forehead. A good chef always respected another's personal space, but then again, Vince was unlike any other chef I'd met before.

Vince gestured at the pan. "May I?"

I raised an eyebrow. "What, am I doing something wrong?"

He grinned and took the wooden spoon from me. "No offense, Tessa, but you stir like an old lady. And I can already tell that the sauce needs something."

"Maybe your expertise?" I quipped, and then gestured grandly toward the stove. "Please, be my guest." I didn't know whether to laugh or be insulted by his remark, but I was curious to see him in action.

Vince poured half a cup of chardonnay into the mixture. "Come on, Tessa. You're Italian and a chef. You know that wine works wonders. Even your award-winning sauce benefits from it. Wine makes *everything* better."

The innuendo in his statement was obvious, but I pretended not to notice. "My tomato sauce is the award winner. But my carbonara and pesto are pretty darn good, too."

"I love a chef who isn't modest," Vince teased. "Like me." He continued to stir the sauce with one hand while refilling my glass with the other before I could stop him. He added another shake of pepper flakes. "You always look like you're plotting something when you stir."

His comment almost made me choke on the wine.

"Actually, it's sort of like therapy for me." I paused for a moment. "Especially since Dylan died."

Now it was Vince's turn to be apologetic. "I'm sorry. I didn't mean to sound insensitive."

"It's okay, really." The sauce smelled heavenly. Vince filled a pot with water and set it on a burner. "You have pasta ready to go?"

I moved toward the freezer and removed a ziplock bag of noodles. "Yes, I made a fresh supply the other day."

"I'd expect nothing less of you," he chuckled.

"Don't you miss cooking?" I asked.

He shrugged. "I still dabble. As a matter of fact, I'm looking into opening my own catering business. With any luck, I'll have it off the ground in the next couple of months. That's why I've been going back and forth to New York City so often. I have contacts there who've been instrumental in helping me."

I leaned against the counter, in fascination. "What type of catering? Business lunches? Dinner parties? Italian cuisine? Should I be worried about competition?"

His eyes twinkled as he poured himself some more wine. "No, I wouldn't do that to you. These are private dinner parties I'll be catering. I have an associate from my former restaurant who is willing to relocate and work with me. I'm only interested in doing the gig on weekends. If it's as successful as I think it will be, she'll share some of the duties and even host a couple of events during the week."

"She?" My interest was piqued. I started to reach for another sip of wine and then stopped myself. The glass was nearly empty, and one was my limit. I still had to drive home later.

Vince's mouth twitched. "Yes, she's a woman. Victoria and I have been friends for a long time."

"Is she married?" Cripes. What was with all these questions? Why did I even care? Maybe it was the wine.

A grin spread across his face. "Divorced. Why are you asking?"

Why indeed? "No reason." I was taking sleuthing to a whole new level. I liked Vince. When we'd worked together briefly at Slice, he'd been rude, arrogant, and constantly tried to downplay my culinary skills. But he'd had his reasons, and after Dylan's death he had apologized for his treatment of me.

I didn't believe in holding grudges, and since then, Vince had done everything imaginable to show me that he was a good guy. Anything's Pastable wouldn't have happened without his help.

"Come on and taste the sauce then." Vince cajoled me like a little boy as he dropped the pasta into the boiling water. After thirty seconds, he removed it. "Ah. Delicioso al dente. This restaurant is going to be a huge success, mark my words."

With interest, I watched as he layered the sauce over a bowl of the linguini, twirled it on the fork, and then held it out to me. Heat rose in my cheeks, but I opened my mouth while he fed me the pasta. Holy cannoli. The sauce was spicier than usual, thanks to the addition of the red flakes and wine, but what a sensation. My mouth was ready to burst from the flavor, and I savored it for as long as possible.

Vince folded his arms over his chest, obviously pleased with himself. "Well? What's the verdict?"

I reached for a napkin on the counter and waited until I had swallowed. "It's fantastic."

He beamed and gave a gallant bow. "Thank you, kindly."

"Almost as good as mine." I couldn't help myself.

His eyes grew wide with astonishment, then he barked out a laugh. "A little full of yourself, aren't you, Chef Esposito?"

I reached for a glass of water on the counter and accidentally brushed my hand against his in the process. "Look who's talking." I was so thirsty that I swallowed the entire glass.

"I like that in a woman." His voice was low and husky. "Confidence. And it doesn't hurt when she's beautiful as well."

"Thank you." Silence emanated through the room.

Vince gazed over the rim of his glass at me, his dark eyes staring intently into mine until, embarrassed, I looked away. Finally, he spoke. "Did you like the flowers?"

"Oh." How embarrassing that I'd forgotten to mention them. "Yes. They're gorgeous. Thank you."

"My pleasure."

My skin was growing warm. Fortunately, the phone at the hostess station started to ring. It was a beautiful sound to my ears. "Oh, my gosh, maybe it's a reservation!"

Vince laughed and waved me on. "Go, Miss Pastable. I'll hold down the fort in here."

I hurried into the dining area and exhaled a long, slow breath that I'd been holding for what seemed like an eternity. Vince was clearly still interested in me, and I didn't know how to feel about it. He was fun to be around, and

I enjoyed talking shop with him. But as I'd told Justin, I wasn't ready for a relationship with another man and didn't need distractions right now. Frankly, I had enough to contend with.

"Good afternoon, Anything's Pastable." I spoke cheerfully into the phone.

"Oh, sorry," a woman's voice on the other end said. "Wrong number."

Disappointment spread through my chest. I was trying not to panic, but it was difficult. Why weren't people calling? Did they really think I could have killed Daphne with my cannoli? I was worried about Gabby's bookstore surviving, but my business wasn't off the ground yet and was even more susceptible.

As I made my way back toward the kitchen, I heard a male voice that didn't belong to Vince and froze. *Lorenzo.* What was he doing here?

"Sorry, I didn't mean to interrupt anything," he said.

Vince's voice floated through the air, as smooth and rich as a fine alfredo sauce. "No problem. She'll be back in a minute. What'd you say your name was?"

"Lorenzo Garcia. Are you Tessa's boyfriend?" he asked.

"No. Not yet," Vince answered smoothly.

My mouth fell open in amazement as I listened. *Where do you get your nerve, Mr. Falducci?*

I forced my face into a neutral expression and entered the kitchen. Lorenzo was leaning against the back door, while Vince poured sauce into the container I'd left on the counter for that purpose.

Lorenzo moved in my direction. "Hello, Tessa."

I gave him an encouraging smile. "Hi, Lorenzo. How's everything?"

He glanced uneasily from Vince to me. "I need your help. The cops—they keep badgering me. They found out some things and—" His eyes shifted to Vince again.

Vince got the message. "I think I'll be shoving off now." He raised an eyebrow at me. "Unless you'd prefer that I stay?"

I knew what he meant. He didn't know Lorenzo's situation and was concerned for my welfare. "No, I'm fine. Thanks for the cooking lesson."

The sexy bad-boy smile was back in place. "Anytime, chef."

I walked Vince to the door and watched from the doorway as he revved the engine to his Harley. He placed the helmet over his messy, dark curls and then looked back over his shoulder to shoot me another sly grin. Good grief.

Vince Falducci should come with a warning sign—*Danger Ahead.*

With a shake of my head, I shut the door and faced Lorenzo. "So, what exactly are the police doing?"

Lorenzo's nostrils flared. "There's some guy—not your cousin—who's called me back in twice for questioning."

"Detective McDermott."

"Yeah, that's the name. He thinks that I killed Daphne." Resentment sounded in Lorenzo's tone. "I got so mad that I almost rammed my fist down his throat."

His words made me cringe inwardly. I had hoped that Lorenzo's hothead days were over. "That would be about the worst thing you could do. Do you want to go to jail for assault?"

He hung his head. "Can't your cousin do something? You've all known my parents for years. This isn't only affecting me. Mama's losing business. People won't buy from her now because of me—what they think I did. I overheard her talking to my father about it. She's worried about all the bills coming in. I don't want my parents to have to suffer for this."

"Did you find out about the baby yet?"

He didn't answer right away, so I pressed him.

"Lorenzo, it's none of my business, but you asked me to help. We need to know if you were the father."

Lorenzo ran a hand through his hair nervously. "Okay, yeah, I know. I'll find out tomorrow." He exhaled sharply. "Maybe I should go away."

"If you leave, that will make the police even more suspicious. You can't go anywhere right now."

He startled me by slamming his fist against the door. "This really bites. Big time. I feel trapped—trapped in my own hometown. Nice, huh? It's not bad enough that Daphne lost her life, but mine is being destroyed, too. When you see your cousin, will you give him a message?"

Oh, boy. This couldn't be good. "What is it?"

"Tell him to get that McDermott guy to stop stalking me," Lorenzo raged. "He's been following me around on the sly. I don't appreciate it."

"Gino talking to Paddy probably won't do any—"

Lorenzo cut in, his dark eyes blazing with animosity. "The entire police department needs to stop harassing me. If someone pushes me too hard, I will push back. Don't doubt it for a second."

He opened the door and slammed it behind him, without another word.

Sometime in the middle of the night, I was awakened by a scratching sound. I clicked on the lamp next to my bed and saw Luigi sitting on the windowsill, meowing and pawing at the panes of glass.

"Hey, buddy. You okay?" I rubbed my eyes and sat up. Luigi yowled and continued to scratch the windowpanes. I'd never seen him act like this before. Yawning, I stumbled to my feet and went to stand beside him, peering into the night. The road was dark, except for a streetlight casting a faint glow several houses away. A car was turning off my road and then disappeared. I wondered what would make someone get out of bed at three o'clock in the morning.

Luigi looked at me and meowed again. He must have spotted a squirrel or bird in the darkness. How I wished I had his X-ray vision.

I laughed and scooped him up into my arms. "It's a little early for bird-watching. Come on and cuddle with me." I placed Luigi on Dylan's pillow, where his loud purrs resonated through the room. I stroked his head and then shut the light off. "Such a good boy," I murmured and immediately fell back to sleep.

The sun streaming through the half-open blinds awakened me. I glanced at the clock and blinked once, then twice. Eight thirty. Holy cow. I never slept this late. It must have been the wine. Luigi was on the floor, looking up at me expectantly. He jumped onto my stomach, causing me to groan. Now that he had my full attention, he began kneading my arms. His meow this time was full of disapproval. It clearly said, *You had one job. My breakfast is late. Get moving.*

I moved Luigi off me and rolled out of bed. He trotted after me down the stairs and into the kitchen where I filled his dish with food and gave him fresh water. While he ate, I brewed a cup of coffee in my Keurig and glanced down at my phone left on the counter from last night.

There was a text message from Penelope. She'd attached a credit card receipt but had blocked out the numbers. The name on the card read Marta Eldridge. Before I got too excited, I shot off a quick text to Gabby. Do you know Marta's last name?

Her reply came back instantly. Elder or Eldridge I believe. Something like that. Preston told me when he introduced me to her. Why?

I'll fill you in when I see you today, I shot back.

Gabby wrote, Okay. I'm at Gino's for breakfast. I'll stop over at the restaurant on my lunch break.

I'd been expecting to see Sylvia's name on the slip, but it was believable that Marta had bought the groceries. Heck, she did everything else in that house, so why not?

So Marta had bought the chocolate and used it in the cannoli. And Sylvia may have been the one who added that little extra ingredient that resulted in Daphne's death. I needed to get back in the house and have a chat with Marta when the others weren't around.

I fixed myself some toast, brewed another cup of coffee, and then went back upstairs to take a shower. I was expecting a produce delivery, but fortunately it wasn't due to arrive until around noon. I also wanted to experiment with a new vodka crème sauce and try it out on my family tomorrow for taste testing.

After I pulled on jeans and a T-shirt, I grabbed my keys and gave Luigi a hug. After locking up, I walked toward my car in the driveway and immediately froze.

Almost every inch of my new black SUV had been covered with green spray paint and graffiti. The words made me blush upon sight. No one had ever called me names like that before. There was one particular message that caught my attention on the driver's side of the car. *Back off or die.* It was the same message that had been attached to Gabby's rock.

I glanced up and down the street, almost as if I expected to see the culprit. A tremor of fear shot through me, and I ran back into the house and dialed Gino's number. He answered on the second ring.

"Nancy Drew's starting early today, I see." He sounded like he was in a good mood for a change.

"Gino." My breath came out in gulps, and I was afraid I might burst into tears. "Can you come over to my house right away?"

"Tess, what's wrong? Are you okay?"

"Someone vandalized my car. And I think it was Daphne's killer."

SIXTEEN

AS I'D EXPECTED, GINO'S MOOD HAD turned foul when he arrived. "You two never should have gotten involved in this," he said. "For the last time, you're not detectives. I was afraid someone might make it personal, and now look."

My nerves were already on edge, and I bristled at his comment. "What do you expect us to do? Detective McDermott thinks that Gabby and I are involved somehow. You and Lou can't work the case. What other choice do we have?"

He narrowed his eyes. "The killer's got you in their sights now. Seems to me I've seen that before."

Gabby, who had followed Gino over from his house, slung a protective arm around my shoulders. "Tess, this is all my fault. You've been through enough already."

"Don't blame yourself." We were standing in the

driveway, and I tried to avoid looking at my vehicle, but it was impossible. I'd managed to anger a killer again. Someone had destroyed my property and, if given the chance, probably intended to harm me as well. Gabby didn't want me in danger, and the feeling was mutual. At some point, we must have spoken to Daphne's killer. But who was it? Preston, Sylvia, or Lorenzo? Someone else who had a link to one of them?

I thought back to Luigi's behavior last night. He must have seen the person spray-painting my car. How I wished cats could talk.

I showed Gino the text I'd received from Penelope earlier this morning, but he was unconvinced. "Just because Marta bought the same kind of chocolate that was used in the cannoli doesn't make Sylvia a killer, Tess."

Gabby rolled her eyes toward the sky. "You're always giving people the benefit of the doubt. Come on, bro. Her husband was sleeping with Daphne. That's enough of a reason for Sylvia to want her dead."

"Anyone else could have bought that chocolate," Gino remarked. "Amazon sells it, right? If they bought it online, you wouldn't know unless you had access to their credit card records. Sylvia is a chef and probably—"

"Sylvia's not a chef!" Gabby snapped. "She's a phony. She followed Tess to Justin's the other night and tossed that rock through my front window."

Gino stared at his sister, dumbstruck. Gabby's face flushed and she put a hand to her mouth. "Whoops."

"Why am I just hearing about this for the first time?" he asked.

"Because I thought it might be some kids fooling around. Until we saw the note attached, that is."

Good grief. She was making things worse for herself.

"What note? Did you touch it?" Gino demanded. "Where is it now?"

"I called Lou when it happened. He brought the note to Paddy, I think." She looked faintly embarrassed.

Gino cursed under his breath. "This is just great. My own sister and her boyfriend—a coworker of mine—are keeping secrets from me. Wait until I talk to Lou."

Gabby wrinkled her nose. "Lou's out of town. I didn't ask him to keep it from you."

"But you didn't happen to bring it up when you were at my house this morning, did you? Look, I don't know what you're trying to prove but—"

"There was a piece of stationery with the rock that we

think belonged to Sylvia," I cut in, hoping to steer Gino back to the investigation and from choking Gabby. "It said 'Back off or die.'"

Gino glanced over at me and then at my car, sheer exasperation on his face. "Well, it's obviously the same person who did this. What have you two been saying to people?" he demanded.

Gabby tossed her head in defiance. "Don't worry. I've been keeping Lou up-to-date on what we've found out. We talked to Lorenzo, Sylvia, and Willow. And of course, Preston decided to go see Tessa unannounced last night."

"We didn't get much of a chance to chat," I said with sarcasm. "I think we should talk to Daphne's father."

"No," Gino said sharply. "You two are done asking questions. Leave it to Paddy."

"Forget it," Gabby shot back. "I don't trust that guy. He's got it in for me and couldn't care less about my bookstore or Tessa's restaurant. I have no customers, Gino. How long do you think a business can survive without customers? You can't do this to me."

Gino's features softened when he looked at her, and he almost smiled. "Oh, yes, I can. Remember, little sis, I'm the law, not you, and I'll do whatever it takes to keep you both safe. Family over everything." He hesitated for a moment. "I've been thinking about that a lot lately."

Gabby drew her eyebrows together. "What's going on? You've been acting weirder than usual this week. Spill it."

He flashed us a mischievous smile. "All right, but promise you won't let Lucy know that I told you. She wanted us to tell the entire family together, at Tess's grand opening. But I can't wait any longer."

Gabby and I looked at each other and then recognition dawned. "A baby?" I asked with delight. "Is Lucy—"

Gino beamed as he nodded. "She wanted to wait until she was officially three months along next week but—"

"Oh, my gosh!" Gabby burst into tears as she threw her arms around her brother. "This is wonderful."

When she was finished, I hugged him as well. "I'm so excited for you both. Are you hoping for a girl this time?"

"As long as the baby's healthy, that's what's important." He stroked his clean-shaven chin and grinned at me. "But yeah, a little girl would be wonderful. We haven't told Rocco and Marco yet, but I'm sure they'll be thrilled."

Lucy had the patience of Mother Theresa. I adored their boys, but they could be little devils at times. Luigi hated it when they came to my house and always ran and hid from them.

Gino opened the door to his sedan. "I've got to get back to the station. I have to tell Paddy about this, so don't be surprised if he wants to speak with you both again."

"Great, can't wait," Gabby mumbled.

Gino ignored her comment and addressed me. "Do you need a body shop recommendation for your car?"

"I already called someone. Thanks for coming over."

"Anytime. Please be careful. And don't forget, not a word to Lucy about you-know-what."

Gabby chuckled. "Remember, they say once you have one set of twins, the chance to have another pair doubles."

We watched as the smile faded from Gino's face. He mumbled something under his breath, started the engine, and drove away.

Gabby drew a tissue out of her jeans pocket. "I can't believe I'm going to be an auntie."

"You're already an auntie," I gently reminded her.

"Oh, you know what I mean." She sniffed. "It's a new experience all over again."

"If you and Lou tie the knot, you could be next," I said teasingly as we went inside my house.

Gabby made a face. "Let's not rush things, okay? Besides, I don't know if I want to be married to a cop. I'd spend every night worrying that he might not come home. Lucy deserves a lot of credit, let me tell you. And even though I despise a cheater, it had to be tough on Justin's ex as well."

I moved into the kitchen and started the Keurig. I hadn't planned to tell Gabby, but this was the perfect opening. Besides, I was curious what she'd have to say. "Natalie is back in town."

Gabby, who had reached down to pet Luigi, jerked her head up. "Say what? You're joking."

I handed her the sugar. "No. I saw her come out of his house the other night. Justin told me that she wants to get back together."

Her jaw dropped. "But they're divorced."

We went into the living room with our coffees and sat down. Luigi immediately jumped on my lap. "That doesn't matter. It's happened plenty of times. I believe she's laying a guilt trip on him, and it's working."

She watched me closely. "You're so calm and collected about this. I know you two are close. How do you feel about her being back?"

"I'm not sure. Beyond knowing that Natalie is nothing

but trouble for Justin, I can't process everything while I'm still mourning Dylan and trying to launch my new business. It's a bit overwhelming. Let's not forget the murder investigation, and the fact that we're both suspects."

"I think the graffiti incident might clear you," Gabby remarked. "I can't imagine that even Paddy would think you did that to your own car. But me? The jury's still out on that one. Paddy should be disciplined."

"Except for the intense questioning, he hasn't done anything wrong. Besides, that's not for us to say, and the Harvest Park PD wants him here," I reminded her. "Gino's said they're lucky to have him, even though the guy doesn't want to be stuck in our hick town."

She sipped her drink thoughtfully. "Well, yeah, especially since the police department is overworked and underpaid, as Gino constantly tells me. Look, I should get over to the store, in case someone decides to stop in ever again. Can I drop you at the restaurant on the way? I'm guessing you don't want to be seen in your car until it gets repainted."

"Thanks, but I'm having it towed." There was a tap on my front door. Luigi trotted over to it and then waited expectantly. "That's probably him now." I'd been hoping Gabby would be gone before the man arrived.

Gabby waved me off and went to peer through the peephole, then turned to look at me with an *are you kidding me* look. "Why is Matt Smitty here?"

"Like I said, he's here to tow my car." Matt was my old high school boyfriend, and to put it plainly, he and Gabby couldn't stomach each other. She'd hated it when I'd dated him and had never been shy about telling me so.

She gritted her teeth in annoyance and muttered, "Good thing I'm leaving," as she opened the door.

"Always nice to see you too, sunshine." Matt gave her a playful wink, which clearly infuriated Gabby. Tall and lanky, he hadn't changed much since high school. His wide-set hazel eyes stood out in his face, and the rounded chin and cheeks made him seem much younger than his thirty-one years. A dimple on the right side of his mouth flashed when he smiled at me.

Gabby clenched her teeth together then looked from me to Matt. "Maybe I should stick around. I'm not sure I trust you around my cousin."

"I'm the one who called him," I reminded her.

"Guess who's turning into an overbearing bully like her brother," Matt retorted.

I laid a hand on Gabby's arm. "Come on, you two,

knock it off. We're not in high school anymore." My head still ached, and I was already exhausted from the day, even though it was barely ten o'clock. "Gabs, I'm a big girl, remember? Go open the bookstore. If I need a ride, I'll let you know."

She gave me a hug. "Okay. Call me later. For the record, I still feel like this is all my fault."

"It probably is," Matt said snidely.

Gabby shot him a dirty look but mercifully said nothing further. She pushed past Matt, and we followed her out to the driveway. After she'd turned the car around, she looked at Matt, with a sour expression on her face as if she'd just eaten a lemon.

"Be careful, Tess," she warned me, while giving Matt the evil eye. "There's a lot of unsavory characters around here." With that, she sped off.

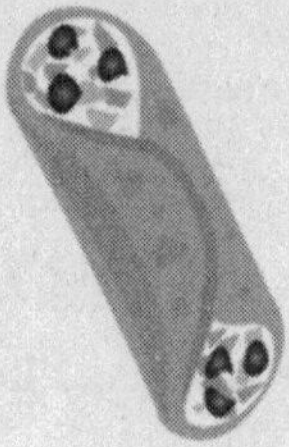

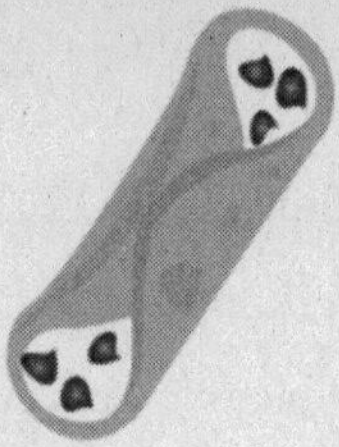

SEVENTEEN

"NICE TO KNOW THAT GABBY'S STILL fond of me," Matt remarked.

"She always has been," I said lightly. The two had never liked each other, not since sixth grade when she'd given him a fat lip for putting gum in her hair. I'd always secretly wondered if Matt had done it to gain her interest, but if so, it had certainly backfired.

He laughed, and then his expression quickly sobered. "Maybe it's more that she'll never forgive me for being a jerk to her cousin, and how I managed to screw up a good thing."

An awkward silence followed between us. I was glad that we were friends again, but not interested in anything more from him. Last fall, much to my dismay, he'd also been a suspect in Dylan's murder.

Matt and I went way back to grade school, and we'd

ruined a perfectly good friendship by dating each other during our senior year. He'd been too possessive, so I'd broken it off. Matt had not taken the rejection well. He'd gotten into drugs and fallen in with the wrong type of crowd. There were rumors Matt had been in rehab after that, but I still didn't know the full story since I'd been away at school. When I returned, he had already started dating a pretty blond from Georgia named Lila. They'd married shortly afterward and had three children within four years.

I studied him as he ran a hand through his dirty-blond hair, pushing the bangs out of his eyes while looking over my obscenity-riddled vehicle. He'd never liked Dylan, but fortunately my fears of him being a killer had been unfounded. Lila had taken their three sons and left town while Matt had been under the cloud of suspicion. I'd felt responsible, but he'd assured me they'd been having other problems. After Dylan's killer was behind bars, Matt came to see me unannounced one day and asked if we could be friends again. Thankfully, he seemed more interested in getting his family back than anything else, and I hoped it worked out for him.

Matt walked around the entire car and gave a low whistle. "Unbelievable. They barely missed an inch, Tess."

"It wasn't a random act," I admitted.

His mouth was grim. "Yeah, I kind of figured that. I can't remember the last time someone spray-painted a person's car around here. People don't do that type of thing in Harvest Park."

Maybe not, but we'd now had three murders in this town within the past year—Daphne's, Dylan's, and another one related to Dylan's killing. Matt's words didn't exactly reassure me. Harvest Park was a picturesque little town with people who were a bit too nosy for their own good but also happened to care deeply about one another. Murder wasn't supposed to figure into the equation.

Matt placed his hands on his slim hips. "I heard about Daphne Daniels, and her body being found in Gabby's shop. Does your car's damage have something to do with it?"

I hesitated, wondering how much to tell him, but news did travel fast around here. "It's possible. Remember how Daphne was always bullying Gabby? Well, it doesn't exactly bode well that she died in her store, so we've been asking questions. I think someone's setting Gabby up to take the fall."

"Yeah, I remember what a jerk she was to Gabby." Matt's jaw tightened. "I asked Daphne out once, you know.

She laughed in my face. It was one of the most embarrassing moments of my adolescent life."

His statement surprised me. "I didn't think she was your type."

Matt's amber eyes brightened. "No, but she was always a knockout, and I was a hormonal teenager. Now when I look back, I don't know why I bothered. There were other lookers besides her—and they were much nicer, too." He watched me for my reaction.

Time to change the subject. "So, what do you think—about the car? How much will it cost me?"

He pursed his lips. "I don't do body work. I mean, I know how, but my place is way too small." Matt owned a two-bay repair shop, the Car Doctor, in Harvest Park. He was an excellent mechanic and thrived at the job. "However, I know a guy who could do it. Gus Bailey owns In-N-Out Autobody." He nodded toward his tow truck, which was parked behind my car, thankfully blocking it and the graffiti from the view of my neighbors. "I could tow it there, if you like. To guess off the top of my head, I'd say around five grand."

I sucked in some air. "My car insurance will take care of it, right?"

Matt shook his head sadly. "Probably not. I mean, you can check with them, but graffiti isn't usually an item that's covered. Sorry that I don't have better news for you."

I tried to steady myself against this newest shock to my system. I had the money, but it was going to hurt. Most of Dylan's life insurance policy had gone to pay for the renovations at the restaurant and to cover my monthly expenses. I hadn't worked at a paying job since my brief stint at Slice last November. Sure, I had counted on things coming up, but not this.

I leaned against the car. The spray paint had long since dried. "You might as well go ahead and tow it. How long do you think it will take Gus to do a new paint job?"

Matt stared down at his phone. "He just texted me back. Gus said a week at most. I have an extra vehicle down at my shop if you'd like to borrow it for a few days."

"No, that's okay." It was a nice offer, but I didn't want to be indebted to him. "What do I owe you for the tow?"

"There's no charge."

I shook my head vehemently. "I have to pay something. You need to make a living, too."

He smiled at me, shading his eyes from the unrelenting sun above. "Well, maybe we could work *something* out."

Oh, jeez. Had it been a mistake to call him? I thought he understood that I had no interest in dating him again. "Like what?"

He grinned wickedly. "Don't look so panic stricken, Tess. I meant maybe a tow job in exchange for dinner at your new restaurant. It opens this week, right?"

Relief flooded through me. "Sure, that's fine. Let me know what night you'd like to come in. That doesn't seem like a fair trade, though." Tow jobs were at least a couple of hundred dollars. How I wish I hadn't let my roadside assistance lapse last year.

He leaned against the car, arms folded over his chest. "Would it be okay if I brought the boys?"

"Of course. I have a children's menu."

"Great. Put the four of us down for opening night, then. Unless you're already booked?"

Didn't I wish. "Oh, I'm pretty sure I still have room. That includes dessert for all of you as well, and anyone else you'd like to bring."

"It will only be me and the boys." Matt's eyes were puffy, indicating a lack of sleep, and his usual ruddy face was pale. "They're staying with me until next week. I'm hoping to get Lila to give me joint custody."

I tried to phrase my question in a delicate manner. “Does this mean you two are officially separated?”

“Lila’s asked me for a divorce. She’s seeing someone else but won’t tell me the guy’s name.” He gave a bitter laugh. “She probably thinks I’d try to go after him.”

“I’m sorry this is happening to you.”

Matt shot me a small, sad smile. “Thanks, but it’s not your problem, Tess. This is my own doing. Someday I’ll learn from my mistakes, right?”

After Matt left, I decided to make sausage and peppers. The situation with the car had freaked me out, and I needed to de-stress and keep my hands busy for a while. Luigi settled himself on a stool at the breakfast counter, observing me in silence and possibly weighing his chances for a tasty treat.

“What do you think, big guy? A piece of sausage for your lunch?”

He made a little chirping noise as he hit the floor, which I took as a yes. I cut up a small piece of the meat and placed it on a paper plate for him to gobble up.

I sautéed the onions with garlic and then added sliced Italian sausage and peppers. It wasn’t long before the comforting smell started to diffuse through the room and helped me to relax. Ah, much better.

Someone banged on my front door, and I let out a low groan. My happy, safe place had been invaded once again. I sighed and turned the burner off, wiped my hands on a dish towel, and made my way into the living room, with Luigi following at my heels. I glanced through the peephole, and the face looking through on the other side made me do a double take. Something told me this wasn't a good omen.

I opened the door and stared out at Lorenzo. "Hi."

He practically jumped at my greeting. "Hi, Tessa." Lorenzo looked like he hadn't slept in days. He was unshaven and there were heavy circles under his eyes. "Can I talk to you for a minute?"

I held the door open. "Of course. Would you like a cup of coffee?" By the looks of him, he could use one.

"No, thanks." He stood there in the vestibule, his anxious eyes darting around my living room. Luigi sniffed at his shoes and then, as if satisfied, jumped onto the arm of the loveseat and nudged my hand with his head. I reached down to scratch him behind the ears. "What's going on?"

Lorenzo shifted his weight nervously from one foot

to another. "I need you to help me. My mother said you would. When the police find out they're going to think I killed Daphne for sure."

Instantly I knew what he was referring to. "You heard back about the blood test?"

"Yeah." Lorenzo's voice was barely above a whisper. Before he spoke again, I already had my answer. He let out a strangled cry and put his head in his hands. "It was—me. I was the baby's father."

EIGHTEEN

A HAND FLEW TO MY MOUTH before I could stop it. "I'm so sorry." My heart broke for him. I didn't know if this would make Lorenzo look guiltier to the police but suspected it wasn't going to help his innocence.

"Daphne was sixteen weeks pregnant and never said a word to me." His voice, devastated and hollow seconds ago, now shook with rage. "Why did she do that? I had a right to know. She must have realized she was pregnant."

For a moment I was tempted to say she hadn't. I'd heard of unusual circumstances where a woman didn't know she was expecting until much later in term, but it seemed unlikely in this case. Daphne had clearly used him. I was convinced she'd planned to pass the baby off as Preston's. Even if it hadn't worked, he may have offered her money to keep silent about their affair.

Lorenzo looked at me as if he'd read my thoughts. "Daphne thought I was an idiot. She used me for a good time. She wanted that author to marry her and was going to lie and say it was his baby."

I placed a hand on his arm. "You need to go to the police and tell them."

"No way. They're going to think I killed her, and my mother will freak." He dropped his face into his hands and the anger died, giving way to another anguished sob. "That was my kid. I'd have been a good father. I would have helped her with expenses, but she didn't care about any of that." He gave me a pleading look. "You believe me, right? I swear, I didn't kill her."

His imploring eyes and heaving shoulders helped to convince me. "Yes, I believe you." But would Paddy and the rest of the police force?

"Tessa, you've got to help me," he begged. "You have to prove that someone else killed Daphne. I'd never do anything to hurt her. I loved her."

As much as I loathed the idea, Gabby and I needed to get back to the Rigotta house and talk to Marta, hopefully when the others weren't around. "I'll do what I can, but you should tell your mother what happened."

His face fell. "This would have been her grandchild," he whispered. "You know she'll be heartbroken."

"It will all come out eventually anyway," I said sadly. "If we can locate Daphne's obstetrician and show them your blood test, maybe they'll share some information with you—say, if she mentioned you by name to her doctor." Or perhaps *another* male name, but I didn't want to say that out loud to Lorenzo. It was like walking on eggshells around him. Daphne's doctor might not share any information because of patient confidentiality, but it was worth a try.

The misery etched in his face had been replaced by raw, stark fury. "Whoever did this needs to pay," he said bitterly, "and I'm going to make sure that they do."

After Lorenzo left, my elderly neighbor Stacia dropped me off at Snappy Rental Cars. One of Gabby's friends worked there and had wrangled me a discounted rate. Afterward, I went to the restaurant and called my insurance company, who happily assured me that graffiti was not covered under my policy, nor was a rental. This was shaping up to be a banner week. Plus, there were only three days until my grand opening and still no reservations. Well, thinking back to my promise to Matt, at least no paying reservations.

I wrote a check for the sign man and organized the pickup station for my waitresses. It would have been a great time to sort through my invoices and do a spreadsheet on the computer, but Lorenzo's grief-stricken face kept appearing before me. Resigned, I called Gabby, who arrived five minutes later to pick me up.

"Where to first, the Rigottas' or Daphne's father?" Gabby asked.

"We should talk to Daphne's father, but I don't have an address for him."

Gabby accelerated. "Wrong. That's where I come in. His first name is Wayne and he lives in an apartment in Albany. He came into the store last year to order a book that I later ended up mailing to him. Unless he's moved, we can find him easily enough and Lou and Gino don't have to know."

"Then we'll worry about the Rigottas later. I'm hoping he'll be willing to talk and tell us if Daphne mentioned her future plans, or maybe even how the Rigottas reacted to her pregnancy news." Both hands on my watch were pointing at the twelve. "Sylvia must be done taping her show by now, and if she sees me, it won't go over well."

Gabby let out a breath. "I'm not exactly in their good graces either, remember. Preston bad-mouthed my store on his Facebook page yesterday."

"Why didn't you tell me about this sooner?" I asked.

"What good would it do? He didn't mention me by name, only the store, but that's just as bad. He said Once Upon a Book was a joke and his publicist died after eating something vile there. He pretty much came right out and said I was a murderer."

"Ugh. What a mess."

Gabby's lower lip trembled. "I've decided to tell Liza I have to let her go."

"But it hasn't even been a week since the signing," I objected.

"What do you want me to tell you?" She looked like she might cry. "Sales have been down for months and now they're nonexistent. Why delay the inevitable? Besides, I'm betting Liza already knows. She told me yesterday that she had a job offer from a bank. I think she doesn't want me to feel guilty."

"Maybe it won't come to that. Don't give up hope yet," I encouraged.

Wayne Daniels lived in a small duplex just outside of Harvest Park. Much like the shabby state of Slice before I took over, his home needed work. The cement steps were close to crumbling underneath our feet as we climbed the small porch. Dark blue paint on his front door was chipped and peeling, windowpanes were dirty, and the roof was covered with a blue tarp, indicating to me that there were leaks in it.

"Holy cow," I murmured as we rang the bell. "Daphne's father must have fallen on hard times. Didn't they own a nice colonial on Autumn Drive before? I wonder what happened."

"He looked sickly the last time I saw him," Gabby remarked. "When he stopped in the bookstore, he mentioned that he wasn't working anymore. Maybe he's not well enough."

No doubt having his only child murdered wasn't helping things either.

The front door opened a crack, and a man dressed in a dingy T-shirt with gray hair receding at the temples peered out at us. He was much older than I remembered, but it was definitely Daphne's father.

He glanced from me to Gabby and then said, "I know you two from somewhere."

"Mr. Daniels?" I asked and he nodded. "My name is

Tessa, and this is my cousin Gabby. We went to school with Daphne."

Recognition dawned in his weary eyes. "Would you like to come in?" he asked. He held the door open wide and Gabby entered first, with me bringing up the rear.

We followed him down a narrow hallway, the once white walls now a yellowish color. Smells of cabbage and cigarette smoke permeated the small home, and the stale air made me wonder if he ever opened the windows.

There was a small television set up on a wooden entertainment stand, a plaid couch, and two folding chairs in the room. Wayne sat in one of them and gestured to the couch. "Please make yourselves comfortable. Can I get you something to drink? I just made a pot of coffee."

We both shook our heads. "No, thank you," I said.

"We're very sorry about Daphne," Gabby put in.

A shadow passed over his face. "Thank you. I appreciate you both stopping by. It's always nice to meet some of Daphne's friends. I knew you two looked familiar."

He must not have remembered Gabby from the bookstore, which was a good thing. An awkward silence followed. What purpose would it serve to tell the grieving man the truth—that Gabby couldn't stand his bullying hateful daughter, and I'd never been a fan of hers either? Why rub salt in his open wounds?

Wayne was slender to the point of being gaunt, his face a milky shade of white underneath a beard tinged with gray. I surmised that he was in his late fifties, but he looked much older.

I decided to get right to the point. "We were wondering if the police had any leads about her death."

He shook his head. "They haven't shared much information with me. But it had something to do with that guy she worked for. I'm convinced of it."

Gabby and I said nothing and waited for him to continue.

Wayne hesitated for a moment, then leaned forward in the chair, propping his elbows on his knees. "Since you're both friends of hers, did she ever talk to you about her infatuation with that author?"

"I don't remember her saying anything to me." Boy, was that the truth. "How about you?" I turned to my cousin.

Gabby shook her head. "Not a word. When was the last time you saw her?"

He stared off into the distance. "Daphne came by a

couple of times every week, just like clockwork. She was a good girl."

"She was?" Gabby blurted out. Irritated, I elbowed her in the side. "Ouch! I mean, oh, yes, of course she was."

A sad smile formed on his lips. "I know that some people thought she was self-centered, but my princess was always good to her old man. She even hired a nurse to come in every day to look after me."

I blinked. That had to have cost Daphne a small fortune, and the gesture made my heart soften toward her. A person who made sure that their parents were well taken care of couldn't be completely bad. Whatever the case, she certainly didn't deserve to be murdered.

Wayne's eyes were focused on me intently. "Look, I'm not stupid. My daughter could be mean and selfish to other people. She made some enemies. I told that cocky detective who came by the other day that I think her hunger for money is what got her killed." His nostrils flared. "That guy was asking me questions like I was the one responsible for her death. Can you believe that crap?"

Gabby and I exchanged glances. Paddy would probably suspect his own mother if the situation called for it.

"But I have to admit, the detective was on the right

track. I am partially responsible. Daphne didn't want me to have to go into a nursing home. She took the first high paying job she was offered from that—*author*." He spoke the word like it was diseased.

My curiosity was piqued. "You don't like Preston Rigotta?"

Wayne looked at me like I had two heads. "What's there to like about him? The guy was a pretentious snob. My daughter was always doing his bidding, even personal errands. She was supposed to have been hired as a publicist, not his maid. And I suspect that he was taking advantage of my little girl, if you get my drift."

Oh, I got his drift all right. Suddenly uncomfortable, I tried to steer the conversation in a different direction. "How did she get the job with Mr. Rigotta?"

"Daphne was formerly an office manager for a small publishing company in the Lake George area," Wayne explained. "She heard from someone that a local author was looking for his own personal publicist."

I'd been under the impression that Daphne had worked as a publicist before landing the job with Preston. Perhaps Sylvia had been speaking the truth when she said Daphne had lied about her experience.

"She had a degree in marketing, so she met with Rigotta and he hired her on the spot." He reached in his shirt pocket for a cigarette and lit it. "I'm betting Daphne's looks, not her experience, are what got her the job. She was a true beauty."

"The police told you she was pregnant?" Gabby asked.

Her words made me wince inwardly. Some days my cousin needed to be a bit more tactful with her questioning.

Wayne stared at her in amazement. "Yeah, the coroner said so, but Daphne had already told me. How did you find out? I thought that was private information."

"Um, Daphne told us," Gabby blurted out.

"She did?" He seemed surprised. "She said that she hadn't share the news publicly."

Oh great. We were getting in deeper and deeper.

"We forced it out of her," Gabby said, and I had a sudden urge to pinch her.

"They didn't tell me who the father was, but I'm betting dollars to doughnuts on that pompous jerk Rigotta." Wayne's mouth suddenly quivered at the corners, as if he had a secret. "But he didn't know who he was up against. Daphne had her own plan in the works. My little girl was a smart cookie."

My heart gave a little jolt. "What did she have in mind?"

He removed his wallet out of his back pants pocket and produced a small folded piece of paper, then handed it to me. "I didn't know all the details. Daphne stopped by last week. I wasn't expecting her and was at a neighbor's house for dinner, so she left me this note."

I read the words that had been written in her fine cursive handwriting. *"Sorry I missed you. Our money problems will be over soon. He'll see it my way, trust me. Love, D."*

I flipped the piece of paper over and saw that Daphne had written what looked like a reminder note. *"Dr. Reynolds. Next Checkup, Tuesday, May 24th."*

My heart pounded rapidly. Was this the name of Daphne's doctor? Maybe her obstetrician? Was there something Dr. Reynolds could tell us that we didn't already know, and might help us learn who had killed Daphne? It might be worthwhile to pay her a visit.

What was even more interesting than Daphne's note was the heading on the piece of paper. The cream-colored stationery had an *S* and *R* intertwined in raised gold letters at the top of the page, exactly like the one wrapped around the rock that came through Gabby's window. The hairs stood up on the back of my neck. If Daphne had access to Sylvia's stationery, who else did?

"What do you think Daphne meant by that sentence? 'He'll see it my way'?"

Wayne drew deeply on the cigarette. "I'm guessing my daughter planned to tell that creep she was carrying his child, and that they'd have to pay her to go away. That snob wife of his hated Daphne. Pure jealousy, I tell you." He shook his head in disgust. "Daphne got in over her head. I warned her. That entire family was awful to my girl, especially Sylvia and that spoiled rotten daughter of theirs." He gritted his teeth in irritation. "Winnie, right?"

"Willow," I corrected.

"Yeah, that's it. Do you know what that brat told Daphne a few weeks ago?" His face turned red, and I worried he might make himself ill. "She accused Daphne of trying to cut her out of her father's business. Told her to stop interfering with the website and making dumb suggestions to her father. She also knew that Daphne was pregnant."

"But how?" Gabby asked in amazement. "You said that Daphne hadn't shared the information—well, with anyone besides us."

A determined gleam came into his eyes. "I don't know how that little snob found out, but I will tell you this. Willow told my daughter that if she tried to push that baby off as her father's, it would be the last thing she ever did."

NINETEEN

"THIS IS RISKY," I SAID TO Gabby as we drove toward the Rigotta mansion. "And if Gino finds out, he might shoot us both."

After we'd left Wayne's house yesterday, we'd traveled to the Rigottas', but Sylvia's BMW had been parked in the driveway. This morning we'd called the television station ahead of time, pretending we had a floral delivery for her, and been told by Liz that she was still taping her show.

Gabby laughed. "Nah, we're family. He can't shoot us. This is the perfect opportunity to catch Marta alone. According to Preston's website, he's at Okay Talk Radio for an interview this morning so we don't have to worry about running into him."

I shuddered inwardly, remembering how he'd grabbed

me the other night. "That man is vile. I'd be happy to never lay eyes on him again."

"After what he did to you, I don't blame you. And he's obviously hiding something. Preston doesn't want anyone to learn he and Daphne were involved. Sylvia hated Daphne because of the affair with her husband and wanted to get rid of her. Sylvia must have known about the baby, too."

"We have plenty of suspects," I said. "What we need is the killer."

"And we can't forget about Lorenzo either," Gabby pointed out. "Every one of them was present for the book signing, at some point. They all could have easily spotted my key ring lying around and removed the bookstore one."

I pointed at the Rigotta mansion as we approached. "No, I don't think Lorenzo killed her. My theory is that the killer lives here. Marta bought the chocolate for the cannoli that killed Daphne, which Sylvia planned to pass off as her own. My car was defaced. Sylvia followed me and might have thrown a rock through your window. Plus, Preston assaulted me and warned us to back off. By the way, Gino texted earlier that Preston told Paddy he never even touched me—I made the whole thing up." Rage simmered inside me whenever I allowed myself to think about it.

"Big surprise there," Gabby remarked as she parked the car across the street from their home and locked it. "What should we say to Marta?" She asked as we dodged raindrops that had just begun to fall.

"We'll talk about cooking," I said smoothly. "We need to get her to mention the cannoli and see where it leads. She might tell us something that will help." My attention was distracted by the envelopes sticking out of the mail slot next to the front door. I took a step in that direction when the front door opened.

Marta stood there, one hand on the doorknob, her face etched with suspicion. I gave a little wave. "Hi, Marta. Remember us?"

Marta started to shut the door, but I stuck my foot in the way. "We're not here to cause any trouble. Gabby only wants a minute of Mr. Rigotta's time—to talk to him about another book order she's placing."

"He is not at home," she replied firmly.

"But he'll be back any minute, right? He's expecting me," Gabby lied. "Can we at least wait in the foyer? I mean, it *is* raining out."

Uncertainty registered in Marta's hazel eyes. "I'm not sure. Perhaps I should call him first to check."

"Oh, please do," I said and then immediately regretted my statement. If she told Preston we were here, he'd become enraged and would call the police. Paddy would be more than happy to provide handcuffs.

To my surprise, Marta merely shrugged, stood back, and allowed us to enter. She grabbed the mail out of the slot and set it on the small receiving table inside the front door.

Gabby gave her an apologetic grin. "May I use the bathroom, please?"

Marta narrowed her eyes and then crooked a finger at Gabby. "This way." She turned to look back at me. "You stay there, please. No more wandering around the house like last time."

Score one for Gabby. I was certain she'd seen me glance toward the mail and knew what I had in mind. Once they were out of sight, I grabbed the phone bill that was lying on the receiving table and slipped it under my shirt. Underneath it was an envelope addressed to Sylvia, with Dr. Reynolds's name in the upper left-hand corner. My heart thumped furiously. What was she sending to Sylvia? Without stopping to think, I slipped that envelope under my shirt as well.

A two-tiered white cake was sitting on the mahogany

dining-room table in the next room. Marta came hurrying back to the foyer followed by Gabby and frowned at me. "I told you not to go anywhere."

Instead of answering, I pointed toward the cake. This was the opening I'd been looking for. "Did you make that, Marta?"

She nodded. "Yes, for Willow's birthday."

"It looks delicious. You do a lot of cooking and baking, don't you?"

Marta gave me a look that told me she wished I'd shut up. "It's part of my job."

"Of course," I said. "I'm a big fan of Sylvia's television show, especially her cooking. How I wish I could make cannoli like hers."

Marta's face relaxed at my words, and I figured I might be gaining some ground here. "Only a talented baker could make cannoli as rich as hers. I'd love to know what her secret ingredient is."

"Mascarpone," Marta replied, and then her face colored. "The homemade version, not what you buy in the store. And the chocolate—there is a special kind you should use called Valrhona. You shave it and then add to the filling. The texture is much richer, but it's very expensive."

"Thanks for the tip. Sylvia was going to bring cannoli to the book signing but she forgot them," I said, before deciding to cut to the chase. "You made them, didn't you?"

Marta pressed her lips together stubbornly. "That is none of your business."

"She's very lucky to have you," I commented. "Sylvia told us how you've made desserts for her show when she's been in a pinch."

"She did?" Marta stared at me, puzzled.

"Of course," Gabby smiled sweetly. "Sylvia said she didn't know what she'd do without you."

Okay, I was worried that Gabby might have gone too far, but Marta's face flushed with pleasure.

"Do you have any cannoli left? I'd love to sample one," I said.

"No, they went fast." Marta smiled proudly. "When I got up the morning after the signing, there were only a few left. Sylvia takes them to the television station sometimes."

A deep, masculine and familiar voice rang out from above. "What are those two troublemakers doing in here, Marta?"

I looked up the staircase and saw Preston's venomous eyes focused on me. There was no remorse in them from the way he'd treated me the other night, but I hadn't expected any. I squared my shoulders and stared back in anger, refusing to give him the satisfaction of looking away.

"Preston," Marta's face paled. "I didn't know you were home yet."

"That's obvious," he retorted and started down the stairs. "I came in through the rear entry. Marta, I thought I told you to keep these women out of my home. Escort them both to the door *now*. They think they're holding an inquisition, and I'll have no part of it."

Marta looked crestfallen at his words. "Of course. I am so sorry."

"We followed her in," I said quickly. "She didn't invite us." There was no reason Marta should have to take the rap for this, and I sincerely hoped Preston wouldn't fire her because of us.

Preston glared at me but pointed a finger at Marta. "Get my attorney on the phone. I'm filing a restraining order against these two. I'd better never see your faces here again. Now go. *Go!*"

Gabby took a step backward and bumped into me, pushing my body up against the door. I managed to turn around and fumbled with the doorknob. We couldn't scramble out of the house fast enough and rushed down the driveway to her car. The rain was coming down harder and pelted our faces. Once we were inside the vehicle we wiped our faces with a towel Gabby had stored in the glove compartment.

"That went well," Gabby remarked as she started the engine.

"Get ready for Gino's lecture." I pulled my seat belt around my wet sweater and turned the heat on.

"At least a two-hour one. It would have been worth it if we'd learned something valuable."

"Daphne must have told Preston she was pregnant and Willow overheard and told her mother, or something like that. I'm betting the entire family knew. And what about that note Daphne left her father on Sylvia's stationery? She was planning on getting a serious cash windfall from Preston. What are you doing?"

Gabby turned the car around in the Rigotta driveway, and I cringed when I saw a curtain move in the upstairs window.

"Someone's watching us." Gabby gulped. "Preston scared me, Tess. You must have been terrified when he forced his way into your house. I can't believe how I once idolized that man."

Gabby's fangirling days were long over. As far as I was concerned, everyone in the Rigotta household was a potential suspect in Daphne's death. Preston was violent and worried that the pregnancy would hurt his career. Sylvia was self-absorbed, hated Daphne for the affair, and worried she might get her hands on their money. And Willow? She just wanted to get away from her parents and had resented Daphne. They'd all had opportunity and motive to do the deed.

When she stopped for a red light, I pulled out both the phone bill and Sylvia's envelope from the doctor's office. "Let's go back to my house and take a look at these gems."

A grin spread across Gabby's face and she high-fived me. "I knew you'd fix this. Way to go, girl."

"I couldn't have done it without you," I laughed.

"Do you think anyone else was home?" she asked fearfully. "Who could have been in that upstairs window?"

"Hard to say. It may have been Preston, making sure we'd gone. One thing is for certain. We've definitely made enemies of that family."

An hour later, Gabby and I sat at my dining-room table, enjoying leftover sausage and peppers with fresh Italian bread. We both had a portion of the phone bill in front of us. The rain had stopped, and Luigi was curled up asleep in the window seat, enjoying the sunbeams and clearly disinterested in our activity.

"This is a family plan," I observed. "Well, two phone lines, obviously cells. Someone in the house has a separate one."

Gabby scrolled through the contacts on her phone. "That bill must be for Sylvia and Willow. I have Preston's private number in my phone. He probably writes his off as a business expense."

"Or makes calls that he doesn't want Sylvia to see," I murmured.

"I doubt Daphne was the first employee he was involved with," Gabby said. "Now that I think about it, he's had several personal assistants or publicists in the past five years since I've been following him, and none have ever lasted that long. I once saw him at a book signing with the woman who Daphne replaced. Dark hair, very pretty, *and* young. Right up his alley."

The more I learned about the bestselling author, the more I detested him.

Gabby made a red X through three of the calls. "These were made to my bookstore two weeks ago so we can rule them out. Willow had questions pertaining to the signing. So, I'm guessing the number ending in 1629 is hers. The one with 5544 must be Sylvia's. See, that's why I didn't even know Daphne had been hired. Willow was always the one to call me."

"Let's pick a few numbers at random numbers to call," I suggested. "But don't use your cell. My landline is private and can't be tracked." I'd made a mistake like this before when checking into Dylan's death, and it had cost me dearly.

The first number I called turned out to be the television station. A woman sounding like Liz answered after the second ring and I murmured, "Sorry, wrong number." The next number was for Sunnyside Up, a diner where I'd once worked. Probably a takeout order.

Gabby's cell buzzed. She stared at the screen, mouthed "Lou" to me, and went into the kitchen to talk in private. I sighed. I didn't want to do this all day and needed to get to the restaurant. I dialed the next number on Sylvia's list and got a recorded message. "You have reached Dr. Reynolds's office. If you are in labor, please hang up and dial 911. To make or cancel an appointment, press 1."

I perked up at the doctor's name. Daphne's obstetrician once again. Had someone at the Rigotta residence been trying to obtain information about the pregnancy? Did they find what they were looking for and, more important, had it led to Daphne's death? I pressed number one. I needed to discover what the Rigottas might have learned, if anything. Perhaps bringing Lorenzo to see Dr. Reynolds with his blood test to prove he was the baby's father would help.

Gabby came back into the room and I put a finger to my lips as a woman came on the line. "Doctor's office. How may I help you?"

"Hi, I'd like to make an appointment to see Dr. Reynolds."

"Name and date of birth, please."

"I'm a new patient." I gave her my information and assured her that no, I wasn't pregnant, I only wanted an exam.

My doorbell rang as she searched for an appointment. I opened the envelope addressed to Sylvia. It was a report from her most recent visit. As I began to scan it the receptionist came back on the line. "I have a cancellation for this afternoon at four o'clock. Would that work?"

That was only two hours away. The restaurant would

have to wait until later, and I didn't even know if I could find Lorenzo within that time frame and convince him to come along. But I heard myself say, "Perfect, see you then," and clicked off.

I looked up to see Gino standing there, arms folded over his chest, a sour expression on his face. Gabby winked at me from behind him. This couldn't be good.

I dropped Sylvia's report into my purse on the chair next to me and then casually moved a notebook over the Rigotta phone bill. "What's up?"

Gino's mouth tightened in anger. "You two have gone too far this time."

"Preston called you," Gabby said quickly, as if afraid I might come up with a different conclusion.

Boy, news traveled faster that I'd thought. "Gino, we can explain—"

"He didn't call me directly," Gino said through clenched teeth. "He called my boss. Warner lit into me big time and so did Paddy. It was embarrassing."

Gabby placed her hands on her hips. "We didn't do anything wrong. It's not like we broke in. We asked Marta about the cannoli, and then Preston came home and went into a rage when he saw us. That's all."

"That's *all?*" Gino said angrily. "Whoever killed Daphne is on to your little game and has already made it personal. Now the Rigottas want a restraining order against you both."

Gabby's nostrils flared. "My store is about to go under. Tess doesn't have one reservation for her restaurant, and it opens in two days. This is our livelihood. Don't you understand how we feel?"

Gino placed his hands on her shoulders, and she dropped her arms. "What about how *I* feel? Helpless and completely useless. I can't work this blasted case because my family is involved. Now you're getting into trouble and putting my job on the line."

I gasped. "The department can't do that, can they?"

"No way." Gabby looked at him soberly. "I never thought your job might be in jeopardy."

Gino's eyes met mine and then flickered back to his sister. "They can do whatever they want. Remember, no one is irreplaceable. Now, I have to get back to work. A word of warning. You're gaining extreme popularity at the police department with this latest antic, and Paddy's got his eyes on both of you."

"That creep," Gabby muttered.

I was overcome with guilt about Gino's situation. This murder had managed to turn all our lives upside down. "How's Lucy? Is she feeling okay?"

He waggled his hand back and forth. "She's had some nausea but other than that everything seems good. She goes back to see Dr. Reynolds next week."

At the mention of the doctor's name, my ears perked up. "Oh, I've heard she's a wonderful obstetrician." Heck, there had to be more than one in Harvest Park, but Dr. Reynolds's name kept popping up everywhere. I couldn't very well tell Gino that I planned to see her this afternoon with Lorenzo in tow, because he'd freak.

Gino eyed me sharply. "Yeah. She's only been practicing two years. Lucy said she took over for her father, who was also an ob-gyn. From what I've heard, Dr. Reynolds was Daphne's doctor as well. For some strange reason, I'm guessing you already know that."

Thankfully, Gabby spoke up. "Has Paddy given you any information about the investigation?"

"No," Gino replied, "and it's doubtful he will now. Look, you both happen to be more important to me than my job, so I've been doing some secret checking on my own, despite Warner's warning. I don't want your lives in jeopardy again like they were after Dylan died." He stepped forward and bussed each one of us on the cheek. "Remember, family over everything."

Gino wasn't usually a demonstrative person, so his actions surprised me. Maybe it was due to his recent fatherhood news.

Gabby hugged her brother tightly. "I do happen to love you—you pesky cop," she said in a choked-up voice. "And don't worry. Nothing like that is ever going to happen to us again."

TWENTY

IT WAS STRANGE TO BE IN an examination room with Lorenzo by my side. He'd reluctantly agreed to come with me and was already waiting in his car when I pulled up in front of the medical building.

We sat in silence across from the examining table, and Lorenzo visibly colored when he stared at the picture of the developing baby during pregnancy and at the separate diagram of female organs. Talk about your awkward moments.

"Relax," I told him.

"What good is this going to do?" he burst out. "When the doctor finds out that I was the baby's father, she'll think I killed Daphne because of it."

I decided to be honest with him. "Maybe nothing. Then again, it might give us a clue as to who killed her."

Lorenzo was gripping the arms of the chair, his body visibly shaking. Perhaps this hadn't been such a good idea. He was too emotional and high strung about the entire situation, and I couldn't blame him. "Did you tell your mother?"

He stared down at the floor and nodded. "Yeah. She took it pretty hard."

There wasn't much I could say to that. Carlita's family meant everything to her. Even if she hadn't liked Daphne, she still would have wanted to be part of the baby's life.

The door opened, and a woman about my age stepped into the room. Tall and sophisticated, she had peaches-and-cream skin with long, blond hair pulled back from her face in a single braid. She looked more suited for the runway than medical school. A white coat covered her pale blue blouse. Even with sneakers on, she towered over my five-foot, four-inch height. She glanced from me to Lorenzo and smiled. "Hi, I'm Eve Reynolds. You're Tessa Daniels?"

"Yes, and this is—*was*—my sister Daphne's boyfriend." I purposely didn't give his name.

She looked confused. "Are you here for an exam? It says that you're a new patient."

I shook my head. "No, I didn't quite know how

to phrase it to the receptionist, but this is regarding Daphne. As you might have heard, she died suddenly last week."

Eve stared at us with pity in her eyes. "Yes. I am very sorry for your loss, but I don't understand what it has to do with me."

"She was pregnant," I said. "We know that she was seeing you for prenatal care."

Eve's mouth formed a taut line. "Sorry, but I can't discuss a patient's condition with you. Even though she's deceased, I'm still not at liberty to do so."

"Yes, I'm aware of that." I'd gone through something similar with Dylan after he passed away. The angst was apparent on Lorenzo's face, and I knew something of his frustration. "This is the father of Daphne's baby. He has a blood test to prove it. We know that you can't disclose medical information, but we hoped you might at least share with us how she felt about the baby?"

Lorenzo held out the envelope to the doctor with a shaking hand. Eve gave him a dubious look but opened it and studied the contents for about five seconds while he shifted nervously in his seat.

With a sad smile, Eve handed the paper back to

Lorenzo. "Again, I'm very sorry for your loss and wish I could help. Unfortunately, I still can't tell you anything."

"Come on! Don't you realize what this is doing to me?" Lorenzo exploded. He jumped out of his chair, and for a second, I was afraid he might lunge for her. Eve backed up, obviously thinking the same thing.

I quickly laid a hand on Lorenzo's arm. "Hey, we tried. I'm sorry."

He drew a long breath and looked at me, his lower lip quivering. "Yeah, right. Let's get out of here."

I kept a hold on his arm as we walked past the doctor. "Thanks for seeing us."

As I reached for the doorknob, Eve cleared her throat. "Daphne was going to have the baby."

Lorenzo and I both turned around. "Do you know if it was a boy or a girl?" he asked.

The cool, confident look had disappeared from Eve's face, and her high cheekbones became tinged with pink. "Normally I might not remember, but I happened to look at her file again after learning of her death. We did an ultrasound a couple of days before she died. It was a boy."

Lorenzo drew a hand to his mouth, and for a second I worried he might start crying. He remained frozen in place, staring at the doctor with grief-filled eyes. I was overcome with sadness for him. Perhaps things wouldn't have worked out with Daphne, but that didn't change the fact he'd never gotten the chance to know his child. As I stared at his stricken face, any lingering doubt I had about him being the killer faded away.

I extended my hand to Eve. "Thank you again."

She studied me. "It's no trouble. You must be the one who called last week asking for details on the pregnancy, right after her ultrasound. I hope the receptionist wasn't rude when I refused to talk to you."

"No, she was fine." I hated to lie, but at least she'd given me the information I'd been looking for, and then some. The date of the ultrasound would have corresponded with the date on the Rigotta phone bill. I was convinced someone was trying to obtain further information about Daphne's pregnancy.

Eve nodded. "Well, if you'll excuse me, I have another patient waiting."

"Thank you," Lorenzo said gruffly, and before I could stop him, he stepped forward and stretched out his hand.

The doctor clasped it between hers. "Again, I'm very sorry for your loss, Mr. Rigotta."

Lorenzo raised his head in astonishment. "*What?*"

Oh boy. I hadn't given Lorenzo's name in hopes that the doctor might throw us a bone, and I wasn't disappointed. She must not have looked too closely at the information on the blood test. I prayed Lorenzo wouldn't give us away.

"Preston," I said slowly and deliberately. "You have to meet with your agent tonight, right? We should leave and let the doctor get back to her work."

Anger smoldered behind Lorenzo's dark eyes. "Yeah. I guess I found out everything that I needed to know."

"Good luck with your books," Eve said. "I'm not much of a reader myself, but Daphne raved about your work. I'll be sure to check one out next time I'm on vacation."

"Bye, Dr. Reynolds." I pushed Lorenzo out into the hall and quickly shut the door behind us. Phew. That had been a close one. Lorenzo was a volcano, ready to erupt at any second.

Once we were safely in the elevator, he glared at me. "You must really think I'm an idiot, don't you?"

His words took me by surprise. "Of course not. I was afraid you might get angry when she mentioned Preston's name."

The elevator dinged, and when the doors opened, Lorenzo strode ahead of me in the lobby, his chin high and erect, hands balled into fists at his sides. Concerned, I hurried to catch up with him. "Lorenzo, wait a second."

Once we exited the building, he turned around to face me. "You know the truth same as I do." He practically spat the words out, as if they were poison. "She planned to pass my kid off as that author's. She told the doctor that he was the father! How could she do that to me? I was in love with her. And she never gave two cents about me."

I tried to reassure him. "We don't know that for certain. Maybe Daphne didn't know either."

Lorenzo cursed under his breath. "Yeah, right. Trust me, she knew. Daphne wanted Preston to be her sugar daddy. Maybe she didn't want to marry him, but she hoped he'd cough up enough money to make her go away. I knew she was devious but didn't think she was this bad. Now she and the baby—*my baby*—are dead because of it."

"Look, let's go somewhere and talk about this. You're upset and—"

My sentence was left dangling in the air like a kite. Lorenzo had stopped dead in his tracks and didn't appear to have heard me. I shielded my eyes against the sun to see what he was staring at.

A light blue sedan was in the center of the semi-empty parking lot, with Paddy McDermott behind the wheel. Another man I knew, Steven, a rookie cop on the Harvest Park force, was in the seat next to him. I stifled a groan. This was not going to end well.

Paddy got out of the car and sauntered toward us, his nose lifted arrogantly in the air. He was wearing beige slacks and a dark blue sports coat. A St. Francis medal hung on a gold chain around his thick neck. He stared from Lorenzo to me, a sarcastic smile playing on his lips. "Well, well. Good day, Mrs. Esposito. What brings you here?"

Lorenzo stiffened. "It's none of your business why we're here."

Paddy's eyes shifted to him in annoyance. "See, it *is* my business. You're both suspects in a murder. Your girlfriend—or shall I say, your lady of the month—was murdered, and I happen to think it was done by someone close to her. A boyfriend, perhaps. Someone who was jealous that she had eyes for another man and became so enraged that—"

"Shut up, pig! You don't know what you're talking

about!" Lorenzo yelled, and before I could stop him, he struck the detective across the jaw. Paddy stumbled backward and quickly regained his balance. He charged for Lorenzo like an angry bull, and with Steven's help, they quickly had him on the ground and in handcuffs. A second later Lorenzo was being read his rights, while all I could do was watch in shock.

Lorenzo shouted obscenities at Paddy as they drove away, and a sick feeling of dread washed over me. A minute ago, I'd been positive that Lorenzo was innocent. He'd loved Daphne and wanted the baby she was carrying. But if he was going to lose it so easily in the face of accusation, could I have been wrong after all?

TWENTY-ONE

"OKAY, TESS, GIVE ME ALL THE dirt. What happened after Lorenzo got carted off?" Gabby asked.

She was helping me unpack the box of menus that had just been delivered. I studied the maroon cover with bated breath and then let out a small sigh of relief. Anything's Pastable was spelled correctly. At least one good thing had happened today.

My sleuthing would be limited after the restaurant opened. Then again, if we didn't find the person responsible, I might not have to worry about customers. There were only two days to go, and despite everyone's reassurances, I was still terrified no one would show up.

"Earth to Tess," Gabby sang.

I jerked myself out of my thoughts. "Oh, sorry. What did you say?"

She rolled her eyes. "I want to know what happened to Lorenzo."

I placed menus at each table. Gabby took a pile and did the same. "I called Carlita after Paddy took him away, and she started crying on the phone. I'm guessing she went to bail him out, because I heard nothing back after that."

"You're convinced he didn't kill her?" Gabby's voice was full of doubt.

"No, I don't think so. It's hard to fake grief like that, Gabs. But he's got such a temper. It concerns me what Lorenzo might do if—"

"If someone pushed him too far," Gabby finished the sentence for me. "Yeah, I know what that feels like. There were plenty of times in high school that I wanted to haul off and smack Daphne when she bullied me, but I was afraid of the consequences. I know that's terrible to say, especially now that she's dead."

"It's understandable."

She groaned in frustration. "Personally, I think Paddy and the police are looking in the wrong direction. I'm not convinced Lorenzo is the killer either. By the time they figure it all out, my store may be done for. I never thought my dream would get extinguished so soon."

"What if I lent you some money to tide—"

"I already told you, no. I appreciate it, Tess, but feel bad enough about involving you in this. Look what happened to your car, for goodness' sake. That's a lot of money to have to shell out, and I know you're watching your pennies, too. I can give it another week or two but then I'll have to close down if things don't improve." She glanced at me hopefully. "If you still need another waitress by then, I'd be grateful if you considered me for the job."

"Of course, you can have the job, but don't give up yet," I pleaded. "We're close, I can feel it."

Gabby draped an arm around my shoulders. "Forget about my problem. What can I do to help with opening night?"

I managed a smile. "Everything is ready to go. I've been working on this for weeks, remember. Like you, all I need is customers. So far, I only have one reservation for Saturday and it's Matt."

"Ew." Gabby sounded like a little kid who'd been served a plate of vegetables. "Thanks for the warning. By the way, I'm never waiting on him, unless he wants to wear his dinner. The reservations will come, or you'll have lots of walk-ins at the last minute. You're a fantastic chef, Tess.

The entire town knows it. If they don't show, that's my fault, too."

"Stop saying that. It's not true." I went back into the kitchen and Gabby followed. I was restless and needed to keep moving. Besides the murder, I was missing Dylan terribly today and distractions helped.

My phone pinged from the counter with a text from Justin. Just got off work. Will you be around tomorrow morning? There's something I need to tell you.

My chest tightened as I read the message. He must have decided to take Natalie back. The decision made me sad for him. Didn't he know it was a mistake? Once a cheater, always a cheater was what I believed, but again, this was his life. I would always be supportive because our friendship meant a great deal to me, and I didn't want to lose it.

With clumsy fingers, I texted back. I'll be leaving for the restaurant at nine o'clock tomorrow morning. See you around eight thirty?

Gabby looked at me quizzically. "Bad news?"

"It's fine," I said hastily, not wanting to get into it, even with her. "Justin's going to stop and see me tomorrow, that's all. Getting back to Daphne's murder, I wonder if there's any way we can find out if Sylvia and Preston had a prenup."

"I thought I told you that they didn't. Sylvia bragged about it on her show one day."

"You've got to be kidding."

She grinned. "Nope. Her guest was some famous divorce lawyer turned chef. She rambled on and on about how their marriage was trustworthy and loving and they never felt the need for one." Gabby stuck a finger down her throat for the full effect. "Why do you ask?"

"Well, we know their marriage had problems. Wouldn't she have divorced him already if there was no prenup in place?"

Gabby shrugged. "Who knows? She could have been lying. Sylvia clearly loves the good life, so it would be difficult for her to walk away from it. Plus, Preston got her the job on the show, remember. He may have had the power to take it away if she divorced him. From Sylvia's point of view, it might have been easier to eliminate the problem—Daphne herself—and stay married to the louse."

A sharp rapping on the back door sounded, and Gabby let out a low squeak. We were both on edge these days. "Who is it?" I called loudly.

"Your favorite cousin," a male voice yelled back.

Gabby went over to open the door. "To set the record straight, I'm the favorite around here."

Gino pointed a finger at me in accusation. "Paddy told me all about Lorenzo's arrest. Assaulting a police detective? Real nice. Why were you with that guy? He may be a killer. I told you to ask the Garcias a few questions—not become Lorenzo's best friend. Why do you refuse to listen to anything that I tell you?"

Gabby's mouth twitched. "She's like my twin, isn't she, bro?"

"Not funny," he growled at her. "Assaulting a member of the police force is a big deal. Poor Carlita had to come down to bail out her son. He's going to have to stand trial for this. And Paddy's convinced now that he killed Daphne."

"He was upset," I said in Lorenzo's defense, "and Paddy was goading him. I don't think he killed her."

"That guy is like a loose cannon, ready to go off at any second," Gino remarked. "Just because he's Carlita's son doesn't make him innocent."

"I'm aware of this. But the woman he loved was murdered. His baby died. How do you think he'd react?"

Gino shook his head in disbelief. "I've learned to expect this attitude from my sister, but not you, Tess," he said reproachfully.

Gabby placed her hands on her hips. "And what's that supposed to mean?"

"How about a cappuccino, your favorite?" I gestured at my new espresso machine with a smile, hoping to ward off another sibling argument.

He gave me a look that told me I wasn't fooling him. "To go, please. I have to get back to work."

As the drink brewed, I asked the million-dollar question. "Is Sylvia being brought in for questioning?"

"Unreal. You never stop." Gino looked both exasperated and worn out, and I couldn't help thinking he'd be keeling over with exhaustion in about six months. "If you must know, Paddy's going to bring her in tomorrow morning. I can't be there of course, but he'll get her to crack."

"Like an egg, I'm sure," I muttered under my breath.

"Jeez, that almost makes me sorry for her and I can't stand Sylvia," Gabby remarked. "But I do think she did it. Her husband was carrying on with a younger woman, and Sylvia wanted her gone. Daphne's father told us that Sylvia hated her. And she wanted me and Tess to stop interfering so she threw a rock through my window and defaced Tessa's car."

I'd been thinking about the rock incident all day. It wasn't sitting well with me. "We can't be certain that Sylvia tossed the rock through your window, Gabs."

She stared at me, perplexed. "What are you talking about? The note was written on her stationery."

"Yes, but it doesn't make sense. Why would she use her own stationery? Clearly anyone who was in the Rigotta household had access to it because Daphne wrote her doctor's appointment on one. Sure, Sylvia had a motive, but she isn't stupid. Someone might be trying to frame her for the murder."

"Maybe Tess should be the one questioning Sylvia," Gabby slyly told her brother.

He snorted back a laugh. "Well, we know that can't happen. If Paddy catches either one of you near the police station tomorrow, we're all going to catch heat."

"Can't Lou sit in on it?" Gabby asked. "Maybe he could let Tessa come too, on the pretense that—"

He glared at her. "No. After the recent stunt you pulled at the Rigottas', Lou can't be present either. And Tessa is not a police officer. End of discussion."

"You let me in the room when you questioned Matt about Dylan's death," I pointed out.

"That was different," he said calmly. "Matt asked for you that time. Don't worry, Paddy can handle her. I know you're hooked on the theory she did it because of the chocolate that the housekeeper bought but—"

I didn't let him finish. "That's only part of it. She must have been worried that we had something on her. Plus she hated Daphne so much that she couldn't even say her name; she kept calling her 'that woman.'" I almost mentioned that someone from the Rigotta household had called Daphne's doctor to try to obtain information on her condition but stopped myself in time. If Gino knew about the phone bill, it wouldn't go over well. "If Preston had another child, Sylvia might worry she'd get less of his fortune."

Gino considered this while he took a sip of his drink. "It's possible, but you two need to leave it alone now and let Paddy handle this. Tessa, you have a new restaurant to worry about. By the way, make sure you reserve a table for me and Lucy and the boys for seven o'clock. Lucy may have an important announcement to make to our mothers. Thanks for the drink." He gave Gabby's hair a tug. "Behave."

After he'd shut the door behind him, Gabby picked up her car keys. "Well, I'd better get over to the store."

I glanced at my watch. "It's seven o'clock. You're not even open for business at this hour. What on earth do you have to do there now?"

"Nothing." She stared at me mournfully. "I want to sit in one of my comfy easy chairs and read a book. Get lost in another world for a while. Savor the precious time I have left there."

"I'm going home within the hour," I said brightly. "Why don't you stop over when you're done? We'll watch an old movie on the TV. Something in black-and-white."

A smile formed at the corners of her mouth. "I'll bring my DVD of *Gone with the Wind.* Our favorite."

"It's a date. And I happen to have some freshly made tiramisu, if you feel up to it."

"If I feel up to it? Is the Pope Catholic?" Gabby's eyes sparkled with new hope. "You're the best cousin ever, did you know that?"

"Well, the feeling's mutual. Hey, take my sweater off the hook. It's getting chilly out there."

She frowned. "But what will you use?"

"I'm fine. I have a spare jacket in the rental."

Gabby obediently put my sweater on and pulled the hood over her head. "See you in a little while, hon."

After she was gone, I started on a lasagna filling for the taste test tomorrow. I had wide noodles that I'd already frozen and would put the entire pan together in the morning.

I kept thinking about Daphne's killer while I worked. Funny how making a lasagna was similar to solving a mystery. You had to have all the right ingredients and layer them with care. It took precision and patience, but we were running out of time. We needed to figure this puzzle out before Gabby lost her dream. Before we both did.

I set the covered bowl in the fridge and picked up my purse. The envelope from the doctor's office caught my eye. If Gino had known I was stealing people's mail, he would have gone nuts. If Paddy had known, I'd be behind bars. I hadn't had time to look at it closely before and studied the contents with interest now.

Name: Sylvia Annette Rigotta. Age: Forty-four. She'd been in for an annual checkup the same day that Daphne had her ultrasound. How ironic. I looked at her previous medical history and the surgeries listed at the bottom of the page. An appendectomy back in 1990. Then there was the note about her hysterectomy. *May 1998*. That would make it twenty-two years ago for the surgery next month.

I placed the paper back in my purse and headed for the back door. Then the realization hit me like a brick wall. That date was impossible. Willow had just turned twenty-one, so how could Sylvia have had a hysterectomy before her birth? Medical records didn't lie.

I sucked in a deep breath, confident I had my answer as to who had killed Daphne. Yes, it all fit now.

My heart thumped away at a furious pace as I left Gino a message. "Hey, it's me," I said into the phone. "Call me back as soon as you can. Hopefully before Paddy questions Sylvia. I've got some new information to share."

As soon as I clicked off, my phone pinged with a text from Gabby. Can you come over to the store right away? I think I twisted my ankle and can't drive home.

Worried, I texted back. Are you okay?

Her reply came within a minute. Yeah. I don't think it's broken but can't put any pressure on it.

On my way. I'd hoped to go to the police station, but my theory would have to wait for a while. Besides, I could bring Gabby to the station with me, or after she was seen in the emergency room. Knowing her, she'd most likely refuse treatment.

As I drove to the bookstore, my thoughts wandered back to Daphne. True, she had been unlikeable, but she also had some redeeming qualities I'd never known about before. Because of her death, her father was now left heart-broken and alone. He needed justice for his daughter, and Gabby needed her business back.

I was relieved to discover that the killer wasn't Lorenzo. The raw emotion in his face when he'd learned about the baby had helped to convince me he was innocent. But up until now, there was a person I hadn't really considered. Someone that I'd been aware of, but unlikely a possible killer. That phrase Gabby had coined last year rang true again: *No one is exempt.*

I pulled my car up in front of the bookstore. Darkness had settled on Harvest Park, and the inside of the store was pitch black as well. I tried the doorknob. Locked. I rapped on the door with a series of sharp taps. "Gabs?" I called loudly. "Can you let me in?"

My phone beeped with a text from her. I unlocked the back door for you. I can't move around much, it hurts.

She sounded like she was in a lot of pain. Concerned, I hurried around to the back of the building, and the knob turned easily in my hand. What a relief. As soon as I entered the room, I knew something was wrong. A strong sense of foreboding shot through me. I took a step back toward the door to retreat, but someone grabbed me and shoved me across the room.

I let out a shriek as I stumbled against the small kitchen table. My head connected with a solid surface near the floor, most likely Gabby's mini-fridge. I landed on my back, groaning with pain. Too stunned to move, I remained there, frightened by the person who lurked in the darkness. And where was my cousin?

I brought a hand up to my forehead, which throbbed with pain, and touched a wet and sticky spot. Blood, no doubt. My other hand connected with something soft and warm next to me on the floor. It was a body. Cold, stark fear settled inside me as I moved my hand over the figure. My fingers connected with short, silky hair. "Gabs?" I let out a low sob.

Her breathing was heavy and uneven, but there was no answer.

My phone was still in my jeans pocket. The screen

shimmered in the dark when I pulled it out. A flashlight shone directly in my eyes, and I winced from the glare. The phone was kicked out of my hand, and I cried out in pain. I turned to see Gabby lying in a fetal position next to me, a large, bloody gash on the back of her head. The light blinked off as I gasped and gently touched her face. "Gabs, can you hear me?"

I moved my back up against the wall. Nausea whirled through my stomach, and I was afraid I might be sick. A low laugh sounded nearby. Anger flickered inside me like a flame. "Coward," I hissed into the darkness. "You don't even have the guts to let me see your face."

The light shone directly in my eyes again, but this time I kept my gaze level at the person behind it. As I'd suspected earlier, the cold, calculating eyes of Marta Eldridge blazed back at me.

TWENTY-TWO

"DON'T PLAY STUPID," MARTA SNEERED. "YOU knew it was me. Do you think I'm an idiot? You lifted Sylvia's doctor's report and the phone bill at the house today. I figured you might put everything together. But I thought it was you leaving the restaurant until Gabby got out of the car."

"I had to get a rental car, thanks to your decorating skills. You'd better pray that she's okay." My head ached from where I'd struck it. The intense brightness of the flashlight added to the discomfort. I forced myself to look at Gabby's unmoving figure.

"Don't try to change the subject," Marta said angrily. "Willow told me she mentioned Sylvia's hysterectomy to you. She tells me everything. It would have been on the report you stole. She had a physical recently."

Gabby's face was warm to my touch. Her breathing

seemed a little more even now. Her eyes were closed, and she looked so pale. She needed medical attention soon. "You hit her on the head with the flashlight when she opened the door, didn't you?" Rage bubbled up inside me.

Marta giggled like a schoolgirl. "Yes. But don't worry. She never even knew what hit her."

I was aware of blood slowly trickling down the side of my head and swiped at it with my hand. "You lured Daphne here after the signing." Everything had suddenly become clear. "You must have called and said that Willow needed to see her about Preston's book, and you brought the cannoli. It was *you* in Sylvia's car that night, following me around. But you *wanted* me to see you and *think* it was Sylvia. Then you used her stationery to write the note that you tossed through Gabby's window. You did everything possible to frame Sylvia for Daphne's murder. But why kill Daphne?"

"She was going to ruin my plans. I heard her tell Preston that she was pregnant with his child. He was mine first!" The flashlight shook in Marta's hands.

So that was it. I had all my answers now. "You're still in love with Preston. And you needed *both* Daphne and Sylvia out of the way to have him."

She sniffed. "You don't understand. He'll see that it's for the best when Sylvia goes to prison. We were always meant to be together. We have a child, for goodness' sake!"

When I didn't reply, she went on. "I know that you were getting ready to go to the police. I've been following you around. But I can't believe you had the gall to come back and bother Preston again today after he said he was getting a restraining order. You just can't take a hint."

"Does Willow know that you're her biological mother?" I blurted out. Now I realized why Marta had looked so familiar the first time we'd gone to the house. Willow might have Preston's eyes, but the rest of her face was all Marta.

She shifted the flashlight so that I could see her face. Her lips trembled, and she brushed a hand across her eyes. "I sometimes think that Willow suspects, but no, she's never asked me, and I promised not to tell. After I got pregnant, Preston said that he couldn't divorce his wife and marry me. He'd built a public persona as a happily married man and author. He said he loved me, but it would hurt his career. I was so crazy for him that I was willing to do anything he asked."

"And you still are," I said quietly.

Marta ignored my comment. "Preston had just had his first bestseller. He wanted the baby but refused to divorce Sylvia. He said she was the type of wife who would enhance his career. Not a young girl like me who had nothing."

My eyes darted toward the door while I waited for her to go on.

"Sylvia." Marta spoke the name between clenched teeth. "She wanted to give Preston a baby more than anything. She'd been trying to get pregnant, then had to have an emergency hysterectomy. Sylvia knew Preston had been cheating on her, and he admitted it. When he told her about the baby, they agreed to let me stay in the house and have contact with Willow as long as I never told her I was her mother. They made me sign my rights away. And I was stupid enough to do it."

Marta gulped back a sob, then turned slightly and jerked open the drawer of the microwave stand, obviously searching for something. The flashlight moved off my face and into the drawer. Although dizzy, I wasted no time charging at her. The room turned upside down, but I managed to catch her off guard for a second, before the flashlight connected with my ear and a stinging pain shot through my head. Marta stumbled backward, and the flashlight shot out of her hands and cracked against the ceramic flooring, leaving us in total darkness. I didn't wait to see what she'd do next. I needed to get help for Gabby. In the darkness, I found the door to the main store and fumbled with the knob, then slammed it shut behind me.

"Get back here!" Marta screamed.

I was surrounded by complete darkness. My heart was in my throat as I moved clumsily through pitch black. I felt the edge of an aisle, moved down it, and then kept walking until I hit the wall. I ran my hands quietly over the bottom shelves until I found a thick hardcover book, which I lifted in my hands. Still reeling from my earlier fall, I forced myself into a crouching position and waited. I could hear Marta moving around in the store, throwing books to the floor and cursing. "Where's the light switch?" she screamed.

I smiled to myself, grateful she couldn't see my reaction. The only wall switch was up by the front of the store, and it would be a while before she found it. I tried to figure out my position in the store and guessed I must be close to the halfway mark of the front door.

Gabby had a hammer behind the front register. I'd seen her use it last week when she was hanging pictures. I'd have to try and find it in the darkness. I didn't think Marta had another weapon on her and most likely was searching for a knife when I charged her. But had she found one?

"You're ruining everything!" Marta's voice rang out in the darkness, and too close for my comfort. "I thought the rock and spray paint would scare you off, but no, you still had to be a pest, trying to figure things out instead of leaving it to the police, like normal people do. You gave yourself away today. As soon as you asked about the cannoli, I knew you were on to the truth. Why couldn't you have left well enough alone?"

There was silence, as if she expected to hear me answer, and then Marta spoke again, more quietly this time. "You see, I didn't have a choice. I didn't want to lose Willow, but I had nothing to give her. No money. No family. If I'd tried to keep her, I would have had to leave the Rigottas' home and employment. Willow would have everything she needed with them. Money, excellent schools, the finest clothes. Every opportunity I never had, and this way I would still get to see her. When I overheard Daphne tell Preston about her pregnancy and that he was the father, I knew it was now or never. I had to act fast."

Her voice had grown closer, as if she was standing directly across from me in the middle aisle. My heart thumped so loudly I was positive she could hear it.

"Don't you understand?" Marta asked, her tone softening. "He'd never have come back to me if Daphne had his child. She would have demanded he leave his wife, and I'd be left with nothing…again. By killing Daphne, I solved the problem. And by framing Sylvia, I'd finally get her out of the way. With Preston alone and grieving the loss of his child, I could have provided the love and support he needed, and he would finally realize that I was the woman he should have been with all along. We could have been a family—me, Willow, and Preston."

But if he'd loved you in the first place, Marta, he wouldn't have stayed with Sylvia. You killed an innocent woman for nothing. It wasn't even Preston's child. Oh, how I longed to say those words out loud, but I forced myself to stay silent. I had to make a break for the front of the store when or if she ever moved away from me.

Marta started breathing move heavily. "Where are you? Come out now. I promise not to hurt you." Her voice sounded closer, and books crashed to the floor again. She was in the aisle to the right of me. I could try to run past her, but it was risky. I hoped she'd move back in the opposite direction.

"God, how I hate Sylvia. I should have killed her, too!" she screamed suddenly. "Can you believe she always made me call her Mrs. Rigotta? She loved the fact that she got the title, and I didn't. She deserves to go to prison. For years, I've had to put up with her ordering me around, doing all her bidding. But do you know why I hate her the most?"

I gripped the bookshelf with my fingers until I was near the middle aisle. Marta's breathing slowed, and I listened to the silence, trying to get a bead on where she was. My heart was in my throat, and then horror of all horrors, a sneeze started to build inside me. I almost dropped the book when I put a hand over my face.

"She can't even boil an egg, but she got all the credit," Marta snickered. "By the way, that's how I knew you were lying. Sylvia never would have told you I made the cannoli or anything else for her precious show. That was one secret she was prepared to take to her grave. But that's not the biggest reason I hate her. It's because of the way she treats my daughter. Like an inconvenience, instead of as a gift, which is what Willow is."

I managed to suppress the sneeze and raised the book

in front of me, ready for action when she moved closer. As I'd hoped, she kept on talking.

"The night of the signing, Willow called and asked if I would come pick her up. She and Sylvia left when Daphne arrived but they had an argument, which was nothing new. So Willow got out of the car and marched back to the bookstore. When I arrived, I went into the back room from the alley and didn't see her. But I did see the key sitting on the counter and picked it up. Then I went back outside to the car in the alley and waited for Willow. She came out of the coffee place a minute later, and we left."

The alley had certainly been doing a booming business that night.

She chuckled quietly in the darkness. "After everyone went to bed, I called Daphne up and said that Willow and Gabby needed to meet her at the store. Some copies of Preston's books were missing pages, and customers were upset. Daphne wasn't happy but said she'd be there."

My head throbbed unmercifully, as I listened, not daring to breathe. I was waiting for that perfect moment—one that I could not afford to waste, as our lives depended on it.

"So Daphne came to the store but instead of Gabby,

she found me." There was triumph in Marta's voice. "I had a tray of cannoli, and she thought they were left over from the ones you made. When I told her Gabby would be back shortly, she immediately started stuffing her face with the pastries. Within a minute, she was lying on the floor, begging me to call for help. She asked me to get her purse and said that she had an EpiPen in it, but I moved it out of her reach. Shortly afterward, she passed out."

Bile rose in the back of my throat. How sick was this woman? She'd not only killed Daphne but had watched her plead for help while dying.

My breathing sounded a bit loud to my own ears, as the whiff of Marta's lilac perfume hit my nose. Sheer panic set in, and I didn't wait any longer. I heaved the book forward as hard as I could in the darkness and was rewarded with a resounding *"Oof."* I moved to the right and hurried through the darkness. For the first time in my life, I had an idea of what it was like to be blind. The loss of such an important sense left me feeling defenseless and frightened. I'd never even liked to sleep in total darkness, always preferring to have a light on in the house somewhere. The blackness was suffocating as I continued to run through it, hoping for a light at the end of the tunnel.

Hope bloomed in my chest as I moved on, aware of Marta's boots clomping after me. I must be close to the front door. I only needed to find it, slide the lock back, run out into the street, and scream for help.

My stomach was heavier than a bag of rocks. Jackhammers pounded inside my head until I longed to scream in agony. My arm bumped into one of the aisles, but I managed to stay on my feet and keep moving. I had to be close to my destination.

At that moment, I crashed into something—most likely Gabby's book cart—and a wave of pain shot through my body. I went down, hitting my face hard against the floor. With a groan, I tried to stand but was immediately hit from behind and shoved back down.

For a skinny little thing, Marta was strong. Within seconds she'd pinned me to the floor with her knees, one resting on my right arm while the other one pressed painfully into my chest. It immediately became difficult for me to breathe. I twisted and writhed but was weak from my fall and couldn't free myself. Marta wrapped both of her hands around my neck and started to squeeze it tightly.

Her face was directly above mine, but I couldn't see it. She was panting heavily, and her foul, moist breath seared my nostrils. My lungs screamed for air. Panicked, I managed to dig the nails of my left hand into her wrist, desperately trying to free her fingers from my throat. She wriggled her hand free and smacked me across the face so hard that my ears began to ring.

My mother's and father's faces flashed before me, then Dylan's. I became lightheaded and knew I was about to lose consciousness. *Heaven help me.* I didn't want to die like this. With my last bit of strength, I managed to lift my knee and thrust it into Marta's stomach. With a gasp, she fell off me. I tried to lift myself off the floor, choking and wheezing, but she found me in the darkness and pushed me down. She began to squeeze my neck again when a loud clanging noise vibrated through the bookstore's walls. Marta let out a groan and released her hold on me.

The room was silent, except for me gasping for air. I couldn't seem to get enough into my lungs and must have lain there for a minute before the light came on. I blinked against the sudden brightness. I was on my side, staring at Marta's limp body next to mine. She was flat on her back and out cold.

Bewildered, I glanced up. Gabby stood a few feet away from me with a triumphant smile on her face, swaying from side to side and looking like she might keel over at any minute. Her dark hair was matted with blood, and her face was a sickly white color. For several seconds, I continued to stare at her in amazement, wondering if my mind was playing tricks on me.

She extended her hand for me to take. In her other one was the steel serving tray I'd used for the cannoli on the night of the signing. I'd forgotten I'd left it here. With her help, I managed to stand, albeit clumsily, and she wrapped an arm around my shoulders to support me. I bent at the knees, still gasping for breath.

"You okay?" she asked.

"Thanks to you," I said hoarsely.

She guided me forward. "Come on. I've got some electrical tape behind the counter." She reached for her phone. "We can tie her up, and then call Gino." A frown creased her face. "You look awful. Can you breathe all right?"

I managed a nod. My throat was sore, my head hurt, and every other part of my body ached. "Thank goodness you woke up in time."

"But I didn't."

I stared at her, dumbstruck. "Wait a second. You mean—you were faking? The entire time?"

Gabby gave a low chuckle as we limped toward the counter. "Not the entire time. She did knock me out for a couple of minutes, and then it took me a few more before I could get up and figure out exactly what was going on. I may have been down," she said, "but I sure wasn't out. You were trying to get her away from me, and then it was my turn to do the same for you."

"We're quite a team," I said.

"Darn straight," she agreed. "As my brother would say, family over everything."

TWENTY-THREE

A BANGING AWAKENED ME FROM A deep sleep. Puzzled, I opened one eye and listened. Luigi was lying on Dylan's pillow staring back at me, his motorized purrs filling the room. When the noise came again, he yawned, stretched, and jumped off my bed.

There was someone at my front door. I glanced at the clock on my nightstand. Seven o'clock in the morning. Ugh. Way too early for visitors, and it felt like I'd just gone to bed. That was partially true—it had been after two o'clock when I'd returned from the hospital.

With a sigh, I found my robe, grabbed my phone off the nightstand, and staggered to the doorway, where Luigi was waiting. I followed him down the stairs, gripping the rail between my hands as the banging continued. By staring at my phone screen, I'd already deduced who was at the front door. The urgent voice that called from outside confirmed my suspicion.

"Tess?" Justin shouted. "Are you okay?"

Luigi waited while I unlocked and opened the door. Justin stood there, looking rugged and handsome in jeans and a gray shirt that matched his eyes. When his gaze came to rest on mine, his eyes filled with relief.

"Thank God." He stepped inside and wrapped me in his arms. "I just saw your text. Sorry—I went home last night and slept for ten hours straight. Are you okay? How's Gabby?"

"We're both fine." When I sent the text from the hospital around midnight, I was aware he might not see it for a while. He'd come off an eighteen-hour shift and had to be exhausted. But I also knew that if I hadn't attempted to contact him, he'd be hurt and upset when he found out later.

He continued holding me in silence for a minute while I let myself drink in the woodsy scent of him that reminded me of the great outdoors. It was wonderful to feel safe and protected again. Justin had always been there for me, but I hadn't felt secure since Dylan died.

"Gabby has a slight concussion, so we were at the

hospital until pretty late. They didn't make her stay over, so she went home when I did. Lou's taking care of her."

He drew back from me and gently touched the bruise on my cheek where Marta had struck me. His jaw tightened in anger. "I'd love to be in a room alone with that psycho for about five minutes."

I squeezed his arm. "It looks worse than it feels."

"I can't believe this happened to you, and I didn't even know about it! Like Dylan being murdered wasn't enough for you to deal with." His voice became gruff. "I'm glad Gabby was there for you, if I couldn't be."

The memory of Marta choking me and the final darkness closing in was enough to make me shudder inwardly. "If Gabby hadn't been with me, I don't think I'd be standing here right now." Somehow, I needed to forget about those few minutes of sheer terror when I wasn't sure if I'd live or die. "Gino said that Marta will go away for a long time."

Justin's expression was grim. "Well, that doesn't bring Daphne back, but I'm thankful you're safe." He took me by the hand, and we sat down together on the couch. Luigi immediately jumped into his lap, and Justin absently scratched him behind his ears. "Is everything still going forward with the grand opening?"

"Yes, it's happening as planned." I brought my hand to my throat, fully aware that Marta's fingermarks were still on display. "Good thing I own turtlenecks. And some cover-up will do wonders for my cheek because I wouldn't want to scare off the clientele."

His eyes were warm and soft as he looked at me, similar to a cuddly blanket. "You have me marked down for a table, right? Reservation for two."

My heart sank into the pit of my stomach at his words, but I tried to act nonchalant. "Sure. It will be nice to see Natalie." I hoped he knew what he was doing but didn't think I could watch her break his heart again. Maybe I'd get used to it eventually. I vowed to be there for him always, no matter what happened between them.

Justin's jaw dropped in surprise. "Who said anything about Natalie? My friend Will is coming with me. You met him at the fire station that time you and Dylan came by last year, remember?"

"Oh, right. Of course." Embarrassment flooded through me, and I rose to my feet. "Would you like some coffee? I'm dying for a cup. It will only take a second to—"

Justin stood as well, forcing Luigi to jump off his lap and go scampering into the other room. He whirled me gently around to face him. "As long as you brought her up, I came to tell you something."

I swallowed hard. "You've made a decision."

"Yes. Actually, I mean no. There never really was a decision to make. She caught me off guard at a difficult time in my life. I told her I'd think about getting back together but knew deep down that I'd never be able to trust her again. What basis is that for a marriage?"

"Not a very good one," I admitted, thinking about Dylan and the secrets he'd kept from me.

He rubbed a hand over his chin where a five-o'clock shadow was prominent. "You probably think I was stupid to even be considering it."

"No. She was your first love. You wouldn't have married her if you didn't love her."

Justin was silent for a minute. "I did love her, but she wasn't the first woman I ever loved. Do you remember when we first met?"

"Of course. At Anna and Ryan's wedding." Anna had been a childhood friend of mine, and I'd come home from college one summer to be in her wedding. Dylan and Justin had been friends of Ryan's in high school, and both had served as groomsmen. Justin and I were paired off to walk down the aisle together, but it was Dylan who had managed to attract my attention.

He grinned. "After the reception, Dylan and I went back to the hotel room we were sharing for the night. We had an argument—about you."

I stared at him in amazement. "Really? Why? Dylan never mentioned it to me."

"I'm sure he didn't," Justin said wryly. "We discovered that we were both planning to ask you out before leaving town."

My jaw dropped. "You're kidding."

He shook his head. "Nope. Why are you so surprised? I asked you to dance three times at the wedding. Did you think it was just out of politeness?"

To be honest, I'd never really thought about it before. Justin had been a nice guy, attractive, and we'd had fun together that night. But he hadn't stood a chance once I spotted Dylan. "What happened?"

"Dylan got so angry at me. He made me promise not to ask you out until he tried first, so I agreed to wait. I was so confident you'd tell him no." He gave me a sad smile. "The worst decision I ever made in my life."

I was speechless for a moment. "I don't know what to say."

He reached for my hand. "You don't have to say anything. I just wanted you to know that I wasn't some jerk lusting after my best friend's wife all those years. You went out with Dylan, fell in love, and got married. I learned to accept it and moved on with my life, met Natalie, and fell in love with her. After she cheated on me, things changed. I started to regret the way things worked out that one summer long ago. But one thing is for certain. I'll always want you in my life, no matter what happens between us."

"Same here." I was relieved that we could talk to each other like this, and it made me feel closer to him. "Does Natalie want the house back?"

"I'm going to buy her out," Justin said. "We should have taken care of this when the divorce happened. My lawyer warned me she'd come back someday and stake a claim for the property, but I wanted her out of my life as soon as possible. I had him draw up an agreement of sorts and then asked Natalie to meet me at Java Time the other night, so she could sign it. That's when I told her that I didn't want to get back together. *Ever.* I deducted money for the years she never paid into the mortgage. She wasn't happy but agreed. It took almost every bit of my savings but was well worth it. I never have to see her again."

Relief soared through me. "Well, that's one less thing I have to worry about."

"Oh, yeah? I like the idea of you worrying about me," Justin teased. "Actually, the last thing I want to do is burden you with any more problems. There was so much going on these past few months it feels like I've been on a roller-coaster, but you've had a far worse ride than I have. With trying to pick up your life and start the restaurant, I didn't want to dump my troubles in your lap as well."

"That's what friends are for. I'll always make time for you." I squeezed his hand. "You've been looking out for me ever since Dylan died. I want to return the favor."

Our talk was interrupted by a plaintive meow, and we both stared down at the floor. Luigi had his paw on Justin's pant leg. Justin laughed and picked him up in his arms. "Seems like someone else is looking out for us too."

TWENTY-FOUR

"WELL, I HAVE TO ADMIT, YOU were right," I said to Gabby as I plated chicken parmigiana and set it on the counter next to the small plastic sign, *Table* 7. "I guess everyone in this town does like to plan things at the last minute."

Renee hurried into the kitchen and picked up the two plates of chicken parmigiana, flashing us both a broad grin. "There's people out front waiting for tables. And both Tables 5 and 10 want more garlic bread."

"Music to my ears," I said.

Gabby laughed. "What—the tables or the garlic bread?"

"Both!" I said joyously.

"I've got the bread ready to go." Stephanie arranged it on top of the red checkered cloths in two wicker baskets and added them to Renee's tray. As soon as she departed through the swinging doors, Judy bounced in. She was a pretty girl with light brown hair and blue eyes. Freckles dotted her cheeks when she smiled. "Tessa, there's quite a line out by the hostess station. Do you want me to seat them?"

Stephanie looked momentarily flustered. "I'm sorry, Tessa. I'll get back out there."

Gabby waved her off. "No worries, I can do it."

I started cutting a tray of cooled lasagna into squares. "Forget it. I want you to enjoy yourself tonight. Go back out to the dining room and sit with our mothers and Lou."

"Oh, stop." She looked happier than I'd seen her in weeks. "Since you saved my bookstore from going under, I'd say I owe you at least one night of unpaid labor."

"It wasn't just me. You played a big part as well. Oh, and there was also that little matter of saving my life."

Gabby placed her hands on her hips. "Funny, I seem to remember you doing that for me once. Guess that evens the score, until next time."

Yikes. "I hope there isn't a next time."

"You and me both." Gabby hurried out the swinging doors and into the dining area.

Stephanie was preparing salads for Table 1 while I

ladled minestrone into bowls for Table 5. "Can you fix a basket of bread for Table 6?" I asked her.

Stephanie stared at me wide-eyed. Her eyes took in the pan of lasagna, dish of eggplant, and pots of penne and soup that surrounded me in my happy little corner by the stove. "I'm on it," she said. "Gosh, I wish that I could multitask like that. You have a real knack for this, Tessa. The best part? You look like you're loving it."

"That's because I am." I arranged a garnish of parsley next to the piece of lasagna, then moved deftly over to Stephanie's work counter to add a piece of garlic bread to the plate. Satisfied, I set the dish next to the sign for Table 4. "I've wanted to do this for a long time." Of course, I'd planned to do it with Dylan. Stephanie didn't know, but if Dylan were still alive, he'd be doing her job—seating people and helping in the kitchen, although he didn't have her culinary skills. He couldn't even nuke anything in the microwave without causing a minor disaster. I smiled at the memory.

My thoughts of him continued as I emptied a package of my frozen sauce into a pot and turned the burner on underneath. We'd talked endlessly about the restaurant and even how we'd cap the first night off—with a champagne toast to celebrate our success. I blew out a sigh and glanced around. Stephanie was fussing with the croutons on a salad, mumbling to herself, and didn't notice me. It was odd to feel so elated but also sad at the same time. No, I shouldn't be sad. Dylan would have wanted me to be happy, especially tonight. He'd be proud of me, and this place never would have happened without him.

Stephanie spoke up. "I know it's impossible, but I'd love to have my own place someday. Of course, I'm nowhere near as good a cook as you are."

"If you want it badly enough it can happen." I removed the sauce from the burner and poured it liberally over a waiting dish of penne. "Remember our slogan."

"Anything's Pastable!" Stephanie laughed. "Hey, is that hot-looking landlord of yours stopping over tonight?"

"No, he had to go to New York City on business." Vince had texted me earlier and apologized but said he would stop by to see me on Tuesday.

Gabby returned to the kitchen. "You need to get out to the dining room, Tess."

"Is something wrong?" I cut up another square of lasagna for a plate and then covered the rest of the pan.

"There's a customer who can't wait." She grabbed my arm, trying to push me away from the stove.

"Gabs, I'm way too busy. Justin knows I'll be out later."

"I'm not talking about Justin." Gabby was relentless, pulling on me. "Someone has asked specifically for you, and you can't keep this man waiting. Take the apron off, chef."

"Go ahead, Tess," Stephanie encouraged. "I've got it covered for now."

Resigned, I gave in. "Well, only for a minute." At Gabby's insistence, I removed my apron and straightened my short-sleeved, pink silk blouse that I'd paired with blue jeans. It would have been silly to get all dressed up since I spent the entire night in the kitchen, but I'd wanted to make some type of effort.

I followed Gabby through the swinging doors. Standing next to the hostess station was a silver-headed man in an immaculate dark blue suit. At his side was a blond woman wearing a belted beige overcoat. A man about my age with glasses stood across from them, a camera strap around his neck.

"Oh!" I said, startled, and grasped the silver-headed man's outstretched hand. "What a lovely surprise. Welcome to Anything's Pastable, Mayor Randolph. And to you too, Mrs. Randolph."

Mayor Randolph beamed at me. "You have a lovely place here. I can already tell it's going to be one of our favorites."

"Thank you so much."

"Mrs. Esposito." The man with the camera in his hands stepped forward. "I'm Jared Elmsby from the *Harvest Park Press*. Can we have a picture of you with the mayor and his wife cutting the ribbon?"

Bewildered, I stared at him. "There's no—" Then I noticed a yellow ribbon stretched across the doorway of the dining room. Red and white balloons that read "*Congratulations*" floated near the ceiling. "This is silly," I laughed. "People have already been seated. You have a ribbon-cutting ceremony before anyone comes in."

"So what?" Gabby said grandly. "It's your restaurant, so I guess you can do whatever you please." She handed me a pair of scissors.

I approached the ribbon, aware of everyone's eyes on me. I hated to be the center of attention, but it was too late to back out now. Jared lowered himself underneath the ribbon with great agility to get the photo from the other side. Mayor Randolph stepped forward and placed his hand over mine as I made the cut. The flash popped in my face, and everyone clapped and cheered.

After chatting with the mayor and his wife for a minute, and then letting Gabby seat them, I walked around to each table, asking everyone if they were enjoying their meal. It was how I'd always pictured it would be. People were laughing and talking, enjoying their food and each other's company. My heart soared with pride.

Gabby was sitting with Lou and Aunt Mona. Gino and Lucy were at the table next to them with Rocco and Marco. When Rocco saw me approaching, he stood up and threw his arms around my waist.

"Aunt Tessa, your pasghetti is awesome!" he shrieked, wearing a giant red stain on his white shirt to prove it.

Marco looked up at me from his seat, a meatball poised on his fork. "Aunt Tessa, Mommy's going to have a baby and Grandma started crying when she told her."

I leaned over to give Lucy a hug. "I'm so happy for you. For both of you."

"Thanks, Tess." She smiled up at me with brilliant green eyes that resembled jewels. Gino winked at me as his arm went around her shoulders. "The place is amazing, but I always knew it would be," Lucy said.

My mother, who had been talking to the mayor, came over. She beamed at me under her dark hair, piled high on top of her head in dramatic fashion. "I'm so proud of you, sweetheart. People have been complimenting the food all night. The restaurant is going to be a great success."

"I hope so." I bussed her cheek.

She cocked her head to the side. "You okay?"

"I'm fine. It's all a little overwhelming, I guess."

My mother was not easily fooled. She squeezed my hand. "He's looking down on you, sweetheart. And he's every bit as proud as I am."

My throat was tight with tears, but I was determined not to cry. "Thanks, Mom. I'd better get back to the kitchen, but I want to have a word with Justin first."

She nodded in understanding. "We'll stop in the kitchen later to say goodbye."

Justin's table was at the other end of the room. He rose when I approached. "Hey there. I knew this place would sell out. How could it not with the best chef in the world cooking? Tess, you remember my buddy from the firehouse, Will."

Will rose to shake my hand. He was at least ten years older than Justin, with wrinkles forming at the corner of his brown eyes, which regarded me kindly. "It's nice to see you again, Tessa. Justin said not to worry. If you burn anything, we're on it."

Justin and I both laughed out loud. "See if I invite you to join me for dinner again," he told his friend.

My eyes scanned the room and I noticed Carlita standing alone by the hostess counter. I placed a hand on Justin's shoulder. "Will you excuse me for a minute?"

"Of course. We'll catch up later, when you're not so busy."

I moved across the room to Carlita, who held a bakery box between her hands. "I'm so glad you're here. Can I get you a table?"

She shook her head. "I cannot stay but made you present. Call it a restaurant-warming." Her brow furrowed. "Is there such thing?"

"There can be, if you want."

Beaming with pride, Carlita lifted the lid of the box and I peered inside. There was a luscious-looking cake covered with chocolate chips and two cannoli on top. My mouth watered at the sight. "Oh, my goodness. Is that what I think it is?"

"*Si*, cannoli cheesecake. Some are inside the cake, too. Theresa, you charge big money for this," she ordered. "At least ten dollars a slice."

I burst out laughing. It was wonderful to see her back to her old, bossy self. "Carlita, thank you so much, but this wasn't necessary."

Her dark eyes gazed directly into mine. "It *is* necessary. My way to say thank you for helping Lorenzo."

"How's he doing?" I hadn't seen him since the day he took off from the doctor's office.

She wiggled her hand back and forth. "He is going to be all right. It has changed him, though. Look like he is finally getting his act together. Lorenzo ask me if he can go full time at the bakery. And he plan to move out and get apartment with friend."

"That's wonderful."

Carlita's expression suddenly became pained. "It makes my heart ache whenever I think about that baby—*his* baby. It will always hurt him."

She was right. Hopefully in time Lorenzo would heal and meet another woman that he loved and could start a family with. "He's lucky to have you."

"May that Marta rot in jail," Carlita seethed. "What those Rigottas say when they find out their housekeeper a killer?"

"I don't know." Gabby had told me earlier the Rigottas

had left their home in Saratoga and rumor had that it wasn't together. Apparently, there were still reporters surrounding it, waiting for their return.

Carlita patted my cheek. "You get back to work. And stay out of trouble. No more murders, okay?"

"You have my word," I promised.

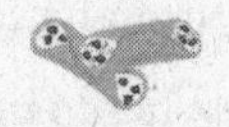

It was close to midnight when I emptied the dishwasher. I'd told Andy to go home before the cycle finished, assuring him I'd put away the dishes. We'd been so busy that none of my staff had managed to leave before eleven, and thankfully they hadn't seemed to mind. It meant more money out of pocket, but I didn't care. The success of the place had been well worth it.

I'd served almost two hundred people that evening—takeout included. Sure, I knew that every night wouldn't be like this, but right now, I was feeling confident about the future of Anything's Pastable.

Stephanie slung her purse on her shoulder and walked over. "Want me to do that before I take off?"

I shook my head. "That's okay, I'm almost done." The counters had been scrubbed, the floors swept, and tables set for Tuesday. I could rest up Sunday and Monday and then the craziness of the restaurant world would begin again. And I could hardly wait.

If the restaurant continued like this, I'd need to find another employee, and soon. Thanks to Gabby helping intermittently tonight we'd managed, but now that her bookstore was back open and had seen some increased traffic today, I couldn't ask her to do this often.

"Sorry that I kept you so late. It won't always be like this."

Stephanie dangled her car keys. "It's fine. I'm so glad everything went well. Your restaurant is going to be the toast of the town."

"Thanks, I hope so." Her words reminded me that I had forgotten something. I placed the last of the glasses in the cupboard above the dishwasher and unlocked the back door for her. "Drive safe and thanks again for everything."

She shot me a puzzled look. "Aren't you leaving?"

"In a few minutes. There's one more thing that I need to do."

"I can wait if you like," she offered.

I smiled at her. "That's okay, I'll be fine. Enjoy your days off and rest up for Tuesday."

Stephanie's face lit up like a Christmas tree. "I'm looking forward to it. 'Night, Tess."

"Good night, Stephanie."

I waited until she was inside her vehicle, parked next to mine, then locked and shut the back door. After another look around the immaculate kitchen, I went to the refrigerator and drew out the bottle of champagne that Gabby had brought me tonight as a gift. I hadn't told her what I planned to do with it—that was my little secret.

As I filled two flutes with champagne, my memories returned to Dylan. Whenever I'd had a free moment earlier, thoughts of him had occupied my mind. I'd felt his presence everywhere. Justin had come into the kitchen before leaving and asked if I wanted to stop by his house for a celebration drink when I finished, but I told him that I'd see him tomorrow. He'd asked no questions and seemed to understand without my saying so that this was an evening of reflection for me.

I unlocked the back door and opened it, leaning against the doorway with the flute in my hand. The full moon shone down from between the trees, which were just starting to fill out after a long and dreary winter. I clinked my glass against the side of the other one on the counter, stared back at the moon, and raised my glass to it.

"We did it, baby." I closed my eyes and pictured Dylan so vividly in my mind that it was as if he was standing next to me. His presence pacified me, calmed me. How I'd have done anything for one more kiss, one last touch.

I clung to the sensation for as long as possible, watching his blond hair blowing in the wind. Dylan's eyes filled with love as his lips touched mine. For a moment, I even heard his voice. His lips were against my ear as he spoke those same words that he uttered every time I was skeptical about something, including our dream restaurant.

"We're going to live our best lives, Tess," Dylan had told me. "Remember, anything is possible, as long as you believe."

I opened my eyes, praying to see him next to me, but I was alone. The cool moist air whipped around me as I listened to the peaceful quiet of the night.

An owl hooted somewhere in the darkness, and I watched a star fall from the sky. "Thank you for loving me," I whispered. "It's made anything possible."

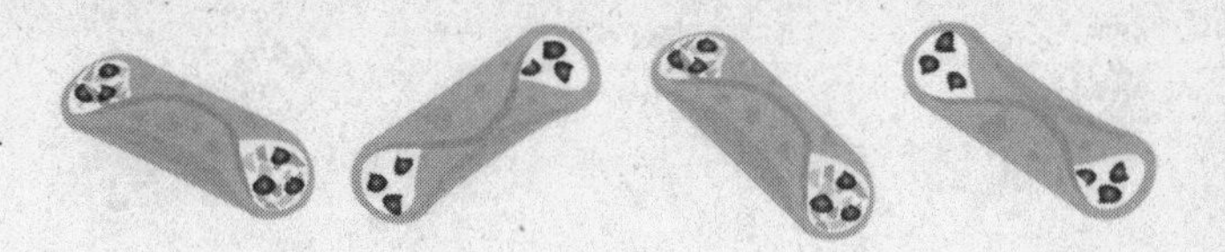

RECIPES

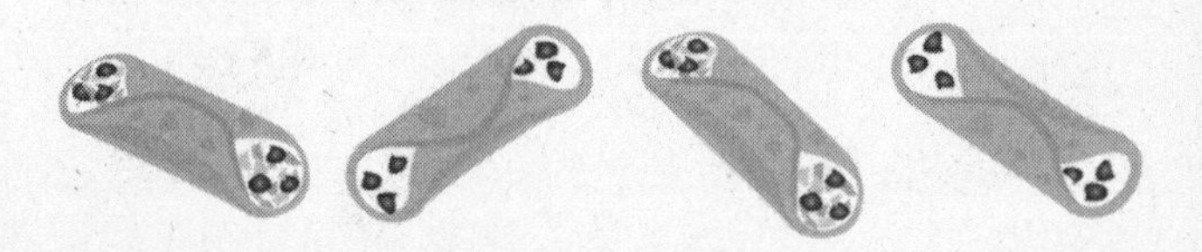

CANNOLI TO DIE FOR

For the shells:

- 2 cups all-purpose flour
- 1 tbsp. dark brown sugar
- 1/8 tsp. salt
- 3 tbsp. softened butter
- 2 eggs, yolks and whites separated
- ¼ tsp. nutmeg
- ¾ tsp. cinnamon
- 2¾ ounces sweet Marsala wine

Mix all the ingredients except for the wine into a bowl with a pastry cutter until crumbly. The butter and egg yolks should be thoroughly mixed. Add in the wine, a little at a time, until you are able to mix it with your hands. Form into a ball and let sit uncovered for 30 minutes. After the dough rests, lightly coat the dough with flour, and roll it through a pasta machine set to the thickest setting. If you don't have a pasta machine, use a rolling pin to roll the dough out as thinly as possible (to about ⅛ inch thick) on a lightly floured surface.

Use a 4-inch, round cookie cutter to cut circles from the dough. Take one circle at a time and pull into a 5-inch oval. Repeat with the excess dough, kneading it back together and cutting it until you have 12 ovals. Place the egg white in a small bowl and set aside.

In a wide pot with a heavy bottom, heat vegetable oil at your choice of temperature, between 350 and 380 degrees, with a heat thermometer. Line a large plate with paper towels. Wrap one oval of dough loosely lengthwise around a cannoli form. Brush one end of the dough with egg white, then pull the dry end over the top and press down to seal. Repeat with three more dough ovals.

Using tongs, carefully lower the dough into the oil and fry until golden brown, turning them as they fry, for 2 to 3 minutes. Remove the shells with the tongs, and transfer them to the paper-towel-lined plate to cool. When the shells are cool enough to touch, remove the molds and repeat with the remaining dough in batches until all shells are fried. Dip ends of cooled shells in melted chocolate if desired, and cool until dry. Fried shells can be stored in an airtight container for a few weeks.

For the filling:

- 32 oz. Impastato or mascarpone (you can buy already made)
- ½ cup granulated sugar
- ½ cup confectioners' sugar
- ½ tsp. vanilla
- 2 cups semi-sweet chocolate chips—optional (The miniature ones work best. Be sure to save some for garnish.)

Mix all ingredients together except for the chocolate. Reserving some for a garnish, melt the chips in the microwave for about 30 seconds and add to mixture. Use a pastry bag with tip to fill the shells. Grate more chocolate over the ends of the shells for a decorative look or dip the ends in melted mini chocolate chips. Refrigerate for at least a couple of hours. Makes at least 12 pastries.

TESSA'S RAGU BOLOGNESE SAUCE

Ingredients:

- 2 tbsp. olive oil
- 2 ounces butter
- 2 ounces pancetta or *guanciale*
- ½ cup carrots, diced
- ½ cup celery, diced
- ½ cup onions, diced
- 3 garlic cloves, thinly sliced
- Salt and pepper, to taste
- 2 cups ground beef (80/20)
- 2 cups ground pork
- 1 ounce all-purpose flour
- 2 ounces tomato paste
- 1 cup tomato puree
- 2 cups white or red wine
- 1 cup water or chicken/beef broth

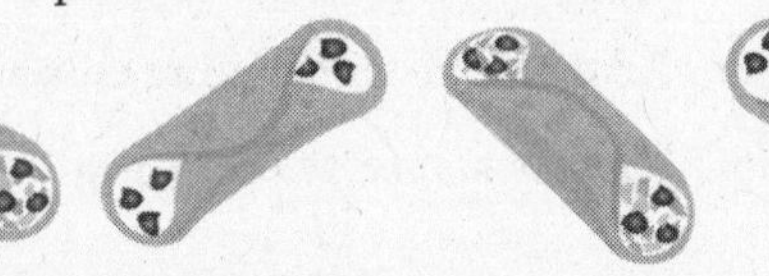

- 1 bay leaf—optional (Do not break the leaf up, because it can be dangerous to eat. Keep it whole and remove before serving.)
- 1 cup whole milk, room temperature

In a braising shallow pan, over medium heat, add olive oil and butter together. Once butter is melted, add pancetta. Sauté pancetta until translucent, about 4 to 5 minutes. Add carrots, celery, and onions, and stir vegetables 8 to 10 minutes. Add thin slices of garlic and stir for about 2 minutes. Add salt and pepper. Push vegetables to the perimeter of the pan and add meats to the center of the pan. Increase heat to medium high until meat browns, around 8 to 12 minutes. Add a little salt and pepper, and combine meat and vegetables. Add flour and cook until completely blended, for about 1 minute.

Make a spot in center of pan and add tomato paste. Sauté 2 to 3 minutes then mix with meat and veggies. Add tomato puree and stir together. Add wine and stir together. Add broth or water and stir together. Bring to a boil and add bay leaf. Simmer for 1 to 2 hours on low, stirring every 10 minutes or so. Add room-temperature milk and bring to a boil. Remove bay leaf, and serve over pasta.

CINNAMON CHIP BISCOTTI

Biscotti:

- ½ cup butter, room temperature
- 1 cup granulated sugar
- 2 eggs, room temperature
- 1 tsp. vanilla
- 2½ cups all-purpose flour (use the lightly-spoon-and-level method)
- 1½ tsp. ground cinnamon
- 1½ tsp. baking powder
- ½ tsp. salt
- 1 cup cinnamon chips

Optional Drizzle:

- ½ cup cinnamon chips*
- 1 tsp. vegetable shortening

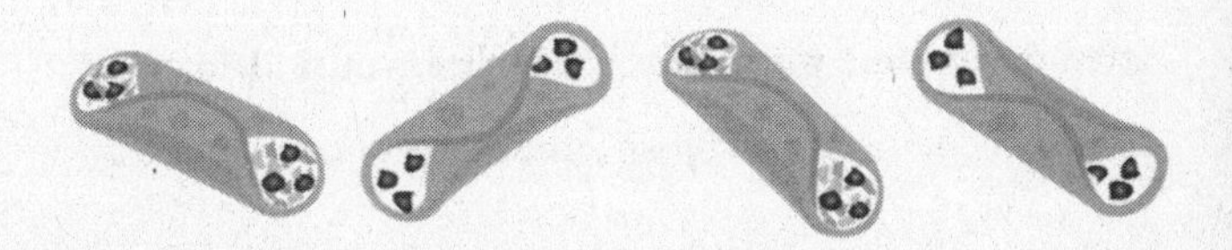

Preheat oven to 325 degrees. **For Biscotti:** In the bowl of a standing mixer beat butter and sugar together until fluffy. Add eggs, one at a time, and beat until thoroughly blended. Add vanilla and blend. In a separate bowl, whisk together flour, cinnamon, baking powder, and salt. Slowly add to butter mixture and mix on low speed until thoroughly incorporated. Stir in the cinnamon chips. Leaving the dough in the mixing bowl, cover with plastic wrap and place in the refrigerator for 30 minutes. Divide dough into 4 equal pieces and shape into logs about 8 to 10 inches long. Long and skinny logs are better than short and wide logs since the dough spreads while baking. If needed, spritz your hands with non-stick cooking spray while handling the dough.

Place on parchment-lined baking sheets, 2 logs per sheet, approximately 8 inches apart.

Slightly flatten the logs then bake 25 to 30 minutes until a toothpick inserted in the center comes out clean. If you prick a cinnamon chip, it won't give you an accurate read. Aim for the dough. Remove from oven and let cool on baking sheet at least 30 minutes. Transfer to a cutting board and cut logs crosswise into 1/2-inch-wide slices. A serrated bread knife works best. Place slices cut side down, on a parchment-lined baking sheet. Return to oven and bake

6 minutes at 325 degrees. Turn each slice over and bake an additional 7 to 9 minutes, until slightly golden brown. Remove from oven and let cool 5 minutes on baking sheet, then remove them from baking sheet and cool completely on a wire rack. Biscotti will harden as they cool.

Optional Drizzle: Be sure to use cinnamon chips for this. Cinnamon Sweet Bits won't work. In a small, microwave-safe bowl, melt cinnamon chips with vegetable shortening for 30 seconds. Stir until smooth. If necessary, heat in additional 10-second increments, stirring well each time. Be careful not to overheat. Pour the cinnamon chip mixture into a piping bag fitted with a small circle tip (or use a small ziplock bag with the corner cut off). Drizzle over the biscotti. Allow the drizzle to set before storing cannoli in an airtight container. Without drizzle, biscotti will last for 2 weeks if stored in an airtight container away from heat. If drizzle is added, consume within 3 days.

*Note: Hershey's makes cinnamon chips but they are typically only found during holidays in grocery stores. King Arthur Flour carries Cinnamon Sweet Bits, and they can be mail-ordered year-round.

ACKNOWLEDGMENTS

I AM GRATEFUL TO MY PUBLISHER, Sourcebooks, for allowing me the opportunity to tell the stories of my heart, and for readers who give me the chance to entertain them. Special thanks to editors Margaret Johnston and Anna Michels, who are both amazing to work with.

To my literary agent, Nikki Terpilowski, for her encouragement, patience, and all the time she devotes to guiding my career. I wouldn't be here without you.

Heartfelt thanks to retired Troy Police Captain Terrance Buchanan, who never tires of my questions and whose conversations constantly spark new ideas for me!

To my awesome beta readers and dear friends Constance Atwater and Kathy Kennedy, who always give it to me straight and never let me down.

Thank you to the talented Kim Davis for the use

of her amazing cinnamon chip biscotti recipe and to Sue Malatesta for her delicious cannoli recipe. Profound thanks to Gio Culinary Studio for allowing me to use their Bolognese creation and Donna Ferris Venturiello for sharing her knowledge of the restaurant world with me!

To my husband, Frank, for putting up with me as I spend many hours in my pretend, little world and often take him along for the ride. Your support means everything.

ABOUT THE AUTHOR

USA Today bestselling author Catherine Bruns lives in Upstate New York with an all-male household that consists of her very patient husband, sons, and several spoiled pets. Catherine has a B.A. in both English and Performing Arts and is a former newspaper reporter and press release writer. In her spare time, she loves to bake, read, and attend live theater performances. Her book *For Sale by Killer* was the 2019 recipient of the Daphne du Maurier award for Mainstream Mystery/Suspense. Readers are invited to visit her website at catherinebruns.net.